Big Trouble for a Little Lady

Big Trouble for a Little Lady

A Sandi Webster Mystery

Marja McGraw

Writer's Showcase
San Jose New York Lincoln Shanghai

Big Trouble for a Little Lady
A Sandi Webster Mystery

Writer's Showcase
an imprint of iUniverse.com, Inc.

For information address:
iUniverse.com, Inc.
5220 S 16th, Ste. 200
Lincoln, NE 68512
www.iuniverse.com

ISBN: 0-595-18180-5

Printed in the United States of America

For Alton—You inspire me, thank you!.

ACKNOWLEDGEMENTS

A special thank you to Jill Shelton (a great editor and daughter), Curt Lyon, Judy Lang-Hope, Louise Darden, Lila McGraw, Mary Lou Whitney, Dale and Carole Keast, Wanda Espinoza, Phyllis Matheus and Boyd Moffitt for your help and encouragement. A very special thank you to Elizabeth Rasmussen for many years of encouragement, idea sharing and caring, and to Mary Blueberg for talking me into trying my hand at writing in the first place.

"...held one's interest and presented an unusual ending which pleased this reader."
Phyllis Matheus, author of *The Valleys of the Walker River*

"...well written. It's a MUST READ book."
Boyd Moffit, author of *Some Good, Some Bad, Some Indifferent*

"Terrific characters in Sandi and Pete...Made for each other."
Elizabeth Lyon, author of *Gaylord Fordyce*

CHAPTER I

If I had known how much my life would change, and how close I would come to becoming a statistic, I might never have left my safe and sane secretarial job. On the other hand, I might have had a pretty boring existence.

I grew up watching old detective movies on television, circa 1930-1950. I lost myself in the heroes, the hard-nosed private eyes who always got their man, and trying to figure out who done it. *The Maltese Falcon* had its effect, as did *The Big Sleep* with Bogart and Bacall, but my favorites were the ones with a touch of humor. Nick and Nora Charles' humor was ahead of its time. Bob Hope gave me more than one chuckle. Red Skelton got into the act with his *Whispering…* movies, and Abbott and Costello managed to visit a haunted house or two.

I watched the comedic and klutzy gumshoes trip their way to conclusions, and I decided a person doesn't have to be macho to be a private detective. I deceived myself into thinking there was no reason a five foot three inch female, weighing in at 115 pounds soaking wet couldn't detect as well as any man. All it would take was intelligence, common sense and good deductive reasoning. My long, dark brown hair, big innocent blue eyes and slight build tended to make people trust me. I felt, overall, they didn't perceive me as a threat, so my appearance and size could actually be a plus instead of a handicap.

So, after thirteen years of working at a government job in Los Angeles and lots of night school classes, I turned in my resignation,

1

withdrew my retirement and opened the Webster Detective Agency. I was thirty-one years old at the time.

My name is Sandi Webster. I knew the name of the agency had to sound masculine, so I just used Webster and left the Sandi part out. Actually, there are men called Sandy, so I had to remember to spell my name with a "y" instead of an "i". I'm not a women's libber, but I do believe in equal rights and hated the fact that I'd probably get less business if people realized right off that I was female. I figured that once I created a good reputation for myself, I could quit worrying.

I also knew I couldn't do everything alone once I got established in the business, but an operative would have to wait for awhile. At least until the money started rolling in, as I knew it would eventually. A positive attitude doesn't hurt.

When I left my job, my friends and co-workers had their doubts about my new venture, and they made no bones about letting me know how they felt. The fact that I used terms like "operative" worried them because it made them feel I was naive, although it did give them a good laugh. I just laughed with them. No big deal. They meant well, and I *liked* the vernacular of my trade. Just the same, they gave me a great send off and wished me the best.

As far as my mother, well, she lived in Chicago and I lived in Los Angeles. What she didn't know wouldn't hurt her, right? Wrong. I knew I'd have to tell her eventually. She'd find out one way or the other anyway. She always seemed to know when I was keeping something from her, and she had a knack for wheedling things out of me. Another asset for my career choice—I'd learned from the best. Mom.

When I finally called and informed her of my new career, she was very quiet.

"Don't you have anything to say?" I finally asked when the silence became too loud.

"I'm not sure you'd want to hear what I have to say, dear," she replied, "so for the moment I won't say anything. Just be careful. We'll keep in touch." And I knew we would. I had no doubt I'd hear from her frequently.

She was quiet again, but finally said, "I've been thinking about taking a little vacation to come see you sometime during the next month, if that wouldn't be an inconvenience." Like being an inconvenience would have stopped her. "We can talk more then," she added.

"Sure, Mom. You know you're more than welcome anytime."

Just what I needed. Well, at least I had somewhere from a day to a month to figure out how to handle her.

As it turned out, I had the whole month to take care of business before my mother arrived. I'd already found the best location for the agency, and had spent the previous six months attending auctions and yard sales looking for office furniture and the equipment I needed. I hung out my sign, figuratively and literally speaking, and waited. I hung my license on the wall, decorated and rearranged the office, and waited. Had I moved too fast in leaving my old job? Of course, but it was too late now. The few prospective clients I was going to start with had left me high and dry. I put an advertisement in the newspaper and in the telephone book, an extravagant expense for me, had a grand opening cocktail party and waited some more. All of this over a period of three weeks.

My mother found time to call me at least once a week, and I continued to wait.

One month to the day after my first career conversation with my mother, she arrived for vacation. She stayed a week. Actually, we had a pretty good time. She kept my mind off the waiting, to some extent. She inspected my office, talked me into changing the locks on the doors and adding a deadbolt, and treated me to a couple of new outfits. Mother always did love to shop. She decided that as a detective I needed a whole different style of clothing, which hopefully meant she was getting into the whole thing. She picked out business suits while I chose Levi's and cotton shirts. We compromised and bought a little of both. We wandered around Olivera Street, a Mexican street bazaar, where she bought souvenirs for her friends in Chicago, then headed over to Chinatown where she bought more souvenirs. She was a little disappointed because both places had changed so much since her last visit to them years earlier, but we still had a good time.

"You've led a pretty sheltered life, even though we went through some rough times when we lost your father, Sandi," she said over lunch. That was an understatement.

Oh Lord, here it comes, I thought to myself.

"How are you going to deal with it if a particularly nasty situation comes up?" she continued.

"Mother," I said defensively, "I'm not all *that* innocent. After all, I'm thirty-one years old and I've seen my share of life. Think how long I've worked in downtown Los Angeles, and in the court system, for crying out loud."

"Right," Mom said, totally unconvinced.

I knew I was a little naive, but that was more in personal relationships. I felt unsure around men, especially after a somewhat strange relationship I had sometime back, but in everyday situations I could handle myself pretty well. It was time for my mother to go home. She had a way of making me feel like a dumb little kid.

She did leave shortly after that, and because there was so little business coming in, she felt pretty good about everything. She seemed to think I'd get bored or go broke and go back to secretarial work. She really should have known better. I did have a stubborn streak, which I inherited from her, and it always worked its way out when she made me feel like that dumb little kid. I wouldn't give up that easily.

The day after Mother left, as I was dusting the frame I'd put my license in, the door opened and I heard my first client walk in. I turned around and was a little disappointed to find it was one of my old co-workers. I figured she was stopping in to see how things were going.

"Hi, Sandi," she greeted me. Janice Jensen had been my supervisor at
one time and I really liked this gal. She was a knowledgeable, fair and
likable person to work for. She made us feel like we were all part of a
group instead of setting herself apart from the rest of us. She made us
feel like valuable employees, not just secretaries. She and her husband
had invited me to their home a few times, and Janice had even tried fixing me up with a blind date. We'd become pretty good friends. Then I
was transferred to another division, and we sort of lost touch.

"Hello, Janice," I replied. She seemed slightly ill-at-ease. "Have a seat
and tell me how things are going. How've you been? I'm so glad to see
you," I said, and meant it.

"I'm afraid this isn't a social call," she stated. "I need your help."

She didn't want to know how I was doing, because she was to be my
first real client. I acted calm, cool and collected, but underneath I was
nervous. It would have been easier if my first client had been a complete
stranger. I knew I'd really have to prove myself to Janice Jensen.

"Oh," I replied. "What's wrong, Janice? What can I do to help you?"

I stood up and walked over to the coffee maker. I poured myself a cup
of coffee, indicating an extra coffee mug to her, but she shook her head.
I sat down behind the desk, all my attention focused on her, ready to
find out what was going on.

"Let me get right to the point," she said, scooting forward in her
chair. "Sandi, you know my husband, Gene. Well, I think he's having an
affair. I've got to know the truth, and I need you to check it out for me."

Great! My first case and it had to be a domestic problem. Where was
all the suspense, the danger. Well, at least the suspense. I'm not sure I
actually wanted the danger. This would just be a lot of snooping. I
wanted to put my deductive skills to work. After all, I'd gone to night
school for a long time to learn my trade, and I knew I could handle
something bigger. Oh well, I needed the work.

"Janice, are you sure you want to know? Sometimes we're better off *not*
knowing," I said hopefully. I honestly couldn't imagine Gene being

unfaithful, and I didn't want to see Janice hurt if I was wrong. Of course, on the other hand, if it was me, you bet I'd want to know the truth.

"I'm sure," she replied. "Things just haven't been right between us for some reason lately. I guess I just need an excuse to file for a divorce."

"Divorce?" I said, surprised. "If you want a divorce that much, just do it. Why go through all of this?"

"That didn't come out right. I don't really want a divorce, but I need to know what's going on. Gene hasn't been coming home until late at night, and he always has these unbelievable excuses. He always looks tired, and he never seems to have time for me. The indications are there. I just need to know for sure. If he doesn't love me anymore, then I'd rather give him his freedom and get on with my life. Right?" she asked uncertainly.

"Wrong," I stated. "If there is anything going on, then you need to fight for what's yours. As I remember, you and Gene have always been very close. In fact, I sort of looked at you two as an example of what a marriage should be like. I can't believe Gene is up to anything, and I'm going to do my best to prove it."

"I hope you're right," Janice said tearfully.

"Now," I continued, "how long has this been going on?"

"About six weeks. Please Sandi, help me with this."

"I'll do my best. Let me get some more information from you and I'll get started on this right away. And calm down until we know something for certain. Don't build this into something it might not be."

Janice reminded me of where her husband worked, told me who his close friends were, and so on and so forth. I assured her I would let her know as soon as I found out anything.

Janice left the office, still crying, and I shook my head as I watched her climb into her car. I just couldn't believe Gene would be unfaithful, but you never know about these things.

I followed Gene for a couple of days. Every night after work he grabbed a quick hamburger and then drove directly to the local bowling alley. On the fourth night I decided I needed a little exercise. Bowling would be just perfect.

I strolled through the lobby, casually looking around. I didn't see Gene anywhere. I was still glancing around as I approached the shoe rental counter, which appeared to be untended. As I turned to look for help, Gene stood up and met me face to face. He'd been bent over, putting shoes away. I didn't have to pretend surprise when I saw him, because I was truly surprised.

"Gene," I said. "What on earth are you doing here? I haven't seen you in ages."

"Hi, Sandi," he replied, looking slightly embarrassed. "I'm working here part-time." So this was where he was disappearing to. I wondered why he couldn't tell Janice, and he quickly supplied me with the answer.

"Do me a favor, huh? Don't tell Janice about seeing me here."

"If you say so," I replied. I looked at him, a little puzzled. "If you don't mind me asking, why don't you want Janice to know about this job?"

"Our twenty-fifth wedding anniversary is next month," he said, sighing. "I want to do something special for her this year. I've saved up some money, but not enough. I've been working here to get the extra cash I need for a cruise to Mexico. I wanted it to be a surprise. Get it?"

"Got it," I said. "I won't say a word. But do me a favor, and figure out some good excuse why you haven't been coming home to her at night. I happened to run into her, and she seems worried that something might be wrong."

"You ran into her? Where?"

"I had to go up to the courthouse on business and saw her there," I lied. "I asked her how you were doing, and she said she wasn't sure because she doesn't see you that much lately." Was I pushing it? I hoped not, but I hated to see this whole situation go bad.

"I get it," Gene said. "I'll take care of it, and even if it kills me, I'll make things right. Starting tonight."

We talked for a few more minutes, and then I bowled the best game I'd bowled in years. Gene had restored my faith in mankind.

The next day I called Janice and guaranteed her that Gene wasn't fooling around. I also made her promise me she'd never let Gene know she suspected him of anything wrong. When she asked what was going on, I told her it was none of her business for the time being, but assured her she'd find out later. She heaved a rather large sigh of relief and said she'd keep quiet.

That was my first case, and the beginning of my career. Since Janice still worked at the courthouse, she started putting in a good word for me wherever possible, and jobs began trickling in. First domestics, and then a few more challenging cases. My big break came when an insurance company decided to give my services a try.

They hired me to investigate a suspected case of fraud. I brought the matter to a close in minimum time and proved beyond a shadow of a doubt that they were right. Mr. Jason Beason was faking injuries allegedly sustained in an automobile accident. The photographs I took clinched the case, and I was on my way.

Word-of-mouth can be very beneficial, and it was my road to semi-success. Within a year I had a reputation for being an accomplished researcher and detective. My caseload grew steadily and I began to consider taking on an operative. It was simply getting too busy for one person to handle alone. Los Angeles has a lot of insurance companies, and plenty of claims to be checked out.

My mother worried less and less about me being a detective, even though things were becoming so busy. When she realized the types of cases I handled weren't life-threatening, it eased her mind considerably. The only thing that really worried her were the domestic cases because they could get sticky. I told her she'd been watching too much television. The people I checked up on never even knew I was around. Overall, her biggest concern was whether I would meet and marry someone before age fifty. We'd covered that territory several times over the past few years. She thought I was being too picky. I called it being selective. She suggested that when I hired an operative, I should be selective by her definition, which meant to hire a single male. I found myself sighing a lot when Mother called.

While I worked at the courthouse, I developed a good rapport with the police department, so I looked to some of my friends there for leads in my search for an operative. The same name kept popping up. They all suggested I talk to Peter Goldberg.

He had to leave the department because of an eye injury which left minor problems. It was a matter of departmental medical policy or he'd still be a cop. They assured me he would be just right for my needs, and that he was a hard worker, intelligent, patient (someone snickered at that one), knew all the tricks of the trade and was currently available.

One of the guys gave me his home phone number, so I called him early the next morning before I left for the office.

"Hello," he barked as he answered the phone.

"Peter Goldberg?" I inquired.

"Yeah, who's this?"

"My name is Sandi Webster, and…"

"I've been expecting a call from you," he interrupted. "A couple of the guys called to tell me you were looking for a partner."

"I'm not looking for a partner, I'm looking for an operative," I corrected him.

"Same difference."

I didn't agree with him, but I wasn't going to argue the point. Between his gruffness and comment, he wasn't making a real good first impression on me.

"Hmm. Well, would you like to meet with me to discuss the job?" I asked with some misgivings. I'd have to trust the judgment of others for the moment.

"Sure. I'm between jobs right now, and I could use the work."

"How about meeting me at the Golden Dragon in Chinatown and we'll have lunch," I suggested. "My treat. It's deductible."

"Deductible. All business, huh? Yeah, I'll meet you. What time?"

"Meet me at one-thirty," I replied. "It won't be so crowded that time of day."

"How will I know you?" he asked. "Will you look like an operative?" he asked sarcastically. He was beginning to tick me off, and I hadn't even met him yet.

"I'm fairly short with dark brown hair and blue eyes. I'll be wearing Levi's and a blue shirt," I replied, choosing not to respond to his crack.

"Okay, see you at one-thirty," he said as he hung up.

After I set the phone down I thought about our conversation. His tone of voice had sounded testy right from the beginning. My fault, I relented. After all, it was seven o'clock in the morning. I'd probably awakened him. Still, I wasn't too sure about him at all. He sounded so…I don't know, I just wasn't sure about him. I'd have to play it by ear.

I finally got myself in gear and put on my Levi's and blue shirt. After a quick breakfast consisting of toast and a glass of milk, I grabbed my briefcase and headed for the door. I'd always wanted a briefcase. It made me feel important and businesslike, although I'd never tell anyone that. I suppose there was something psychological about it. My mother sent me the briefcase for my birthday. Maybe she was really getting into the swing of things.

I drove to the office, started the coffee and sat down to go over some notes on a case I was just closing. I got up and sharpened my pencil, poured my first cup of coffee for the day and was sitting down when the phone rang.

"Webster Detective Agency," I answered. "May I help you?"

"Yes. This is Mrs. Jessica Cushing. I'd like to make an appointment with Mr. Webster for this afternoon, if that would be convenient."

I didn't correct her reference to *Mr.* Webster. Some people backed off when they found out I was a woman, and I had better luck keeping them as clients if they met me first and found that I knew what I was doing.

"Just a moment while I check the appointment book," I said. I paused for effect and looked out the front window, then said, "I see there's an opening at four o'clock this afternoon. How would that be?"

"That would be fine," she replied.

"May I ask what this is in reference to, Mrs. Cushing?"

"My brother has disappeared, and I'm terribly worried about him. It's not like him. He's usually so dependable," she explained, beginning to sound tearful.

"Have you notified the police?" I inquired.

"I'd rather not, for personal reasons," she answered. "If that's a problem, I can call someone else."

"Not a problem," I responded quickly. "I just wanted to know what the status is at this time. Well then, I'll see you at four o'clock."

I hadn't handled a missing person case yet, and I wanted the experience. If I could find this kid, it would be great for business. I put my coffee cup down and chastised myself. This poor woman's brother was missing and all I could think of was how good it could be for my business. While I didn't want to be cold-hearted, I did want all the experience I could get.

I spent the rest of the morning taking care of minor details on a few of my open insurance cases. The type of details that could be taken care of with a quick phone call or short letter. I couldn't afford to hire both an operative and a secretary, so I doubled as my own secretary.

Around one o'clock I ran a brush through my hair and put on some fresh lipstick. I locked up the office, got into my car and headed for Chinatown to meet with Peter Goldberg.

The rave reviews this guy got from his friends, and the guy I talked to on the phone, sounded worlds apart. I was curious about him. I thought fleetingly that I'd probably have to look further before I hired anyone. However, I did want to be fair and at least talk to him.

CHAPTER 2

I arrived at the restaurant a few minutes early and the waitress seated me at a quaint little table for two. Quaint wasn't what I was looking for. I asked her to move me to another table, and she did. I ordered a mild cocktail, I wasn't much of a drinker, and pulled some papers out of my briefcase to review while I waited for Mr. Goldberg to arrive.

I glanced toward the entrance to the restaurant a few times. At one point I looked up and saw an elderly man of oriental persuasion; too old and definitely not a Goldberg. Another gentleman walked in, but he was with a date. I didn't think Mr. Goldberg would be coarse enough to bring a date with him, so I turned back to the papers I'd pulled out. I looked up again as a third man entered, a possible Goldberg, but he waved to someone across the room and walked over to join a group. Next I saw a very interesting man walk in, but he certainly wasn't a Goldberg. This one appeared to be one hundred percent Italian. I checked my watch and saw that it was exactly one-thirty.

I had just turned back to my papers when, out of the corner of my eye, I saw someone approach the table. I looked up to see a swarthy face looking at me.

"Excuse me," he said, "but are you Sandi Webster?"

"Yes, I am. Are you Mr. Goldberg?" I asked, surprised.

"That's me," he said, smiling.

"Please, have a seat," I said as I placed my papers back in the brief-case. "I'm sorry, but you took me by surprise. You certainly don't look like a Goldberg," I said, putting my size six foot into my size five mouth. "Sorry, no offense intended," I added quickly.

"None taken, but what should a Goldberg look like?" he asked dryly. "Never mind," he said, shrugging. "If we decide to work together, I'll tell you about the name sometime. And call me Pete."

I motioned for the waitress, but didn't have much luck getting her attention.

"Gina," Pete called as he motioned to her. She waved and smiled, then brought menus and left us to make our choices.

"Gina," I said. "That certainly doesn't sound very Chinese."

"You have a real thing about names, don't you," he said. "She's about a fourth generation Chinese-American, and her father is Italian."

"Oh. You know her family?" I inquired, trying to extricate my second foot from my mouth. I didn't feel like I was off to a very good start. His opinion of me was probably no better than my opinion of him. Maybe it was time to start fresh.

"Yeah, I know her dad, plus I used to work in Chinatown. Got to know a lot of people down here."

"I see," I said as I turned my attention back to the menu.

I ordered chicken chow mein, fried shrimp, pork fried rice and egg foo young. I knew I wouldn't be able to eat it all, but it sounded so good. Pete told her he'd have the usual. I guess he really had spent a lot of time in Chinatown. Or maybe with Gina.

"Let's get down to business," I said after Gina delivered our food. "Tell me a little about your background and why you think you'd make a good investigator."

After making kind of a snorting noise, Pete explained that he'd been with L.A.P.D. for eleven years, but had left when he'd injured his eye and couldn't pass a departmental eye test. The injury wasn't enough to interfere with his life, only his career with the department. They had strict rules.

He went on to describe what his duties with the department had entailed and told me about the experience he gained while on the job. He also had some impressive schooling in criminal law, psychology, police science and even some forensics. He'd been very busy during his off-duty hours. I'd taken some of the same basic courses, but he had continued where I left off. I made a point of not mentioning that he made better grades than I did. I didn't want to give him an edge. He didn't need to know *everything*, right?

On the personal side, his wife divorced him after three years of police service and two years of marriage. Prior to the eye injury, he'd been shot in the line of duty. It wasn't a serious wound, however, the wife decided she wasn't going to spend her life wondering if he would get through each day in one piece. She packed her bags and moved to New York where she met and married a nice, safe doctor. She and Pete didn't have any children, so after that he buried himself in his work and schooling.

"Now," he said, "how about filling me in on your background."

"Mine?" Somehow his question put me on the defensive.

"Sure. I'd like to know a little about my partner. Excuse me, my employer. I'd like to know what I'd be getting into, too."

"Fair enough," I replied. I filled him in on my schooling, leaving out the part about my grades, and told him what my objectives for the business were, and included some of my reasons for getting into the line of work I'd chosen. I mentioned that while working with the county I'd worked in the court system, so I was familiar with that too. Other than the fact that I was single, I barely touched my personal life. After all, as he pointed out, I was the boss, the prospective employer.

It all boiled down to the fact that his experience had been in the streets, and mine had been later in the process, in the courts.

I was impressed by his background and felt that if nothing else, at least he wasn't laughing at me. Additionally, I was finding his personality didn't seem to be quite as grating as my first impression indicated.

We continued to talk while we ate lunch, and to a small extent, it seemed that our personalities were beginning to click. My gut feeling was that we could probably work well together. I tended to go with my first impressions on most things, but this was one time I was having second thoughts. I was coming to the conclusion that he wasn't quite as gruff as he tried to sound.

I focused more on the man while we sat there, finding Pete to be around five feet, eleven inches or so, maybe 170 pounds and fairly muscular. I assumed that he probably worked out, and was proven right when he mentioned that he belonged to a local health club where he lifted weights and exercised. He had dark brown, almost black hair, and very dark eyes. He was thirty-six years old, had a dark, swarthy complexion, and was already beginning to gray at the temples. There was a small scar at the right corner of his mouth, which added character to his appearance, and his almost, but not quite too large nose had been broken at least once, I was sure. He looked like a man's man, not particularly handsome, but virile in appearance, almost rugged.

I had a sense that if I was ever in a pinch, he'd be the man to help me out.

"Okay," he said as we finished lunch. "What do you think? Can we work together partner?"

"I think so, partner," I replied. "I guess it really is just a matter of semantics, isn't it." It didn't matter what word you used. Maybe I was learning to relax a bit.

"Now you're catching on," he said.

"So! How would you like a job? Can you start right away?"

"I can start today," he said. "I need the money."

I hoped it was more than just the money. I needed someone I could count on to give the business his all.

I opened my purse and pulled out one of my business cards, handing it to him.

"Here's the address. Meet me there in about half an hour."

I picked up the check and we both pushed back our chairs and stood up. He reached across the table and we shook hands.

"See you at the office," he said as he turned to leave.

I paid the check, then strolled out to my car, thinking that I'd made a good choice, and I felt optimistic about finding an operative, or partner, so easily. I decided to let him sit in on my meeting with Mrs. Cushing to get him started. Besides, I could use his input since he probably handled missing persons cases during his tenure as a cop.

*   *   *

I took my time driving back to the office, relieved that I wouldn't be so rushed anymore. Things were booming, at least from my point of view. Some days were pretty hectic, and others were just plain nuts. Very few were quiet like they had been in the beginning, and like the day I met Peter Goldberg.

I remembered his entrance into the restaurant and wondered about the story behind his name, then checked my thoughts as I pulled into my parking space next to the agency. I saw an unfamiliar car parked in the next slot and assumed it was Pete's. As I got out my keys and walked toward the front door, I saw that I was correct. Pete was leaning against the door jam, waiting for me.

"You made good time," I said as I unlocked the door.

"I got impatient with traffic and took all the shortcuts I could. I don't like to waste time."

"Oh," I said. I wondered how that might affect his work.

We entered the office and I showed him around. I'd acquired a second-hand desk the week before, contemplating hiring someone, so I pointed it out to him.

"That's your desk", I said. "I use the coat closet as a supply cabinet. You should be able to find everything you need in there. Help yourself, and if you can't find something, let me know. By the way, are you licensed yet? If not, we need to get busy on that."

"Don't worry, I'm licensed," he said as he glanced from my new desk to his used one. "I planned to get into this line of work anyway. Working for you is just getting me into it earlier than I planned."

He walked over to his desk and studied the chair.

"You got anything bigger than this?" he asked.

I smiled when he planted his large frame on the very old, small secretarial chair.

"Sorry, but it's only temporary. I had to order another chair and it hasn't come in yet."

"Right," he said uncertainly as the chair wobbled.

"I think we'd better switch chairs until the new one comes in. I don't need any workers' comp claims this early in our relationship," I said as I pushed my chair over to his desk.

I watched him as I returned to my own desk. After a moment of looking around, he stood up and sauntered over to the supply closet. He rummaged around and returned with pens, pencils, scratch pad, a stapler and other essentials.

"You're a very orderly woman, aren't you?" he asked.

"Huh?" I had just opened a file and looked up at him.

"Orderly. You're orderly, aren't you. Everything is neatly stacked and in its own special place in the closet," he said, somewhat condescendingly.

"I guess I am. Does it matter?" I asked. Maybe this guy would get on my nerves after all.

"Not to me, but I'd better warn you that I'm just the opposite."

"No problem," I said. "As long as the work gets done, that's all I really care about. And, speaking of work, I have a client coming in at four o'clock regarding her missing brother." I glanced at my watch. It was nearly four. "I thought you could help me with this one. It'll be my first missing person case. I'd be open to any questions or suggestions you might think of while she's here. You're probably more experienced in that area than I am. I'll learn as we go along."

"You're all right," he commented, looking thoughtful.

"Why do you say that?" I asked. It almost, but not quite, sounded like a compliment.

"Maybe you're not quite as pushy as I thought. You seem to be open-minded. I've worked with plenty of women…well, never mind. Things just might work out between us."

I laughed politely, not quite sure from moment to moment how to take Pete. Only time would help me out. I shrugged, mentally.

"It's three forty-five now," I said, "so she should be here any minute. Oh, by the way, her name is Jessica Cushing."

"Jessica Cushing? No kidding," he said, once again looking thoughtful.

"You sound like you know who she is. Is there something I should know about her?"

"Yeah. She's the wife of the biggest import man in town," he replied.

"So?"

"So this. His import business is the proverbial cover. He deals in drugs and illegal guns. No one can get the goods on him though, and many have tried. I can't believe you've never heard of him."

"Oh, *that* Cushing," I said knowingly. "I just didn't make the connection." In all honesty, I'd never heard of anyone named Cushing until Mrs. Cushing called earlier that morning, but I wasn't about to let Pete know that. "I wonder why she called me instead of one of the big agencies."

"Ask her," he suggested sarcastically.

"*You* ask her," I replied. "I wouldn't want to look a gift horse in the mouth. At least I know she'll be able to pay her bill."

"You've had trouble collecting payments?" he asked.

"Actually, it's the type of payment I have a problem with sometimes. The desk you're sitting at? That was partial payment from a man who owns a used furniture store. He told me to come over and take my pick,

I could have anything I wanted. Since I'd already decided I was going to have to hire someone, that's what I picked. The couch and end tables in the lobby were another payment, delivered yesterday afternoon."

"What lobby?" he asked. "There's no lobby in this place. It's a one-room office."

"I prefer to think of the front of the office as the lobby. I've got to use my imagination until I can afford to move to a bigger place and get a secretary. By the way, can you type?"

"Hunt and peck method," he replied, shaking his head.

"Good enough for now. I'll help, but you can do most of your own typing."

"What am I going to type?" he asked.

"Letters to the clients," I explained. "As far as the files, you can fill those out by hand, as long as they're legible."

He looked at me, then the used typewriter (I needed to move into the new century and buy a computer), and finally at the lobby. He was shaking his head again.

Before I could say anything else, the front door opened and a tall red-head with unbelievably long, shapely legs that put me to shame, walked in. Her clothing and jewelry indicated she had expensive taste and money to burn. Her long red hair curled around her shoulders and framed a beautiful, perfectly oval face.

Too made-up from my point of view, I thought as I glanced at Pete and saw that he was practically drooling.

I turned back to her and noticed very long eyelashes, probably false, and the greenest eyes I'd ever seen. No doubt she had on colored contact lenses. I was sure the perfect figure had to have had some help to look that way.

"Mr. Webster?" she asked, looking at Pete.

"I'm Sandi Webster," I said, diverting her attention away from Pete. "Sorry, but there is no Mr. Webster. Please have a seat," I said, trying tc be congenial while pulling in my claws. It certainly wouldn't pay to be nasty, and I realized how petty I was being by picking her apart. So what if she was one of the most gorgeous women I'd ever seen. Big deal! I wasn't exactly chopped liver.

"This is Pete Goldberg," I said, introducing her to Pete. He stood up and they shook hands, Pete appearing reluctant to let go.

"How do you do," she said politely. He mumbled something unintelligible.

"Now," I began, "you said over the phone that your brother is missing. How long has he been gone, and why are you so concerned?"

"I, uh…" She looked at me a little dubiously.

Becoming all business, I leaned back slightly and tried to act like I'd handled a hundred missing person cases.

"Please," I prompted. "We can help you, but you're going to have to answer some questions."

She slumped over slightly and sighed.

"My brother, Robert, hasn't been seen in a week. He's a college student and has been living with my husband and I for the past year. Last Saturday night he went to a party, and no one has seen or heard from him since. When he didn't come home that first night, I didn't worry too much, although it was out of character for him not to at least check in with me. I thought maybe he'd had a little too much to drink and had spent the night with a friend. You know how boys can be.

"By Monday I was getting pretty worried," she continued, "so I called and left a message at the school for him to call me. When he didn't call, I began to feel panicky. I called the school again and they checked and told me he hadn't shown up for any of his classes."

"So you feel something may have happened to him on Saturday night?" I asked.

"Yes," she answered. "I've checked with as many of his friends as I know, but no one has seen him since the party. In fact, they're worried too. They've been keeping in touch with me in case I hear from him."

"What does your husband think about all of this?" I prodded.

"Oh, he thinks Robert's probably just out fooling around, but I know that's not it. Robert is as level-headed as they come, and I know I should have heard from him by now. He's just not the type to wander off and not check in."

"Do you suspect some sort of foul play?" Pete asked. I noticed his eyes were locked in on her knees. What a weasel.

She visibly paled at his question. "If he'd been in an accident or something I would have heard from the police. I've racked my brain and I can't think of one tangible reason why he wouldn't have contacted me during this past week. He's rather shy, and he seems to depend on me a lot."

Pete and I asked her several questions regarding Robert's personal habits, friends, girlfriends and hangouts. We even got into his eating and sleeping habits. You never know what might help. She looked bewildered at times, but answered all of our questions, not hesitating as she had earlier.

"I think that's about all we need for the time being," Pete said as we wrapped things up. "If he turns up or you hear anything, let us know right away. Otherwise, we'll keep you informed of anything we find out."

He was propped against my desk, but stood up and strolled to his own desk where he began writing furiously, glancing up at Mrs. Cushing every so often. I'd just met this guy, but somehow I felt an odd sense of jealousy. Ridiculous! It was just the type of thing my mother would like to hear. She'd have a field day with what I was feeling. I'd have to make a point of not telling her more than the essentials about Pete.

I, being all business, discussed our fees with Mrs. Cushing, then tried to reassure her about her brother and repeated we would keep in touch. She thanked me and left, with Pete hustling over to hold the door open for her.

"Did you get the impression she wasn't being completely straight with us?" he asked, looking thoughtful. "It seemed like she was holding something back."

"Yes. In fact," I commented, "when I asked her if he'd done anything unusual lately, I thought she was going to say something but changed her mind. I wondered about that at the time."

Pete didn't say anything else as he turned back to his notes. I thought about how he'd busted his buns to race, nonchalantly of course, to the door to hold it open for Mrs. Cushing when she left. I thought to myself what an easy mark he was for a woman with good legs. *My* legs weren't all that bad for a short person. In fact, I'd always thought that for a vertically challenged woman I had pretty long, shapely legs. I never thought about what a contradiction that was. Of course, I was wearing Levi's and a shirt, not a short, slinky dress. Well, to be fair, I guess her dress wasn't really slinky, just very short.

I reprimanded myself for my thoughts. This was so unlike me that I felt ashamed. I reminded myself, once again, that I'd only met Pete a few short hours ago, and after all, Mrs. Cushing did seem like a pretty nice person, so why let it bother me.

The phone rang and I picked up the receiver. I heard the sound of a man gasping for breath. When I realized it was just a poor attempt at heavy breathing, some pervert, I turned to Pete.

"It's for you," I said.

"Me? No one knows I'm here," he said as he took the receiver.

I turned back to my work. We women have our ways, I thought.

CHAPTER 3

"I can see what kind of relationship this is going to be," Pete said as he hung up the phone, a look of disgust on his face.

No sense of humor at all, I thought to myself.

"I'll make a few calls to Robert's friends and see what I can find out," he said.

"Okay. I'm going to take a run out to the college to see what I can find out up there." I opened the bottom drawer of my desk and withdrew my purse. I needed to look into buying a backpack. It would be so much more convenient.

Taking a key off my key ring, I tossed him a duplicate of the office key.

"By the way, you'll probably need this. It fits both the regular lock and the deadbolt," I explained.

"Thanks," he said. He slipped it into his pocket.

"See you later," I called, walking out the door.

On my way to the college I tried to give Pete some serious thought. I'd only met him a few hours ago I reminded myself, so why did I feel a touch of jealousy at the attention he paid Jessica Cushing? I wanted his attention, but I wasn't sure why. I suppose it might be an initial physical attraction, although that feeling sure didn't seem to be returned. In the past few hours all we'd done was spar with each other. Just as well, it wasn't a good idea to get involved with someone you worked with anyway. I tried that once before with disastrous results. It's uncomfortable to face someone every day at work when you've broken things off. With some difficulty, I put the whole thing out of my mind and tried to concentrate on the task ahead of me.

     *   *   *

I arrived at the college campus and headed straight to the Administrative Offices. I introduced myself and explained that I wanted to look at Robert Cushing's school records because he was missing and his family had hired me to find him, and I hoped to learn something about him from the records.

"Absolutely not!" declared the secretary, tightening her lips. "You'll have to come back with some very official paperwork. Better yet, come back with a police officer."

"But…", I started.

"I said, no way, Jose."

I looked at her in surprise. Maybe this was one Pete should have handled. I'd have to start learning more about being sneaky, maybe watch more episodes of *The Rockford Files*.

I started to say something nasty to her, but before I could open my mouth I heard a familiar voice coming from behind me.

"I think we can show Miss Webster the file, Frances." I turned to find one of my old teachers, Professor Welch, standing in the doorway.

"Professor,…" Frances began hesitantly.

"I said to show her the file," he repeated, using the authoritative voice I recalled from class. "You can hold me responsible if she crosses any policy lines."

"I most certainly will," she said as she grudgingly handed me the file she'd pulled from one of the file drawers. I had to pull to extricate the folder from her hands.

"Thank you," I said a little too sweetly.

I turned to Professor Welch. Somehow it was reassuring to see a familiar figure standing next to me. He taught night school at the community college as well as his regular college classes. He was in his late sixties, stood ramrod straight, still had a thick head of hair and didn't look anywhere near his age. He also had an attitude. People automatically tried to stay on his good side.

"Follow me to the conference room," he directed. I followed without comment.

"I've been hearing some good things about your agency," he said. "Congratulations! It looks like all your hard work paid off. I knew you had a feel for this type of work."

I was surprised not only at his compliment, but at the fact he'd heard anything.

"Thank you, Professor Welch. It's good to know word is getting around. I appreciate you letting me know."

"What's going on with this Cushing fellow?" he asked.

"His sister hired me to find him," I replied. "He disappeared about a week ago. Other than that, I don't feel free to say anything else right now."

"Splendid! Splendid! You were actually listening in class when we discussed client confidentiality. You'll go far in your chosen field if you remember that part of the course. One of the easiest ways to lose a client is to talk too much. Well, you go ahead and look through that file," he said as he turned and stood looking out the window.

I discovered from the records that Robert was an outstanding student, he might even make the Dean's List. He was taking a few general courses, but was majoring in archaeology. He was studying work similar to mine in a way, only he'd be looking into the past, and I was working on the present, I mused.

I made a list of his professors' names, intending to call and make appointments to meet with each of them. Anything I could find out might help in the search for Robert.

I'd found out all I could, so I thanked Professor Welch for his help and returned the file to him. He could deal with Frances, because I had no intention of stopping by her desk on my way out.

Other than the fact that Robert was a good student, his records hadn't told me much. I headed back to the office with the hope that Pete had found something out. One could always hope.

He was just hanging up the phone as I walked in.

"I spoke to Cushing's closest friend, Ray Peterson," he said.

"Anything interesting come up?" I asked. I had stopped at a local store on my way back to the office and picked up the backpack. I started transferring things from my purse to the backpack while we talked.

"According to him, Robert's been acting strange for the past couple of weeks. He said he's been jumpy, like he was afraid of something. He said Robert started acting that way shortly before a dig they've been working on. Apparently he and Robert are taking the same archaeology class. That's how they met and became friends."

"A dig? What's that?" I asked.

"You know, an archaeological dig. They have spots they work on to get practical experience. They're searching for artifacts," he explained. Archaeology wasn't something I'd ever taken a real interest in.

"Oh, *that* kind of dig. I knew that," I bluffed.

"Like I was saying, these guys have a few classes together," he continued. "They ended up spending a lot of time together and got to know each other fairly well."

"Uh huh. Well, I've got notes here from his school records. He's an excellent student according to the records."

"Yeah. Anyway, he said that when they were driving back from the dig on Saturday, Robert seemed quieter than usual. That's when it dawned on him that Cushing's behavior had been different for awhile. They went to the party that same night, and Ray says Robert was withdrawn from everyone. At some point during the evening, Robert got into an argument with a guy named Frank Samuels. Ray said it had something to do with an envelope Robert grabbed out of Samuel's hand. That was highly unusual for Robert. He normally got along with everyone. I guess Samuels was pretty angry and said he'd get even with Robert. At the time, Ray wondered why Robert had even bothered to go to the party."

"He didn't have any ideas about what was wrong or why Robert took the envelope?" I asked.

"Nope. Not a clue. He asked him about it, but Robert beat around the bush and wouldn't give him a straight answer. In fact, he wouldn't give him a straight answer about anything."

"I wonder why Mrs. Cushing didn't mention Robert's change in attitude," I said. "You know she must have noticed. You and I both thought she was holding something back when she was here.

"By the way," I went on, "if Robert is Jessica's brother, then why is his last name Cushing. I mean, it should be whatever her maiden name was, right? Something doesn't seem right here."

"According to Ray, Robert is actually Mr. Cushing's brother," Pete explained. "John and Robert Cushing don't get along very well, but Robert and Jessica have developed a close relationship. He's like the little brother she never had, I guess. Anyway, she refers to him as her brother and doesn't make a distinction."

"My, you've done your homework, haven't you," I said. "But back to my original question, I still wonder why Mrs. Cushing didn't mention his change in attitude. She must have noticed it."

Pete shrugged his shoulders. "We'll have to see what we can come up with on our own. Obviously there's something she doesn't want to talk about."

"Did Peterson have anything else to say?" I asked.

"He said around nine-thirty, while they were at the party, Robert said he had to go somewhere. He made a phone call and left, telling Ray he had to tend to some business. Ray also confirmed what Mrs. Cushing said, that no one has seen him since."

"Were you able to get in touch with Samuels? I'd like to know what that was all about."

"No. Ray said he hasn't seen Samuels since the party. I guess he doesn't really know him that well from what he said, although he did mention Samuels seemed different than normal too."

"I think we really need to reach Samuels and find out what's going on. If they've both been acting different, then there could be a connection. We need to look into every lead we can."

"I'll keep trying to find him," Pete replied.

"Well," I said, changing the subject, "it's almost five o'clock. We might as well close up and go home."

"Eight to five in a detective agency? That's unusual," Pete commented. "I would have thought you'd work late around here."

"No eight to five here, but I'm hungry and there's not much else we can do tonight. Besides, I've got an early date," I informed him. Now why had I said that? I didn't have an early date, or any date at all. I hadn't had a date in quite a long time. I'd been so involved in the business that I hadn't even thought about dating. At least not very much.

"Okay. I have a few more calls to make, so I'll lock up when I leave," he said as he reached for the phone.

I said good-night and left. Why was I so anxious to get his attention? What on earth was wrong with me? I had to keep reminding myself that I'd just met him. You don't fall for a man in a matter of hours, it just doesn't happen that way. There were so many contradictions about him that maybe I was just fascinated by his personality. Granted, he had some sort of strange charisma, but this was just silly. I had to put him out of my mind. I'd lose myself in the business. I was pretty good at doing that.

I drove home and freshened up a little, deciding I didn't feel like cooking. I opted to drive across town to a coffee shop and let myself be waited on for the second time that day. Naturally, I took what few notes I'd accumulated on Robert Cushing with me to study while I ate. We sure didn't have very much to go on. There was a lot of work ahead of us on this one.

After being seated I looked around the coffee shop. It was typical of about thirty years ago. Brown carpeting, orange vinyl booths and chairs, and bamboo shades on the windows, just like every other old diner in town. There was a juke box playing music. I almost felt like I'd stepped back in time.

I gave my order for a hot roast beef sandwich with mashed potatoes and gravy to the waitress, pulled out my notes and began going over them. I added the information that Pete had given me to my notes.

I was deep in thought, trying to determine without benefit of enough information what could have happened to cause Robert's change in behavior, and ultimately his disappearance, when I suddenly got a strong and instinctive feeling that I was being watched. I could feel eyes boring into the back of my head.

I casually turned around, saw where the stare was coming from and wanted to crawl under the table. I could feel my stupid, tell-tale face turning red. Of all the places in L.A., why had he chosen this diner!

"So, Sandi, is this the type of place where your typical date takes you?" Pete asked as he slid into the booth. "This guy obviously has lousy taste or not much money. You don't mind if I join you for a few minutes, do you?" It was a rhetorical question, and he was grinning from ear to ear.

"Hi, Pete. Won't you join me?" I asked needlessly. "My date had to leave town suddenly, a family emergency, and I didn't feel like cooking for myself." The lie sounded hollow, even to my ears. Pete was at least tactful enough not to comment on it, although the smile did broaden even more. He picked up a menu and looked it over, trying to decide what sounded good to him.

The waitress delivered my food and turned to Pete.

"Hi there, Pete. Where've you been keeping yourself lately?" she asked. The expression on her face said she wanted to jump his bones right there in the middle of the diner. How tacky. Honest, but tacky.

"What's up, Gracie?" He smiled again. "Good to see you."

They talked for a minute and he gave her his order. Looking over her shoulder, she really swished those hips as she walked away. Pete didn't miss a swish either. You would have thought he was at a tennis match judging by the way his head was moving around.

"Oh, brother!" I mumbled.

"I like the ladies, okay?" He laughed. "I'm just fortunate enough to have them like me back. Works out nice that way."

"Yeah, right."

"Aw, come on. Don't try to tell me you don't watch a good-looking man when he walks by," he said, winking at me. "I've seen women watching men from behind when they think no one is looking."

"Not with the lecherous look I saw on your face," I retorted.

"Ah, so you do take your work home with you," he said, changing the subject, as he slid my notes over to his side of the table. He began perusing the notes I'd been making. "Come to any conclusions, Sherlock?"

"No, I'm just trying to figure out at what precise moment Robert began acting different. Do you think it could have possibly had anything to do with the dig? I can't imagine what could happen at a place like that. But, of course, Ray Peterson said he was acting different before the dig."

"I don't know, it could be any number of things. They'd been working in that particular area for several weeks before the day Ray realized there was a difference in Robert. We're just going to have to do some digging, no pun intended, and see what we come up with," Pete replied.

"Not to change the subject," I said, "but from the way you talked I thought you were stone broke. How can you afford to eat out?"

"Actually, it's none of your business," he replied. "However, I've got a few bucks stashed away. I just don't want to touch it right now, but I do have to eat, and I didn't feel like cooking either. I'm glad your 'date' had to go out of town." He just had to throw that in. "I'm glad to have company while I eat."

"You don't need me. I'm sure Gracie or some other skirt would be more than happy to eat with you."

"Touché," he said.

Talk about timing. Just then a brunette in a skin-tight mini-skirt with a tight off-the-shoulder sweater and matching four-inch heels walked by and said, sensuously of course, "Hi, Petey. Haven't seen you around lately. Give me a call sometime. I've missed you," she gushed. Apparently, I was invisible at that moment in time, not that it mattered to anyone..

"Sure," he replied, trying to keep a straight face.

She walked on by and he turned to me with large, dark and innocent eyes.

"I used to work this beat, too."

"Tell me where you *haven't* worked and I'll start hanging out there," I said irritably. I didn't want to start running into him all the time.

I was feeling a bit testy, but decided it was just as well. I was realizing what a womanizer this guy was. That helped to stifle the feelings gnawing at my insides. Once I came to that conclusion, I relaxed and found I could almost enjoy his company.

"Petey? Petey?!" I started to laugh. "Now that's really cute. Hi, Petey," I said, wiggling my fingers at him.

"Whatever," he replied, not sounding in the least perturbed.

Gracie finally brought Pete's dinner, and as we ate we got back to the business at hand, Robert Cushing. We had a long way to go with this case, and very little information to go on.

"I think we should talk to all of the people who worked at the dig," he said. "And we should probably talk to them as soon as possible."

"You're probably right. I think I'll start with the professor in charge of the dig, and we can work from there," I said.

"While you're talking to the professor, I'll start contacting the rest of the students involved," Pete suggested.

"By the way," he added, "after you left we got another call. Some guy says he's being followed. He wants to find out by who and why. He's coming in tomorrow morning at ten o'clock."

"Now I feel like real gumshoe," I said. "A missing person case and a man being followed, all in one day."

"'Gumshoe?'" Pete echoed in disbelief. "I haven't heard that word in years. Not since the last time I watched an old movie on TV."

"*The Thin Man*," I said dreamily. "I just loved Nick and Nora Charles. Especially Nora. She was so witty."

"You're a little weird, you know?"

I sighed, ignoring him.

"I grew up loving mysteries. I watched old movies and read a lot of books. When I was a kid I read all the *Nancy Drew* and *Hardy Boy* books. I wanted to be a part of their mysteries. I've always wanted to solve a good mystery. So here I am, Sandi Webster, Private Detective. I'm sure you wouldn't understand, but it's what I've always wanted to do."

"Oh, I understand all right," he chuckled. "*Dragnet* was one of my favorites. I used to watch the reruns faithfully."

We finished eating and as I left the coffee shop I looked back in time to see him stop and talk to good ol' Gracie. She could have him. I no longer felt even a twinge of jealousy. The feelings I'd gone through that day were foreign to me. I wasn't normally a jealous person. Oh well, we all have off days. I guess this was one of mine. I hadn't dated in a long time, which was my own fault. I'd been too tied up in getting the business off the ground. Enter one virile man, and my knees got weak. Ridiculous!

CHAPTER 4

The next day, Thursday, I arrived at the office earlier than usual and was surprised to find Pete already there and hard at work.

"Morning," he grumbled as I put my backpack away. "Coffee's already going."

"Okay, how long have you been here?" I asked.

He picked up his mug, walked over and poured himself some coffee.

"Since around six o'clock. I do my best work early in the morning. It's quiet, and it helps wake me up."

"You're not exactly a morning person, are you," I commented.

"What gave me away, my mood?" he asked. "Anyway, I hope you don't mind, but I pulled some of your files to familiarize myself with your work and open cases."

"Good," I replied. "I'm glad you took the initiative. How'd you find the key to the filing cabinet?" I thought I had it well hidden.

He poured a second cup of coffee and handed it to me.

"You're going to have to be more imaginative about your hiding places. Putting the key under your potted plant wasn't too hard to figure out," he scolded.

"Thanks," I said as I took the coffee mug. I ignored his potted plant comment, already thinking of where else to hide the key.

"I thought that after our ten o'clock appointment we could get back to Cushing," I suggested. "I'll talk to the professor and get a list of everyone who was at the dig while you finish talking to his buddies."

"I talked to all of them except Samuels last night after I left the coffee shop," he informed me. "He's supposedly out of town, so I'll talk to him when he gets back."

I was surprised. I assumed he'd spent his evening with either the waitress or the brunette in the tight skirt.

The phone rang and Pete answered it. "That was Robert's friend, Ray Peterson," he said after talking for a few minutes and hanging up. "He said he remembered something that he thought we ought to know.

"He didn't think about it at the time, but the last day they were at the dig Robert disappeared for about twenty minutes. When he came back, he looked pale. Ray asked him what was wrong, and Robert said he'd probably had too much sun. Ray's been thinking about it since we talked yesterday, and he's come to the conclusion that it had nothing to do with the heat. He said that first of all it wasn't all that hot, and secondly Robert seemed more nervous than sick. He thinks that something happened to Robert during that twenty minutes. He forgot about it until I got him thinking with all my questions."

"That's interesting. I wonder if anyone saw where he went," I said.

"Ray had no idea, but he said he'd ask around to see if anyone else knew anything. One of us will need to check that out too."

We spent the next couple of hours working on files. I went over some of the current cases with Pete and showed him a couple of the more interesting closed cases. He made some comments and gave me a few tips on investigation, the kind of tips you only learn through experience, but overall he sounded pleased with what I had done. I felt proud of myself when I considered how much more experience he had with the police department than I'd had during my brief career. It didn't really matter what he thought, but it was nice to get a pat on the back from time to time.

Unfortunately, he pulled his chair over to my desk, and I felt that animal magnetism again. I began to understand why women seemed to fall all over him. It was something that oozed out of him, not something he did intentionally, and not something that you could put your finger on. I stood up and walked over to get another cup of coffee, and to pull myself together. I thought I'd resolved everything the night before.

"Okay, idiot," I thought to myself. "This is ridiculous. You can't get involved with someone you work with. Besides, he's not interested in you and he's not your type. He may be a man's man, but he's also a woman's man. One complication you don't need in your life right now is a guy who seems to get around as much as he does. On top of which, you've only known him for about a day. Besides, mom would never let up if she knew you were interested in someone." It always helped to think of Mother.

I remembered my thoughts from the night before about dating. That's probably why I was going through the confusing emotions. It was obvious to me that I needed to start dating again. I returned to my desk with my feelings well under control.

Before I knew it, it was ten o'clock and Mr. Stanley Hawks fell through the door, literally, landing on his knees.

"Sorry," he apologized. "I must have tripped on something." He looked at the floor like he was hoping he could find something to blame it on.

"Are you okay?" I asked.

"Uh huh," he answered.

Pete got a grip on his arm and helped him up, showing him to a chair.

"I'm Stanley Hawks," he introduced himself. "I called yesterday about a man following me." He sounded like he was distracted, and he kept brushing the knee of his pants with his hand. I noticed he had a slight tic in his right eye.

Stanley was a relatively small man, probably in his mid- to late forties. He was thin and small-boned, slightly bent over, had dull brown hair and he was beginning to go bald. He was light-complected, giving the appearance of someone who seldom saw the sun. With his horn-rimmed glasses he looked like a book-worm. The thick lenses in his glasses made his hazel eyes enormous. I noticed there was a small tear in his trousers, probably from the fall he'd just taken.

"We've been expecting you," I said. "Please make yourself comfortable and tell us why you think you're being followed."

"I don't *think* I'm being followed, I *am* being followed. And I want you to find out the who and why of it." His eye twitched a little harder.

"Mr. Hawks, you'll have to be more explicit so we can help you. Tell us what's been going on," Pete prodded.

"Yes, yes. I'm sorry. This whole thing has unnerved me," Mr. Hawks replied.

He proceeded to explain the situation to Pete and me.

"It started about a week ago. I was leaving for work one morning, and totally by chance I noticed an automobile pull away from the curb at precisely the same time I pulled out of the parking lot.

"I'd forgotten my lunch, and since I was running early that morning, I decided to drive back and get it. As I pulled into the parking lot of my apartment building, I saw that same automobile pull up to the curb. I still didn't give it much thought until I tripped coming out of my apartment door and heard him laugh. At least you didn't laugh at me. Anyway, that's when I really began to take notice of him. When he laughed at me." His expression was somewhat downcast.

"He followed me to work that morning, and he followed me home that evening. He's followed me to the store, and if I go for a walk he even follows me on foot. He's always there, no matter where I go." As he spoke, the pitch of his voice got higher. His twitch was more pronounced, too.

"I'm so worked up that I'm not getting any sleep, and I'm exhausted." True, there were dark circles under his eyes.

There was a short lull in the conversation, so I asked, "May I get you a cup of coffee, Mr. Hawks?"

"I usually drink herbal tea," he said, "but yes, coffee would be nice, thank you. Black, please."

"What do you do for a living, Stanley?" Pete asked as I poured Mr. Hawks' coffee.

"I write," he replied.

"And what do you write?" Pete questioned him further.

"Verses for greeting cards."

"It certainly doesn't sound like this might have anything to do with your job," I commented, handing him the cup of coffee.

He took a sip and grimaced.

"Hot," he said. "You'd be surprised how competitive the greeting card business is," he added while blowing on the coffee.

"Be that as it may, can you think of any reason why someone would be interested in your comings and goings?" I asked.

"No. Let me be frank about myself. I'm a quiet man and I lead a quiet life. I don't bother anyone, and until now no one ever bothered me. My idea of entertainment is to read a good book. I don't have many friends and I keep to myself. So unless the librarian has started sending out the Book Police because of overdue books, I can't think of a single thing that would call attention to me."

Book Police? I loved it. I saw that he was about to spill his coffee so I reached over to steady his hand.

"What does this man look like?" I asked. "Would you please describe him for me?"

"If you look out the front window, you may see him for yourself," he whispered. "He was right behind me when I parked out in front. He's in a brown Chevrolet, the one with the dent in the right front fender."

Pete and I jumped up in unison and ran to the window. Once we got there we tried to look casual. I glanced out the window, but I didn't see a brown Chevy.

I watched as Pete stepped out of the door. Still trying to appear nonchalant, he stretched his arms and shoulders and rotated his head like he was trying to work out a kink. As he did this, he looked to his right and left. He turned to his left and strolled slowly down the street. I lost sight of him. I returned to Mr. Hawks.

"He must have seen something," I informed him. "He walked off down the street. You were about to tell me what this man looks like," I prompted.

"Ah, yes. He's about six feet tall, with dark hair and dark eyes. He's got a thin build, acne scars on his face, and I noticed he has a perpetually grim look on his face, even when he laughs. It's that face that gets to me, that expression. I guess he kind of scares me." Hawks' twitch was going ninety miles an hour by that time.

"He's got very thick eyebrows that nearly meet in the center of his brow line, so it's almost like one long eyebrow. Also, his eyes seem somewhat sunken and he's got dark circles under them."

I didn't move quickly enough, and he finally managed to spill some coffee on his trousers.

"Oh!" he started.

I jumped up and found a paper towel to mop up with.

"Please continue," I said as he mopped up his slacks. He seemed to be smearing the coffee instead of cleaning it up. "Does the man have any distinguishing marks, scars or anything other than the acne scars?"

"Only the eyes and eyebrows. They make him look quite sinister."

I began to wonder what had happened to Pete, but just about that time he walked in the door.

"He was out there," Pete said, "just like Stanley said he'd be, but when he saw me coming, he took off. I got his license number though."

We talked to Mr. Hawks for a few more minutes. I took some personal information that we'd need on him, and he left, tripping again on his way out the door. I heard him mutter to himself, something about being a clumsy oaf.

"Poor little guy," I laughed after he was gone.

"Yeah. A real loser," Pete said.

"Not a loser, just a klutz, and he was nice."

"From what I could see of the guy in the Chevy, he looked like a hood."

"Not the boy-next-door type, huh?"

Pete laughed sarcastically. "Hardly. His face looked vaguely familiar though. I've seen him somewhere." He looked thoughtful, rubbing his chin, a frown line crossing his brow.

"Okay," I said as I started a file on Stanley Hawks, "you follow up on the familiar face, and in the meantime I'll go talk to Cushing's archaeology professor. Let's get both of these cases rolling."

"Yeah," Pete said absently, still frowning.

I picked up the phone and dialed the number of the college Administrative Offices, hoping I wouldn't have to talk to Frances. Unfortunately, she answered the phone.

"Administrative Office," she said.

"This is Sandi Webster," I said. "Would it be possible to speak to Professor Smythe?"

"Absolutely not," she said, coldly. "He's in class at the moment."

"May I leave him a message?" I asked, my voice at least as cold as hers.

"Yes," she said, managing to sigh loudly.

We were both very formal, and I left a message for Professor Smythe to call me back. Somehow the name Smythe fit my idea of an archaeologist.

After I hung up I made a couple of calls regarding other cases, taking notes while I talked, which I placed in the files. I had learned early on that most of my detective work was boring, plain and simple. Only once in awhile did I find anything of real substance and interest.

"See you later," Pete said, startling me as he jumped up and ran out the door.

"Wait! Where…" But I was too late. He was already gone. I had a feeling that maybe he'd remembered where he'd seen our mysterious stranger with the one long eyebrow.

The telephone rang, and after I greeted the caller I heard a deep male voice say, "This is Richard Smythe. I have a message to call a Ms. Webster. Is she in?"

"This is Sandi Webster. Professor, thank you for returning my call. I'm investigating the disappearance of one of your students—a Robert Cushing—and I'd like to make an appointment with you to discuss the matter. Could you possibly make time for me this afternoon? Say between classes or something?"

"As a matter of fact, I'll be free all afternoon," he replied. "My last two classes have been canceled for today. Can you meet me here at the college at one o'clock?"

"That would be fine. Where should I meet you?" I asked.

Professor Smythe gave me a room number and directions on how to find it. I thanked him and hung up.

I tried to call Jessica Cushing but all I got was an answering machine. I left a message asking her to call me at the office after four o'clock. I wanted to pin her down about Robert's recent change in behavior.

By that time it was noon, so I ran a brush through my hair, put on fresh lipstick and drove to the nearest hamburger stand. I ate my hamburger as I drove out to the campus. I'd be lost without fast foods. Sometimes dinner was the only meal I had a chance to take my time with.

By the time I arrived at the campus and located the classroom it was ten to one. The door was closed and locked, so I leaned against the wall and waited. By one-fifteen I was irritated, just about ready to go in search of the good professor. Oh well, I'd give it a few more minutes. I honestly didn't want to run into Frances.

At one-twenty I heard running footsteps behind me. In Los Angeles, the sound of running footsteps coming up behind you can mean trouble, so I whipped around ready to defend myself. All I saw was one of the school jocks flying towards me. To my surprise he stopped in front of me.

"Hello," he said, bending with his hands on his knees and taking a couple of deep breaths. "Are you Ms. Webster?"

"Yes," I replied hesitantly, a little disappointed. The professor had obviously sent this guy to tell me he couldn't make our meeting.

"Sorry I'm late," he apologized as he took another deep breath.

"Professor Smythe?" Naw, couldn't be.

"At your service," he replied as he unlocked the classroom door and held it open for me.

I was indeed surprised. My first impression had been of a very young man in jogging shorts and shirt, probably one of the football players. After I had a closer look at him though, I realized that he was in his late thirties with blonde hair and sparkling blue eyes. He was deeply tanned and appeared to be in great physical shape. I had to look up to meet his six foot two inch gaze from my five foot three inch height.

"I must apologize," he said as I passed by him and entered the room. "To be perfectly honest, I almost forgot about you. I was out jogging when I remembered our appointment. I hope you'll excuse my appearance."

"Apology accepted," I said casually, pretending I hadn't been the least bit irritated with his tardiness. As far as his appearance, it was great.

"You said you wanted to discuss Mr. Cushing?" he reminded me.

"Yes, Professor. His sister is terribly concerned. No one has seen him in a number of…"

"Please call me Richard," he interrupted.

"…days," I finished.

"Hmm. He hasn't been in class all week either," he said, glancing at a book on his desk. "Let me think. Oh, yes. I saw him out at the dig we're working on, but I haven't seen him since then."

"Did you notice anything odd about his behavior that day? Or did you notice anything else unusual?" I asked.

"No," he said slowly, "but then things were pretty busy. I wouldn't have noticed much."

"Did you happen to notice if he disappeared for any length of time?"

He looked so deep in thought that I was afraid I'd lost him for a moment. Was this the absent-minded professor you always hear about?

"Now that I think about it, there was the errand I sent him on," he replied, speaking ever so slowly.

"The errand," I prompted.

"Yes, I asked him to run to my car to get some brushes I'd forgotten. He was gone for quite awhile, probably twenty or thirty minutes. I remember because I was irritated by the delay he was causing."

"Did he seem all right to you when he came back?" I asked.

"Now that you mention it, no. I think I asked him if anything was wrong, because he seemed rather shaky and pale, as I remember it. Oh yes," he said, taping his finger on the desk. "He said the heat was getting to him, although I don't remember it being a particularly warm day."

"Do you have another student in your class by the name of Frank Samuels?" I asked.

"Sorry, never heard of him. Is he involved in Robert's disappearance?"

"I don't know, it's just a name that popped up. I'm trying to get a line on him."

While we talked he began moving things around on his desk, like he couldn't stand just sitting and talking. He had to be moving. He cleared his throat continually as he talked. And he continued to tap that finger.

Common sense told me what was wrong. I just didn't know why.

"Am I making you uncomfortable, Prof...Richard?"

"No, no." A pause. "Well, yes, in a way. You're a very attractive woman, you know."

I was slightly embarrassed, but highly complimented at the same time. That was the last thing I expected to hear, but after being around Gina, Gracie, the brunette in the tight skirt and Jessica Cushing, I needed to hear it. I mumbled a thank you. Now we were both uncomfortable. Ever heard of a pregnant silence? Well, the next few moments were the perfect example. You could have heard a pin drop.

I finally pulled myself together, asked a few more questions and wrote furiously in my small notebook as he answered me, not looking up.

"I'm sorry," he said. "Again. This time for embarrassing you. But you are lovely. Over the phone, when you said you were a private investigator, I pictured a big, muscular woman with a faint mustache and a deceptively feminine voice. It was a pleasant surprise when I saw you standing by the door waiting."

"I have to admit, you don't exactly fit my idea of an archaeology professor either," I replied. "I guess we shouldn't stereotype people."

"Listen," Richard said, "Robert Cushing is one of my best students, and one of my favorites too. He's a decent young man. If there's anything I can do to help, will you let me know?"

"There is one thing you can do to help me," I replied. "If you have some free time tomorrow I'd like to drive out to the site of the dig and have a look around. You could show me where your car was parked and where Robert was working, and maybe answer any questions I come up with."

"I'm not free tomorrow, but if you could make that Saturday, it's a date."

"Saturday is fine. Shall I meet you here?" I asked.

"I'll give you my home address. It's closer to the site than the college."

He gave me his address and phone number, and I handed him one of my cards, asking him to call me if he remembered anything else. He walked me to the door and I left, almost reluctantly, but not quite. I had a feeling that this could be a very interesting man.

I drove back to the office, deciding that I was losing my mind, pure and simple, or in the alternative, I was just plain weird, like Pete thought. I'd met two men in a couple of days and was attracted to both of them, which was unusual in itself. Neither one was my type, or at least not the type which had interested me in the past.

I was looking forward to Saturday as if it were a real date, not just business.

"Now come on, stick to business girl," I told myself. "You can't afford to get involved with anyone right now. You don't need complications in your life. Your hands are full trying to run a business. Besides," I said to myself, "you've never been interested in anyone after just one meeting. You're too careful for that."

On the other hand, maybe the professor would get my mind off Peter Goldberg for awhile.

CHAPTER 5

I returned to the office and found that Pete wasn't back yet. I sat down and added a few notes to the Cushing file, then leaned back to relax.

Stretching my arms up over my head, I looked around the office and decided that I wasn't doing half bad. I'd gone from being a county employee to owning my own business. I'd begun building the business up on my own, with no help. I'd furnished the office so it looked fairly professional to anyone coming in and, I thought, I *was* a professional. I was making enough money to avoid starvation, even though most of my cases were insurance frauds, most of which weren't all that interesting. I'd reached a point where I needed to hire help. I felt good about my decision to follow through with my dream. Maybe I wasn't quite as naive as everyone thought.

The ringing of the phone brought me out of my reverie.

"Webster Detective Agency," I answered.

"Drop the Cushing thing!" I heard a threateningly quiet voice warn.

I sat up straight, surprised by the call.

"Yeah? Is that a threat?" I asked belligerently.

"Take it any way you want to, bitch. Just stay the hell out of it! That is, unless you want more trouble than you can handle." My anonymous caller hung up on that cheery note.

I sat staring stupidly at the receiver which was still in my hand. I hung it up, not knowing what to do next. I sat for a couple of minutes, just taking the call in. I definitely felt anger brewing inside of me.

About the time I decided I was really angry, a large rock came crashing through the front window. It startled me, to put it mildly, and I jumped for cover, knocking the phone off the desk.

"What the…," I said loudly. I was pretty sure the rock was meant to tell me that my caller had meant business. Now I'd have to put out the money for a new window. Funny how your mind latches onto something as ridiculous as the window at a time like that.

One of the reasons I make a good detective is that I don't scare easily, I thought to myself as I tried to ignore my shaking hands. So the rock hadn't done its job. I might be shaking, but there's a difference between shaking and quivering. After peeking out the window to make sure the coast was clear, I got out a broom and pan and swept up the broken glass. I picked up the rock and set it on the edge of my desk. I tried to do some work, but found my eyes kept wandering back to the rock.

It looked like this was going to be my first major case. With the phone call I received, I now knew Robert Cushing's disappearance would prove to be more than anyone had wanted to believe.

"What happened to the window?" Pete asked as he strolled through the door about twenty minutes later.

"Some fool called and said we'd better back off the Cushing case. Then a rock came flying through the window, for emphasis I guess."

"Great," he said. "Oh well, a warning is a warning. We'd better let people think we're treading softly for awhile. We'll have to be more discreet with our questions."

"You're right, even though I think throwing a rock is a childish way to get our attention," I added.

"I wouldn't think in terms of childish at this point. Be careful."

"He sounded pretty nasty over the phone. I think something really has happened to Robert," I said.

"That's an understatement. I don't think this is as simple as a kid running off for awhile to have a good time."

"We may be able to help Stanley Hawks though," Pete said, changing the subject. "I knew that slime ball's face was familiar. I drove over to the department and talked to my old partner."

"And?" I said impatiently.

"And," he continued, "we pieced it together after picking each other's brains. The guy is a small-time hood. He blew in here from Chicago when things got too hot for him there. His name is Al Sands. He's no big deal. He does odd jobs, usually illegal, for some of the slime around town," he explained. "I don't know who he's working for, but at least we got a break in knowing who he is."

"My partner and I arrested him a couple of times on a 647f," he added.

"647f?" I questioned.

"Drunk in public."

"647f. I'll have to remember that one." I didn't know why I might ever need to know that particular code, but it never hurt to store information away for future use.

"Believe me, he gets pretty raunchy when he drinks."

"I'll take your word for it," I said. "So where do we go from here? Are you going to talk to this guy or what?"

"Nah. I'm going to look into this some more first. See if I can maybe find out who he's working for. I've still got a couple of snitches who owe me."

"Okay," I said. "By the way, I talked to Cushing's professor this afternoon. He couldn't add too much to what we already know, but I'm going out to the site of the dig with him on Saturday. I'll see if I can turn anything up there."

"What about talking to the other students?" Pete asked.

"What a jerk!" I said.

"Huh?" Pete looked surprised.

"Not you. Me. I forgot to ask the professor for the list of names. I'll call him and see if he can bring a list with him on Saturday. I did ask him if Samuels was in one of his classes though, and he'd never heard of him."

"I'm sure Ray can give us some of the names, too," Pete said. "That way we can get started. As far as Samuels, Ray said he's just some guy who shows up at some of the college parties. He's a friend of a friend, or something like that. He couldn't add anything to what he's already told us about the kid."

"Okay," I replied. "I also called and left a message for Jessica Cushing to call me. I'm going to try to corner her about Robert. If she wants us to find him, she's gonna have to be honest with us."

Pete made a sort of grunting noise as he picked up the phone to call Ray.

The other line rang and I answered it. It was Jessica Cushing. I glanced at my watch, surprised at how late it was. Somehow it had suddenly become four-thirty. The day had flown by.

"Miss Webster, I should have told you." She sounded shook up. "My husband doesn't know I've hired you. I convinced him that you were an old friend after he heard your message, so if you call and get the recorder again, would you please play along?"

"Sure. But why didn't you tell him? Robert is his brother, so he must be anxious too," I said.

She laughed, a hard sound. "Anxious? No way. He and Robert don't get along. Robert doesn't like my husband's line of work. My husband couldn't care less about Robert's disappearance. Besides, he thinks I'm being ridiculous. You know, the old 'boys will be boys' line of thinking. He figures Robert is just out somewhere having a good time, and that it won't hurt him any. He thinks Robert is too straight-laced for his own good and that he should get out and live it up more."

Before she could say more, I interrupted her. "Mrs. Cushing, why weren't you honest with us about your brother-in-law's recent change in behavior? You had to notice it. Everyone else has."

She was quiet for a moment, then said, "Okay. I'll level with you. I know there's something wrong, and I think it's possible that my husband might be involved, or at least he knows something. He's been acting strange too. When I approached him about hiring a detective, he absolutely refused, said he'd take care of it and to mind my own business. Don't you see? I'm stuck between a rock and a hard place."

"But," I said, "you're sure Robert *isn't* okay, right?"

"Right. You can almost slice the tension around here with a knife. I love Robert as much as I could ever love a real brother. I've got to know what's going on. I'm begging you, *please* help me." She started to cry softly, all the hardness gone.

"Mrs. Cushing, calm down," I soothed. She continued to weep, building up to a real sob. "Mrs. Cushing, Jessica, we will find out what happened. Try to relax." Apparently she was a more sensitive woman than I'd given her credit for.

It took a few seconds, but she finally managed to downshift from sobbing to mere whimpering. I truly felt sorry for her.

"We'll help you," I said. "If you think of anything specific that hasn't occurred to you yet, or if you hear anything, call me. Otherwise I'll contact you when we come up with something."

"Thank you," she said as we hung up.

"Did you get any names from Ray?" I asked, turning to Pete.

"A few. At least enough to start with. He said there were three classes at the dig."

"Wonderful," I said hopelessly. "Three classes. We could be talking to kids for the next month."

"Whatever it takes," he replied.

Before I could say anything more, the phone rang again.

"Busy day," I said as I answered it.

"Is Mr. Goldberg there?" a female voice asked.

I pointed at Pete and he picked up the receiver on his phone. Goldberg. I thought about his name as he talked, remembering he said he'd tell me about it sometime.

"Pete," I said after he hung up, "You mentioned yesterday that you'd tell me the story of your surname sometime. How about now?"

"You don't want to hear that story," he said.

"Sure I do," I replied. "Obviously you're not Jewish, but your name is. What's the story?"

"My grandparents came to America from Italy," he explained. "They couldn't speak a word of English when they got here. My grandfather was persistent though and landed a job on the docks in New York right away. The owner was another Italian. He and my grandmother were able to get an apartment and settle in faster than most of the immigrants.

"My grandfather decided if they were going to live here, then they were going to learn English and be real Americans. Being a real American included having an American name. He wanted things to be right.

"It seems the neighborhood they lived in was predominantly Jewish. There were a lot of Goldbergs in the area."

"Oh no," I said, starting to laugh. "So they thought Goldberg was a typical American name."

"They sure did," he continued. "He had the family name legally changed to Goldberg."

"What was his original name?" I asked.

"Marino," he replied. "Mario Marino became Mario Goldberg. They were the only Catholic Goldbergs in the neighborhood."

"Actually, I like it, Pete. The story's got warmth to it. What a lovely thing they tried to do."

"If you say so."

His story opened a door for us, and we sat talking for awhile, getting to know each other. I'd called someone to come repair the window, and he showed up while we were talking, taking care of at least one of my problems.

"Come on, let's go get some dinner," Pete finally said. "I still don't feel like cooking."

"I don't either. Let's go," I said, grabbing my backpack out of the desk drawer.

We drove to a coffee shop in a part of town where he'd never worked. I made sure of that. No Gracie-types to bother us.

We had a leisurely dinner, discussing both the new cases and personal subjects while we ate.

"Do you carry a gun?" Pete asked unexpectedly.

"No," I replied.

"Yeah, well, I think you'd better get one," he suggested.

"Why should I? I don't need one, believe me. These insurance cases I've been handling certainly don't require a gun."

"Think about it. You got that call this afternoon, and the rock is nothing to turn your nose up at. Just to be on the safe side, you ought to have some protection. What if that wasn't just an idle threat? You've got to be sensible about this."

"I *am* being sensible. If I carried a loaded gun around, I'd probably end up shooting myself."

"You're a detective, haven't you ever handled a gun before?" he asked.

"As a matter of fact, I'm a sharpshooter. But shooting on a safe and sane range and shooting out on the streets are two different things. I tried carrying a gun for a short period of time, but I found I didn't like it. Okay?"

"No. I still think you need some protection, but there's not much I can do to change your mind, is there," he said grudgingly.

"I've got pepper spray in my backpack," I said defensively.

"A lot of good that'll do if someone's shooting at you. Besides, I can just see you trying to get that thing off your shoulder and get the pepper spray out. 'Hold on a sec while I get into my backpack'. You'd have every bad guy in town laughing at you."

"If someone shoots at me, I'll duck. Now let's change the subject. I don't want to talk about this anymore, and I mean it," I said, beginning to lose my patience.

"You're hiding your head in the sand, you know," he said.

"It's my head and I'll hide it wherever I want to. Besides, I'm just being sensible. We're getting dangerously close to an argument here," I cautioned.

We dropped the subject altogether, instead discussing music, books and movies. We both enjoyed the same types of books and movies, but had different tastes in music. He liked country-western while I liked easy-listening rock.

We finally paid the check and headed back to the office where I'd left my car. As Pete pulled into the parking lot, his headlights swept across my car.

"Oh no!" I wailed as he braked and I jumped out of the car. "I don't believe this!"

I walked slowly around my car, taking in everything I saw, but not quite believing it. The front and rear windows had been smashed in, there were dents in the front fenders and "Back Off" had been spray-painted across the hood.

I began to cry. "Do you have any idea how long I saved to buy this car? I scrimped and cut corners because I wanted to pay cash. I wanted it to be all mine!" I looked at my once beautiful red car and cried harder. It was the first car of choice I'd ever purchased, always buying used and only what I could afford in the past.

"Don't cry," Pete soothed as he put his arms around me.

"Don't cry?" I said as I pulled away. "I always cry when I'm this angry. Don't stop me, it's a good outlet. Besides, it's either cry or eat. I eat when I'm upset too, but this time calls for crying."

I kicked the tire, still angry, and sat down on the asphalt to massage my aching toes.

"Uh, I hate to pull you away from your car, but I think we'd better check the office to see if it's still in one piece," Pete suggested.

"Oh no! I didn't even think about the office," I said. I quit crying and ran to the door, my keys already in my hand. There was no need to unlock the door, because it was standing open. I flipped on the light switch and the tears started rolling again.

"Can't you turn that off?" Pete asked, referring to my crying, as he surveyed the damage. "Looks like they did a thorough job."

All the files were scattered around the floor. Everything had been pulled out of our desks and was scattered around the room, including the drawers. The phones were on the floor, in pieces. The closet was open and supplies were strewn everywhere. The filing cabinets had been tipped over. It was a catastrophe. About the only thing they hadn't done was paint graffiti on the walls, like they'd done to my car.

"I'll go down the street to the gas station and call the police," I said. I decided to look into cell phones at the first opportunity.

"Yeah, you do that, but be careful. I'm going to look around to see if I can figure out exactly what happened."

"I think that's pretty obvious," I said sarcastically, but Pete was no longer listening to me.

I called the police and they showed up about half an hour later. I was amazed when they showed up so fast.

Both of the responding officers knew Pete and somehow that seemed to make things go a little faster. He pointed out to them how and where the intruders had entered. They'd come through the rear bathroom window so they couldn't be seen from the street. Apparently they didn't care if they were seen leaving, since the front door had been left open.

The police took a report and checked for fingerprints. There weren't any clear ones, which Pete fully expected. Apparently, the idea of usable fingerprints is highly overrated. They said if we ran across anything substantial during our cleanup efforts to let them know. Pete assured them he could handle things and that suited them just fine.

"Well, shall we get started?" Pete asked as they left.

"No," I replied. "Would you give me a ride home? Let's board up the window for tonight and leave the rest for tomorrow. I just can't face this right now."

We boarded up the window and drove to my place in silence. I wasn't in the mood for small talk, and Pete recognized that. As I got out of his car, I asked him to pick me up in the morning, and he told me to be sure to lock up tight for the night.

"Sandi," he added. "Be careful. I was right about the phone call being more than a threat. I'll watch 'til you get inside. Blink the porch light to let me know if everything is okay."

I nodded. After I'd done a cursory search of the apartment, I flashed the porch light to let him know nothing was out of place.

After Pete left I sat down and had a couple of cups of coffee. I thought about how I'd better toughen up if I really wanted to be a detective. Maybe Pete was right about the gun. Nah! But I'd sure had a rude awakening after my cozy, comfy insurance fraud cases. Maybe I hadn't thought things out as well as I should have. Maybe I should stick to nothing but the insurance cases. They paid the bills. No! I wasn't giving up this soon.

I watched television for awhile, unable to sleep. My thoughts kept returning to Robert Cushing. The way all the files had been pulled out of the drawers, I knew the intruders had been looking for the Cushing file. It only made sense on top of everything else that had happened. Fortunately, I'd taken my briefcase with us when we went to dinner, and the file was in it. I wondered if they'd be back for another try.

CHAPTER 6

The next morning I awoke on the couch. I'd closed my eyes for just a moment, and promptly drifted off.

I stood up and stretched, moaning as I did so. It was unseasonably chilly and I'd stiffened up from sleeping on the couch. I headed for the kitchen to make fresh coffee, then changed my mind and showered instead. I'd had enough coffee over the past few days to last me a month.

After I showered and changed clothes I sat down to wait for Pete, munching on a piece of toast to kill the time. I wasn't too awfully hungry after the events of the previous night.

I heard a horn honk and looked out the window to see Pete waiting for me. I grabbed my backpack and briefcase with the Cushing file, and ran out the door. I flew down the stairs, wondering what I was in such a hurry for.

"You look like hell this morning," Pete greeted me.

"Thanks a lot," I snapped at him.

"Sorry. Rough night, huh?"

"You could say that."

Role reversal. I was in a bad mood and he sounded pretty chipper. At that point in time I really couldn't handle "chipper".

We arrived at the office where I took another look at my car and pounded my fist on the hood. They'd slashed all four tires on top of everything else. I hadn't noticed that in the dark, even when I kicked the tire. The poor car definitely looked worse in the daylight. I shook off the anger, remembering I needed to harden myself against the things that were happening.

"I took the liberty of stopping and picking up new phones on my way to your house," Pete said.

"Thanks, Pete. I'll reimburse you as soon as we can find the checkbook. I'm sorry," I said apologetically. "I dread the mess we've got to face in the office. Let's get the phones hooked up and I'll call the insurance company. Then, of course, I'll have to call someone about replacing the bathroom window. I'm almost too embarrassed to call the same guy from yesterday. Oh well, he did a good job. We're also going to need to get some new supplies. Oh yeah, and I've decided we should get some cell phones."

"Let's get started," Pete said, heading around the building to the office. "This place isn't going to clean itself."

"I wonder if they were looking for the Cushing file," I said as we entered the office.

"I'm sure they were," Pete replied. "Especially when you consider the personal note they left on the hood of your car. It certainly wasn't a love letter, and it certainly isn't some kind of joke."

"Yeah, I thought about that. It doesn't seem very likely that this happened because of the Hawks case, and none of the other cases are that big of a deal."

"Ah, but what's not a big deal to you could be a big deal to someone else," Pete commented.

"True, I hadn't looked at it like that. Nah, my cases aren't that involved."

Cleaning up the office proved to be a long and tedious task. Pete got the phones hooked up while I started picking up files. One of the phones had an answering machine, so that took care of another problem, since the old machine had been ruined along with the phones.

I finally sat down to call the insurance company. They took a report and said they'd send someone out to look at the car. The young woman I talked to told me to get at least two estimates on what it would cost to repair the damage. They were much more cooperative than I'd expected.

Pete was exceptionally nice to me, sympathetic to my mood. As we cleaned, he looked everything over to see if he could find any clues as to who'd created the disaster that I'd once laughingly called my office. Nothing turned up, which didn't surprise either one of us.

I called the college around ten o'clock and left a message for Professor Smythe to call me. I still needed that list of students' names. Fortunately, Frances didn't answer the phone. I really didn't want to talk to her again.

It was noon before Pete and I finished putting things away and got rid of all the trash. We went to lunch and on the way back we stopped so I could pick up some of the supplies we needed. That was the day it dawned on me that I'd never taken out insurance on the office equipment. I'd talk to my insurance agent as soon as we returned to the office.

As we walked in from lunch, the phone was ringing, but the caller hung up before I could answer, and he didn't leave a message.

"You know," I said thoughtfully, "I think from now on we should keep the Cushing file with us instead of leaving it in the office. There's not that much in it, but I'd hate to lose what little we have. It was just luck that I had it with me last night. And I still think that's what they were looking for."

"I think we should go a step further," Pete said. "Let's make up a dummy file to leave in the office. At least it might keep them from wrecking the place again. We've got to start using our heads about this situation. Besides, if we do it right, we can make them think we're on the wrong trail."

"We're not on *any* trail," I reminded him.

"We must be getting close to something," he replied, "or none of this would have happened."

"Good point," I responded. "And I like the way you think. A dummy file is an excellent idea."

We rigged the fake file, making it look like we were a couple of buf-
foons, added a few false clues, and filed it in the drawer. It was a little
sobering when we realized that we really didn't know much about what
was going on. I was beginning to feel like a buffoon, even it wasn't our
fault. We were pretty much clueless and couldn't do anything about it,
at least not yet.

Professor Smythe returned my call at three o'clock.

"This is the first chance I've had to call you," he said. "I just finished
my last class."

"Uh huh. Well," I said, "what I need, Richard, is a list of all of the students who were at the dig on the Saturday in question, plus anyone else
who might have been there. Can you help me?"

"No problem," he replied. "I use a sign-in sheet, so I'll make you a copy."

"Would you please bring it with you tomorrow?" I requested.

"Of course." He paused briefly. "Miss Webster…"

"Call me Sandi," I interrupted.

"Yes, I suppose it is rather silly for me to call you Miss Webster when
I've got you calling me Richard. Anyway, I was wondering, if you're not
doing anything…oh, never mind. I'm sure you're busy." He sounded
almost shy.

"What were you going to say?" I asked, my pulse quickening a bit.

He hesitated again, then said, "I wonder if you'd like to go out to dinner tonight, but I'm sure you've probably already got something else
planned. I know how last minute this is."

"Actually," I said, smiling, "I don't have any plans for tonight, and I'd
love to go out to dinner with you."

Pete, who could hear my end of the conversation, made a face at me
and I signaled him with my hand to buzz off. He laughed.

"Terrific!" Richard said. "I'll pick you up at seven."

"Seven is fine," I said. I gave him my home address.

"I look forward to seeing you," he said, and we hung up.

"Got a real date tonight, huh?" Pete said, teasing me.

"Mind your own business," I said.

"Take is easy. I think it's just fine that you've got a real date. Those phantom dates never seem to go anywhere." He was getting a kick out of the whole thing, and getting on my nerves in the process.

"Did I mention that as a new employee you'll be on probation for the first six months," I said threateningly. "Keep it up and you'll find yourself back in the unemployment line. Real fast."

"Now that scares me," he said, laughing. "I couldn't help myself. All kidding aside though, I'm sure you don't lack for dates as a rule. You're a bright, lovely," pause, "short person."

It seemed like he always had to get a crack in, so I ignored him.

"Hey, kid," he said.

"Look! My name is not Short Person, nor is it Kid. My name is Sandi. Use it!"

"Ouch. A little touchy today, huh?"

"Enough is enough," I said, beginning to seethe. People can joke with me about a lot of things, but not my dating habits. He'd crossed a line and gotten too personal, and he needed to know it.

"Okay, I'll stop. Anyway, what I started to say was that Stanley Hawks gets off work at four o'clock, so I'm going to drive up there and follow the guy who's been stalking him. It's gonna be a regular parade, with me stalking the stalker, who's stalking Stanley. After Stanley is safe at home, I'm going to continue following this Al character to see if he meets up with anyone."

"I guess I'd better not count on you to give me a ride home tonight with all this stalking going on," I surmised.

"I doubt if I'll be back in time," he confirmed.

The door opened and a tall thin guy with a mustache and wearing a cheap suit walked in. He was going bald so he'd combed his very long back hairs all the way up and over his head and over his forehead to make it look like he still had some left. I'd hate to be around if a strong wind hit him from the front. In my own personal opinion, bald men are much sexier without the long hairs as a rule. When were men going to realize that most women would rather see a bald head than a few wisps of hair grown too long and combed where they don't belong.

"I'll grab a taxi home tonight," I said to Pete. "You can still pick me up in the morning, can't you?" Maybe I'd better start being nicer to him. I needed a ride to the professor's house.

"Sure," he answered. "I'll be there the same time as today," he said as he walked out the door.

"Can I help you?" I asked, turning to the stranger.

"Hi. I'm Fred Rice. I'm here from the insurance company about your car. I need to inspect it."

"Oh, good. I'm glad you're here. I'd just about decided you weren't coming today."

"We've had a rash of vandalism lately. Sorry to be so late. Let's take a look at the car," he suggested.

"It's out in the parking lot," I said, standing up. "Come on and I'll show you." I hoped there wouldn't be any problems.

He followed me out and clucked as he walked around and examined the damage. He stopped looking every so often and made a note on the forms on his clipboard.

"Does this graffiti on the hood mean anything to you?" he asked. "It sounds like it might be personal."

"I don't know what it is," I lied, not wanting to confuse the issue any more than necessary. The message was job-related. Could that be a reason not to honor my claim? I didn't want to take the chance, so I stuck with the lie. I'm not a good liar, so I hoped he couldn't read my facial expression.

"Hmm. These vandals are really getting out of hand. You wouldn't believe some of the cars I've seen recently." He clucked his tongue again.

"Well," I said as he walked around the car for the third time, "what do you think?"

"Oh, you're covered," he said, much to my relief. "But I'll need a copy of the police report. I'll pick that up myself since I'm headed to the police department on another matter anyway."

"Thanks. I'll get the estimates for fixing the damage right away, just like your office told me I should."

"You won't need estimates," he said.

"But when I called this morning, they said I had to have them," I replied. "In fact, she was adamant about my getting estimates."

"You may have talked to someone new. We have a big turnover in the insurance business. Anyway, you don't need them. We have two authorized dealers near here who'll do the work and bill us. Here," he said as he handed me a sheet of paper, "these are the dealers. Call either one and give them the claim number I'll be giving you. You shouldn't have any problems."

"Is this going to make my insurance premium go up?" I asked. The last thing I needed was a larger insurance payment.

He shrugged, not knowing or caring. "Probably. That decision is up to someone else."

"Well, thanks for your time, Mr. Rice. I'll call right away and get this taken care of."

As soon as he gave me the claim number and I signed some papers, he left and I called one of the dealers. They wanted me to bring the car right in. I'm not sure if I wanted to laugh or cry, but I was afraid I'd do one or the other. I took a deep breath.

"I don't think so," I said. "It's got no windows and four flat tires." I went on to explain how much damage there was.

"Okay," the voice on the phone replied tiredly. "We'll pick it up. It's near closing, so I'll get someone over right away."

"Thanks. How long do you think it'll take to do the repairs?" I asked. "I need the car back as soon as you can get it to me."

"With what you've described, you'll be lucky to have it back to you in a week," he replied.

"A *week*? I can't get along without a car for that long. I really can't! I've got a business to run."

"We've all got our problems, lady. Hold on a sec," he said. He covered the mouthpiece of the phone and I could hear muffled voices. There was quite a lengthy discussion at the other end of the line.

"Yeah, okay," he said as he got back to me. "I'll have someone follow the tow truck over and leave you a loaner to use. We just got one back. But don't expect nothing fancy though."

"Don't worry about fancy, and thanks a lot. You're a lifesaver," I said. "You really are."

We hung up and I sat back to rest for a minute, but the phone rang almost immediately.

"Webster Det…," was all I could get out of my mouth.

"Ms. Webster," said a familiar and panicky voice. "This is Stanley Hawks. I don't know what to do." His words began coming faster and faster as his panic accelerated. "Now I'm being followed by *two* men. Oh, oh, I just don't know…"

"Mr. Hawks," I interrupted.

"…what to do," he finished lamely.

"Mr. Hawks," I repeated a little louder, trying to get his attention. It didn't work. He was too excited to listen to me.

"One was bad enough, but now there are *two*," he repeated, ignoring me altogether. "What should I do?" His voice sounded shrill, and I knew I had to get his attention quickly.

"Mr. Hawks!" I said sternly. "Listen to me for a second."

"Yes, yes. What is it?" he asked impatiently. I heard a loud clunk as he dropped the receiver.

I could hear a lot of fumbling and background noise, and when he came back on the line I asked, "Where are you calling from, Mr. Hawks?"

"A pay phone outside of my office," he reported.

"Okay. Now I want you to be as nonchalant as possible, but take a good look. Could the second man possibly be my partner? Mr. Goldberg? You remember him, the dark-complected Italian guy?"

"Just a moment, please," he said.

There was a long pause, then, "I think you're right, it is him. What a relief. Oh," he added, "I was careful in my observations so as not to give him away. I certainly wouldn't want the man who's following me to know we're on to him."

"Very good," I complimented. "You did the right thing. Now, just go about your business as you always do. Don't make the man who really is following you suspicious," I instructed him. "Mr. Goldberg is there, as you saw, so you don't need to worry. He'll take care of things."

"Oh my," he said uncertainly. "I surely hope so."

"Trust me," I soothed him.

He said good-bye and hung up without another word. Odd little man, I thought to myself.

I was surprised that Pete had let himself be seen though. He should have been more discreet.

The dealer finally showed up to pick up my car and drop off the loaner. It was a piece of junk, certainly not fancy, but better than nothing. At least, that was my first impression.

The driver's parting words didn't do anything to cheer me up.

"Be sure you pump the brakes on that thing when you come to a stop," he mumbled.

"Hey, wait!" I yelled, but he was already on his way down the street. If I'd had anything besides the car keys in my hand, I probably would have thrown something at him.

Just great! A junky car with bad brakes. Hadn't they ever heard of lawsuits? And I thought it'd be better than nothing. What else could go wrong?

I got my things together and locked up the office wondering what good locking it would really do. There was still the broken window, and obviously my locks weren't all that much help. If someone wanted to get in badly enough, they could always find a way. I shouldn't even ask myself what else could go wrong. It just might happen.

I climbed into the loaner, anxious to go home and get ready for my date. I started the engine, not sure which groan was louder, mine or the car's. I took my time driving, familiarizing myself with the car and not trusting the brakes. I pulled into my assigned parking space at the apartment building and turned off the ignition. The loaner dieseled, not wanting to shut off.

"Die, sucker," I muttered. With its last breath it let out a backfire as loud as a cannon.

I slid down in the seat, embarrassed by the looks I was getting from my neighbors. Their accusing expressions, as they peered out of their windows, seemed to say I'd scared them on purpose. They all thought I was a little nuts anyway, what with my line of work and all.

CHAPTER 7

I tried to slink into my apartment unnoticed, but my landlord yelled at me from his doorway.

"Where'd you get that hunk of junk? Hope you're not keeping it."

"It's just a loaner," I yelled back apologetically.

The first thing I did after shedding my clothes was call Pete's house to let him know he wouldn't have to pick me up the next morning. I left a message on his machine.

That done, I showered and put on a dress. It had been ages since I'd worn a dress, preferring casual clothes for sleuthing. There had actually been a few times when I'd found it necessary to go through trash cans and the like, so when I say casual, I mean casual. On rare occasions I met with clients for lunch, but even then I opted for nice slacks rather than a dress. I didn't want anyone to get the mistaken idea that I was "too feminine" for the job I was doing. It paid to think of things like that. On this occasion, however, I wanted to look feminine.

The dress I wore was a light peach color with a flat white collar, a little tight on me because I'd put on a few extra pounds over the past year. I wore only a simple gold chain necklace with matching bracelet and earrings to accent the outfit. I put on low-heeled white sandals and spritzed on a little cologne.

I was critical of myself as I took in my image in the full-length mirror. My reflection showed a small, slightly pale woman who appeared to be quite tired. I decided to use an old trick I'd learned to brighten my eyes and get rid of the dark circles. I soaked two tea bags in water and placed them in the refrigerator to cool. When they were cold I'd hold them against my eyes for a few minutes, then redo my eye make-up.

I stood, leaning on the edge of the sink, daydreaming. My mind wandered to the subject of tea, of all things. What a wonderful thing tea is. It has so many uses. Besides tasting great and helping dark circles, I'd learned years before that the way to relieve a bad sunburn was to throw a few tea bags in a tub of tepid water and soak in it. It really took the sting out. One of mom's tidbits.

My mind seemed to snap when I thought of mom, and I wondered what I was doing wasting time thinking about tea.

I turned back to my reflection and decided not to worry about my appearance, except for my tired eyes. So what if I was a tad pale. At least it was a healthy pale, a naturally light complexion, not a sickly pale. I liked to think of it as alabaster. Besides, the sun certainly wouldn't do my skin any good. I did put on a tiny bit of blush though, just to add some color. Richard must have seen something in me he liked, or he wouldn't have asked me out in the first place.

While the tea bags cooled I changed from my backpack to a purse and tuned in the nightly news. I walked to the kitchen, and as I took the tea bags out of the refrigerator and pressed them against my eyes, I heard the newscaster mention the name Cushing. Wondering what could be going on, I dropped the tea bags in the sink and ran out to the living room to see what was going on.

Turning up the volume I heard the words, "…tragic death of John Cushing. His widow, Jessica Cushing, was not available for comment."

"We'll return after this message," he informed the viewing audience.

What could have happened, I wondered as my heart began to do a tap dance. I didn't have to wait long for an answer.

The phone rang and I grabbed it before it could ring a second time.

"Sandi, this is Pete." He sounded excited.

"Pete, have you heard about John Cushing? What's going on?"

"I'm not sure. I'm at the office right now, and there's a message on the recorder from Jessica Cushing. She sounds hysterical."

"I heard the news about Cushing's death on the car radio, but there were no details," he continued. "I thought I'd call you before calling Jessica to see if you'd heard anything."

"No," I answered. "I just caught the tail end of the story, none of the details. I don't know what's going on either. Call her, then call me back. I won't leave until I hear from you."

"I'll call back as soon as I can," he assured me as he hung up.

I had a bad feeling in my stomach. It was one of those gut feelings that says things are worse than you thought. With John dead, I was more concerned about Robert than ever. Could John's death have been an accident? I believed there was a lot more going on here than we'd bargained for.

The phone rang and I grabbed it thinking it was Pete calling back, although we'd just hung up. He hadn't even had time to call Jessica yet.

"Hi, sweetheart," a very familiar voice said.

"Hi, Mom," I said, disappointed.

"What's wrong?" she asked.

"Nothing, why do you ask?

"You sound almost breathless. You sure everything is okay, honey? You know I'm always here if you need someone to talk to."

"Honestly, Mom, there's nothing wrong. I'm in the middle of getting ready for a date, and I just heard on the news that something unexpected has happened on one of my cases. Someone has died."

"You have a date?" she asked cheerfully. Somehow it didn't surprise me that she missed the rest of what I said.

"Yes, Mother, I have a date. Don't start planning the wedding though. I just met this guy."

"Sandra! Don't get smart with me," she admonished.

"Oh, Mom. Don't get so excited just because I've got a date. Nothing will probably come of it. I barely even know this guy. I think you worry more about my social life than I do."

"Well somebody's got to worry about it. Now I know you've had a couple of bad experiences with men, especially the one who was so obsessed with you. I thought you'd never get rid of him. But they aren't all that way. Trust me on this, Sandi, I know what people are like."

"I know," I replied. "Don't worry so much. I'm doing just fine. Anyway, let me call you back in a couple of days. I've got to finish getting ready for this date." Mom's calls were usually poorly timed.

"Okay," Mom said with a very audible sigh, "go get ready for your date. But don't be too quick to judge him. Give him a chance. You never give men much of a chance before you dump them."

"Yes, Mother. Bye."

I felt a little guilty about being so abrupt with her, but I wasn't in the mood for all the things I knew she'd have said to me. No one but my mother would have bothered to remind me of Flakey Jake, as I so fondly refer to him. We met and had dated for only two weeks when he started planning the wedding. (After one week, I would have broken up with him, but someone told me I was being picky and I should give the poor guy a chance. Unfortunately, I listened to the advice.) He wanted me to meet his family and friends.

When I told him he was moving too fast for me, it really hurt his feelings. I told him I thought it would be better, and healthier, for both of us if we quit seeing each other. That's about the time he started acting obsessive.

If I went to the grocery store, when I came out he'd be waiting near my car. At the mall he followed me all through each store. He'd call me and cry, wanting to know what he'd done wrong. He called so often that I didn't want to answer the phone or check my messages. He would send flowers and I'd turn them down, sending them back to the flower shop. It got pretty hairy for awhile, but my persistence in repeatedly saying no to him finally paid off.

I thought about reporting him as a stalker, but in this case I'd been able to handle it myself. I later found out he'd done the very same thing to a couple of other women. It pays to be careful as far as I'm concerned. Sometimes it's best to go with your gut feeling.

I retrieved my tea bags and returned to the living room to open the window and get some fresh air. I needed some after the thoughts that had been going through my head. I held the bags against my eyes, feeling even more tired, and welcoming the cool sensation on my eyes. I breathed deeply as the breeze wafted through the window. I was listening to the television, hoping there would be more news about Cushing.

I dropped one of the tea bags. I bent over to pick it up and heard what I thought was a bug hitting the screen, and simultaneously a thud against the wall opposite me. I glanced at the screen, and noting a hole I turned my head and looked at the wall where I'd heard the thud. There I saw a second hole.

Sometimes a person can be amazingly calm, or is it dense, under the worst of circumstances.

"No bug here," I said aloud. "That's a bullet hole. No doubt about it." Had I lost my senses? I was too calm.

At that point my initial calm was replaced by complete panic and I threw myself on the floor. Another bullet whizzed over my head. I crawled to the door and locked it, keeping as low as possible. Then I crawled back to the window and stood up beside it, pulling the cord to close the drapes. Why make myself such a visible target? I couldn't decide whether to sneak a peek or not.

I waited, but nothing else happened. I stooped over and made my way to the lamp, switching it off with a click. After a moment spent catching my breath and hoping my heart would slow down, I moved back to the window. I gently moved the drape and peeked out, but there was nothing to see. After waiting for what seemed an eternity, I opened the drapes a little further. Nothing happened, so I figured the gunman was gone. At least, I sincerely hoped so.

I hadn't heard the crack that goes with gunfire so I had to assume there was a silencer on the gun.

I grabbed the phone and dialed 911. With shots having been fired, it didn't take long for the L.A.P.D. officers to show up. I didn't know either of them, so it took a little longer to explain things to them. I'd been hoping someone I knew would show up. They took the report along with some photographs of the screen and wall, and said they'd take a look around outside before leaving. They said there wasn't really anything else they could do for the time being, except take the report. If nothing else, I figured if anyone was still hanging around, the cops being there would scare the perpetrator off.

The doorbell rang about twenty minutes later and my heart started pounding again, harder than the first time, if that was possible. I briefly wondered if I could have a heart attack from all this beating heart stuff.

"Who is it?" I asked cautiously.

"It's Richard," came the reply.

I ran to the door and jerked it open.

"Come in quick," I said as I yanked on his arm.

"I sure didn't expect this kind of a welcome," he said, laughing. He stopped and took a closer look at me. "Wait a minute. Something's wrong, isn't it. Are you all right? You look like a ghost."

So much for using blush on my cheeks.

"Look at this," I said as I turned on the lights and pointed at the holes in the wall and screen.

"What are those?" he asked, the innocent college professor showing through.

"Those are bullet holes," I explained. "Someone's been taking pot shots at me, if you can believe that."

"My God! You could have been injured." That was definitely the understatement of the year.

"I think that was the general idea. If I hadn't bent over to pick something up, I'd probably be dead right now."

"Someone actually shot at you," he said incredulously. "I didn't know being a detective was really so dangerous. I thought they just made it look that way on television."

"Me, too," I thought to myself.

"I saw a police car pulling away as I drove up, but I had no idea they were here because of you."

"Yeah, well…what can I say. Have you heard the news tonight?" I asked, desperately needing to change the subject. "Something has happened to Robert Cushing's brother. He's dead, but I missed most of the news report."

"To tell the truth, I was so busy that I missed the news altogether tonight. Sorry I can't be of more help."

"Oh well, I guess Pete will fill me in. I hope you don't mind, but we can't leave until he calls me back. Would you like something to drink while we wait? I don't usually drink, but I'm afraid I need something to help me stop shaking."

"No, thank you. Pour yourself something though. You're right, you need it after all that's happened to you tonight. Do you think someone might still be out there? Do you mind if I smoke?" He sounded nervous, and was probably wondering what he'd gotten himself into. After all, the life of a college professor didn't involve getting shot at.

"No, I'm sure whoever it was is gone by now," I assured him. "I'm surprised to find out you smoke. You don't look like a smoker. I'll get you an ashtray." Of course, what did a smoker look like? I hoped I hadn't offended him. I guess we all have our little vices.

As it turned out, I'd reassured myself as well as the professor. My heart slowed down and I began to feel fairly calm. The shaking mostly subsided, though not completely. I found an ashtray in the cupboard and as I reached for it, wondered how I could calm down so fast after having been shot at.

"You amaze me," Richard said, as if reading my mind. "You've just been shot at, and yet you're busy, politely waiting on me.

"Uh, by the way," he added, "If you don't mind my asking, who is Pete?"

"Pete?" I said dumbly. "Oh Pete. You haven't met him yet, but he's my operative."

"Operative?" he questioned. Why couldn't people just accept the terminology. It was really so simple.

"Yes, he works for me. He's my investigator," I explained.

The phone rang as I handed the ashtray to Richard. I jumped again, almost dropping it in his lap.

"Maybe you're not as calm as I thought you were," he commented.

I nodded as I answered the phone. The instant I heard Pete's voice I interrupted him with a torrent of words, trying to tell him what had happened. I couldn't get the words out fast enough.

"Whoa," he said. "Slow down and tell me again. What exactly happened? Did I hear you right, that someone shot at you?"

I took a deep breath and spoke very slowly, enunciating more carefully than was necessary.

"Yes, someone tried to kill me. I was standing in front of the window and someone took two shots at me. Is that clear enough?"

"Damn! I'll be right over," he said.

"No. Don't come over. I'm okay, and Richard is here anyway. Don't worry, the police have already been here."

"Ha! Of course I'm worried. John Cushing fell, or was pushed, seven stories to his death. He was working through his lunch hour at the office and no one else was around. The people on the street heard a crash and a scream, and John came flying out of the window."

"Suicide?" I asked.

"I doubt it. I called and talked to a friend of mine at the Department. He said they're working on the theory that he was pushed. At least there's an indication of a struggle in his office. Not to mention the force with which he flew out the window. It doesn't look good."

"Anything else?"

"Isn't that enough? The only other thing I can tell you is that Jessica Cushing is a basket case. Her husband is dead and her brother-in-law is still missing. A friend is going to stay with her for a few days.

"So," he explained, "you can see why I'm worried about you. People dying, disappearing, and now you getting shot at. And don't forget what they did to the office and your car."

"How could I forget? I can't believe how much has happened in such a short time."

"I mean it, you be careful," Pete warned. "You know, we still haven't located this Samuels character, and there's always the possibility he's behind this. We don't know what his involvement is yet."

"I wish we could find this guy and talk to him," I said.

"You and me both," Pete replied.

"What about Stanley Hawks?" I asked. I was starting to feel nervous again and wanted to change the subject. I was getting good at that. "Anything going on there?"

"Yeah," he replied, "but we'll discuss that later. Why don't you stay home tonight and I'll come keep you company. I still think you should start carrying a gun, especially now that all of this has happened."

"No gun! I'll be okay. Unless Richard wants to back out, I'll be out with him tonight." I looked at him and he shook his head. He wasn't backing out and I was relieved. I didn't want to stay home by myself.

"By the way, I left a message on your machine. I got a loan car, so I won't need you to pick me up tomorrow. I'll talk to you later." I hung up and turned to Richard, grateful he hadn't been scared off.

We left shortly after my conversation with Pete. Richard took me to a quiet little restaurant near the beach with lots of calming atmosphere. Over dinner he commented on how lovely I looked as he placed his hand on mine. He also commented on how exciting the evening had become. I wasn't sure if he meant my company or the shooting.

Unintentionally, I found myself being somewhat coy with him, maybe using the shooting incident to my advantage.

We both had the filet mignon, delicious down to the last morsel. The salad was cold and crisp, the vegetable hot and tasty, the baked potato perfect, and the bread served with dinner tasted freshly baked. It was an ideal meal between the food and the company, and yet I couldn't enjoy it. My stomach seemed to have a mind of its own, and I felt like I was on a roller coaster.

After dinner we drove along the coast, enjoying the cool night air. We stopped by a deserted stretch of beach and walked side by side, getting to know each other. It was soothing to talk quietly with the sound of gentle waves lapping against the sand in the background. It would have been perfect, and should have been perfect, but I couldn't stop looking over my shoulder, frequently. I didn't think Richard noticed, and if he did he didn't say a word.

As we talked I learned that Richard came from an "old money" family. He need never lack for anything. He wasn't too talkative on the subject, almost sounding embarrassed about it. I, on the other hand, had come from an above middle class family, a family I was proud of, regardless of an indiscretion on my father's part. I didn't explain my father to Richard. My parents had been hardworking, fun-loving people, for the most part. My father had died of a heart attack a couple of years earlier and that's when my mother moved back East. We had family there. Now that she didn't have my father to worry about, mom put all her efforts into me.

We eventually returned to my apartment where I invited him in for a nightcap. He readily accepted, so I found a bottle of wine in the refrigerator that I'd been saving for a special occasion. I needed the evening to be a special occasion.

"So how did you get into teaching and archaeology?" I asked as we sat down on the couch.

"The zest for the mystery of it all. The search, the find, the knowledge to be gained. You can't imagine the thrill of a find. It's positively intoxicating."

As he spoke his face became animated, his eyes sparkled. He almost filled the air with a charge of electricity. I could feel his excitement as he spoke.

He told me about his first find on an expedition to South America. He'd been the one to discover an ancient grave site, and from there the expedition had gone on to find relics of a little known civilization. He said he couldn't describe the feeling his first find gave him. He didn't sound like he was bragging, but like he was very excited.

I got caught up in his excitement and before I knew it the time had slipped away. I looked at the clock and saw it was after two o'clock. I needed to get some sleep. His gaze followed mine.

"I'm sorry," he apologized. "I can get carried away sometimes. I'd better go so you can get some sleep. I'll see you in a few hours anyway, when you come over to go out to the site with me."

"You're right. It's been a lovely evening though, Richard," I said as I walked him to the door. "I really enjoyed myself. And in all honesty, I was glad to have the company after what happened earlier. Thank you."

"I'd like to do it again sometime," he said hopefully.

"I'd like that too," I replied, feeling like a kid on her first date.

He stood quietly for a moment, looking at me with an expression I couldn't quite read. Then he put his arms around me and kissed me, tentatively and somewhat clumsily. I was ever so slightly surprised.

"Good-night," he said softly, and let himself out.

I strolled to the window and gazed up at the star-filled sky. I thought what a stroke of luck it was that the smog was light and I could actually see a few stars. I heard Richard whistling in the parking lot, but I didn't look down as he got into his car and drove off.

I thought about his kiss. It certainly wasn't the best I'd ever had, but then it had been brief, and he probably had visions of being shot while he stood by the door. That would make anyone clumsy. However, it was nice to be around someone who wasn't so aggressive for a change.

I locked things up and went to bed. Surprisingly, I slept soundly, not even dreaming. It was as if nothing in the least unusual had happened to me. If only that were true.

CHAPTER 8

The alarm began buzzing all too soon. I dragged myself out of bed and fixed one of those hearty breakfasts, usually reserved for Sunday mornings. I very seldom have more than a glass of milk or bowl of cereal. I cleaned up the dishes after eating, and headed for the bathroom to get showered. As I passed the living room window, I happened to glance out. What I saw made me angry.

"PETE! WHAT ARE YOU DOING OUT THERE?" I yelled out the window. He was leaning on his car, looking up at me.

"SOMEONE'S GOT TO LOOK OUT FOR YOU," he yelled back. He grinned. Then, quieter, "Shh! You'll wake your neighbors."

"Get up here!" I ordered, trying to keep my voice below a scream.

"Coming, dear," he said as he strode towards the stairs.

I slammed the window shut. I wondered how long he'd been out there. As if I couldn't take care of myself. The nerve of that man!

When he knocked on the door I was ready and waiting, tapping my foot impatiently. I opened the door with a jerk.

"Just what do you think you're doing?" I demanded.

"I think I'm standing here admiring a woman who seems to have forgotten she's still wearing her extremely short nightie," he said, leaning against the door frame. His eyes were doing a bit too much wandering.

"Oh! Get in here," I said, pulling on his arm. He laughed as I ran to my room to put on my robe.

"How long have you been out there?" I asked, returning to the living room.

"Since around eleven o'clock last night. I got worried that you might get shot at again, or worse, but when I saw you come home with your date I found myself worrying about your good name instead." That silly grin of his made me even angrier.

"Knock it off! My dates are none of your business."

"Just looking out for my own interests," he said casually. "I'd hate to see you make a fool of yourself. Everything you do could reflect on the business, right?"

"I'm not making a fool of myself, okay? You don't even know Richard, so why not mind your own business. Besides, who are you to talk? You sure seem to be well-known by certain women in this town."

"You did say you called the police last night, didn't you?" he asked.

"Of course I did."

"It wouldn't have surprised me if you'd forgotten," he said. "You seem to be out in left field somewhere, and therein lies the problem. I'm doing all the thinking, and you're not thinking things through at all."

Somehow we'd changed places. Now he sounded angry, and I was on the defensive.

"Okay, okay," I said grudgingly. He was right. I didn't know what was wrong with me. Normally I'm a very level-headed person, always using my common sense, but that common sense had flown out the window. I didn't seem to be working anything through.

"Sit down and tell me about Mr. Hawks while I fix you some breakfast," I invited. We needed to move on. While I cooked, he told me about the fiasco of the day before.

"First of all, Sands isn't too bright. It's obvious that Hawks knows he's being followed, but Sands keeps trying to hide himself anyway. Every time Hawks turns around Sands ducks into a doorway, or turns his back and looks the other way.

"The next thing I know," Pete continued, "Sands starts looking over *his* shoulder, and I had to start stepping into doorways. I think Hawks may have seen me, but I know Sands didn't."

"You're right," I confirmed. "Do you remember Hawks using the pay phone outside his office building?"

"Yeah."

"Well, he was calling me. He didn't recognize you at first and he panicked. He thought that he had two men following him. It really shook him up until he realized it was you."

"I thought he saw me," Pete said. "But the important thing is that Sands didn't. I have to admit I felt ridiculous jumping into doorways every few minutes, but I could tell that Sands at least sensed my presence because of the way he kept turning around."

"So aside from playing Hide & Seek, what else did you boys do?" I asked.

"Hawks made several stops on his way home," Pete continued, giving me a contemptuous look, "and Sands stuck with him all the way. Hawks finally arrived home and Sands hung around for about an hour. He seemed to be waiting until he was sure Hawks was in for the night.

"Sands took off and I followed him to a sleazy bar. He had a few drinks and left with some broad, and I use the term loosely. I thought that was the end of it, but he only drove about four blocks and let her off at another bar. I continued to follow him and he stopped at a coffee shop over on Second Street. I think I would have given up, but he kept looking at his watch. He was waiting for someone, or something, so I decided to hang around."

"Let me go call Richard," I interrupted. "I want to let him know I'll be a little late. I want to hear the rest of your story before I leave."

"Yeah. You go call Mr. Wonderful while I finish eating," he said caustically. He really sounded like he didn't like Richard.

I made the call, then turned to Pete to ask him about his attitude.

"Why do you talk as though you don't like Richard? You've never even met him."

"I don't dislike him," he replied. "He just sounds like a wimp."

"Didn't you see him when we got home or when he left last night?"

"No. When you pulled in last night I was parked where I couldn't see him, which made me realize I'd better move the car. Then I fell asleep around one o'clock. I woke up when he started his car, but it was too dark to see him."

"Too bad you missed him. He's anything but a wimp," I said defensively. Then I smiled one of those knowing smiles that I knew would drive Pete nuts.

"Right. Do you want to hear the rest of the story or not." Pete was becoming impatient.

"Pardon me," I said with a wave of my hand. "Please proceed."

"Okay, so Sands was waiting for something. The jerk spent an hour and a half in that coffee shop. He took one last look at his watch and got up to leave. I knew he was going to meet someone then.

"As he walked past the waitress, the creep pinched her butt. That did it. An argument ensued and the owner called the police because Sands started getting rough. They ended up arresting him for disturbing the peace."

"And…?" I questioned.

"End of story," Pete replied. "All that time spent following him and he never got to keep his appointment. So close, yet so far away. I'm positive he was going to meet someone."

"I don't know what to say," I said.

"There's nothing to say. I'll just have to try again later," Pete said.

"By the way, Pete, I need a favor. The locksmith and the glass company are going out to the office today. Could you be there to meet them please? I know it's your day off, but…"

"Sure. That's the least I can do after this breakfast. It's been a long time since I've had bacon and eggs that weren't greasy, and toast that wasn't burned."

"Poor baby," I commiserated.

⋆   ⋆   ⋆

Pete left and I hurried with my shower and got dressed. I wore old Levi's and hiking boots since I assumed we'd be traipsing through dirt and more dirt. It was still fairly early and already becoming a warm day, so I wore a tank top with the Levi's. With the exception of mascara and lipstick, I didn't bother with make-up. I just put on some sunscreen.

By the time I got to Richard's house it was almost ten o'clock and he came outside as soon as I pulled up to the curb. The trusty old cannon went off as soon as I turned off the engine, or at least I tried to turn it off. It sputtered quite a bit before it finally died.

"Being a detective isn't very lucrative work, is it," he commented as he looked at the car.

"It's a loaner," I explained. "My car is in the shop being repaired."

"Oh, did you have an accident?" he asked.

"In a manner of speaking. Are you ready to go?"

"All set," he said. "But let's take my car. I heard you coming a block away, and I want to be sure we get where we're going."

He drove the most gorgeous blue Mercedes I'd ever seen, but then, I wouldn't have argued with him anyway.

It took us about an hour and a half to reach the site of the dig. It was quite a ways out of town, in a rather isolated area. Surprisingly, there were grassy knolls and plenty of trees. I'd been expecting a more desert-type place.

Richard had packed food and soft drinks in the trunk of his car, intending to make it both a business and pleasure trip. He'd even thought to bring a blanket to sit on.

"Where do you want to start?" he asked.

"First, why don't you show me where everyone was parked and where you, in particular, were parked that day."

"We were all parked in this general area. I was over that way," he said as he pointed toward a group of trees. "I remember because I wanted to park in the shade." I noticed there was a small hill just beyond the trees, more of an incline than a hill. We walked over to the shaded area.

"I was parked in the middle, right here," he said indicating a shady spot. "You can see how if you pull the car up far enough, you'd have trees on each side and in front of the car, so there'd be shade just about all day.

"Now that I think about it," he added, "I'm going to move the car over here. I'll be right back." He took the keys out of his pocket and turned toward his car as I began walking around looking at the ground, not knowing what I was looking for.

The sun glanced off something in the dirt and I stooped down to see what it was. It was only a button. I picked it up absent-mindedly, rubbing it between my fingers as I continued my search.

I looked up to see Richard pulling the car into the shade. He climbed out and opened the trunk while I stuck the button in my pocket to free my hands so I could help him unload the food and drinks.

"Now what do we do?" he asked.

"I'm not really sure what I'm looking for to be honest. It seems like something may have happened while Robert was here working. Why don't you show me the site of the dig."

"There are actually two digs. We were working on one during the weekend in question, and the other one is an old one that didn't pan out," Richard explained.

"Show me the most recent one first," I suggested. "By the way, did Robert ever work on the first dig?"

"Only briefly. For a time we had a third dig working at another location. He was at the other location and only worked here when we were short-handed."

"I see. Well, lead on," I said.

We had to do a little hiking, but the site wasn't too far. We climbed two small knolls, passing the first dig which was between the knolls, and then came to the second site at the bottom of the second hill. I looked over my shoulder and made a mental note that the parking area and the other site were completely out of view.

"Watch where you walk from here on out," Richard instructed. "Don't step inside the roped off areas unless I'm with you."

"High security area?" I joked.

"You could step on something," he said seriously. "Tread lightly. We're nearing an area that we feel may contain artifacts, and I wouldn't want you to undo any of the work we've done so far."

"I understand," I said soberly. "I'll be careful. Would you please show me where Robert was working?"

"Let me think about where he was working that day," Richard replied. He closed his eyes, as if trying to visualize the scene. "Oh yes. Now I remember. He was at the west end. Come on." He took my hand and led me to the section where Robert had been working.

"There's no problem at this end," he said. "Robert was doing some clean up work here. Feel free to roam around."

"Good. Like I said, I don't really know what I'm looking for. Maybe you'd be willing to help me. You know what should be here and what shouldn't. If you see anything that looks out of place or unusual, let me know."

I turned to my right, Richard turned to his left, and we began rummaging around, looking through some equipment that had been left at the site, and even taking trowels to do a cursory search of small piles of dirt.

"I feel like I'm working the dig instead of helping you," Richard said after about forty-five minutes. "It's tedious for you, isn't it."

"It sure is. I guess you'd have to be pretty dedicated to get into this type of work. Of course, it would help if we knew what we were looking for."

Another fifteen minutes went by.

"Richard, come over here," I called out. "I think I've found something." I was kneeling on the ground by a mound of dirt. He walked over to see what I'd discovered.

"Look at this," I said.

"Look at what?" he asked.

I pointed behind the mound. His gaze followed the direction I indicated and he saw an envelope lying on the ground. It was dirty and a little weather beaten, but I could see the name Robert printed on the upper left corner.

"Robert," I said. "Not Bob or Rob or any other form of Robert. I've noticed that everyone calls him by his proper name. Let's take a look."

I picked up the envelope and turned it over. It was sealed, but I could feel something inside. I took a deep breath and said a silent prayer that whatever was in the envelope would give me something to go on. Could this be the envelope Ray Peterson saw Robert take from Samuels?

"I might as well open it," I said, sighing. I ran my finger along under the pasted flap and opened it. What I found was what I least expected.

The envelope held a small plastic bag which contained a white substance. I don't know much about drugs, but I knew instinctively that it was an illegal drug I held in my hand.

"Drugs," I said as I turned to Richard. I paused, thoughtful. "You know, something doesn't seem right here. From everything I've heard about Robert, I can't imagine him being involved with drugs of any kind. He sounds too straight to get involved with this stuff. Besides, I understood that he and his brother didn't get along because of his brother's involvement in this type of thing."

"I have to admit that Cushing does seem an unlikely candidate for drug abuse," Richard agreed, "but then you never really know, do you."

"I suppose you're right. It's just that I had this nice, neat picture of Robert built up in my mind. In my line of work I should always expect the unexpected. I sure didn't expect this, though," I said as I opened my clenched fist to reveal the small bag. Could Robert and Frank Samuels have had an argument over drugs? I didn't know about Samuels, but it didn't seem like something Robert would be involved in.

"Come on," Richard said. "Let's take a break and go eat. It's way past noon and I think you need to relax for a few minutes."

We strolled back to the car and Richard spread the blanket under the trees. He'd brought fried chicken, potato salad and watermelon, all kept cool in an ice chest. I didn't think I was very hungry, but after I began to eat I realized I was famished.

"This is delicious Richard. You cook too?"

"I'd like to say yes, but I'll be honest with you. There's a great deli near my house where I bought the potato salad. The chicken is from, well, one of those chicken places, and of course I can't take any credit for the watermelon. Uh, I've got some pastries in the cooler too, compliments of the local bakery."

I laughed. "Well, at least you know the best places to go for food. That's something."

We ate like it was our last meal. I laid down on my stomach and propped my head on my hands. Richard plopped down on the blanket next to me.

"That really hit the spot, didn't it," he said.

"Sure did," I said lazily.

Everything was quiet for a few minutes, just the sound of a few birds singing. I began to think about Robert Cushing again.

"What are you thinking about?" Richard asked.

"Robert," I replied.

"Terrific! I thought maybe you had me on your mind."

"I'm sorry, Richard. I still feel surprised about what we found. It just doesn't seem to fit in anywhere. Not after all the things we've learned about him."

"Forget it for awhile," he said as he reached over and took hold of my arm. "Come here."

I looked at him and knew what was on his mind, which brought me back to the moment. He pulled me to him and kissed me, sending a shiver down my spine. It was definitely a different kiss than the one I'd received the first time. I was lying on my back by that time and when he ended the kiss his face hovered over mine.

"Look around you," he said softly. "Green knolls, trees shading us, blue sky with wispy clouds overhead. No one around but us and the ants for miles and miles." He paused to brush an ant off his arm. "It's warm and there's a comfortable breeze whispering through the trees. What more could we ask for?" He kissed me again, more gently.

His tender kiss and soft-spoken words lulled me into a state of near total relaxation.

"Seems like the perfect place to make love, don't you think?" he asked, bursting my bubble. It seemed out of character somehow. Up until now I had the impression he was pretty reserved.

Old conventional me began to feel uncomfortable. I should have been more cautious.

"Richard, I don't think…"

"Hush," he whispered. He cut off my words with another kiss.

"No," I said as I pushed him away and sat up. "Richard, the time and place just aren't right. Besides, I hardly know you. I knew you were going to kiss me, but…maybe I'm sending the wrong signals here. I don't want any more than a kiss right now."

He sighed, a very disgusted sound, making me think he was like so many other men I'd been out with. I couldn't believe I'd misjudged him as much as I had. Yeah, he was just like the rest of them.

"I'm sorry," I said, not at all apologetically, "but that's the way I feel."

"What would be the *right* time and place," he asked sarcastically.

"Hey! Not here and not now, that's for sure. My opinion of you is rapidly changing. Just back off, will you?"

"Back off? That doesn't sound like the sweet young thing I thought I was getting to know."

"Richard!"

"Okay," he said quietly. "I'm sorry, Sandi. I guess my timing is all wrong. How about if we just forget it and get back to work."

"I don't think there's anything else to go over today," I said with a slight chill in my voice. "We may as well pack up and get back to town."

It was a quiet drive back to Richard's house. Once in awhile he'd say something complimentary, making me feel as if he were trying to make up for being so pushy. Somehow it was almost endearing, the way he was trying to make up to me.

"Richard, leave it alone," I finally said. "It's okay. No damage done. I still like you, and I'm sure it's not the first time you've ever been turned down." Whoops! Shouldn't have said that. "I'd like to see you again, but let's take it a little slower, okay?"

"I'm glad you feel that way," he said, relief sounding in his voice. "I do want to keep seeing you. I don't know what came over me this afternoon. I'm not usually so, well, forward with women. I should have been more sensitive to your feelings."

"Well, don't make a federal case out of it. You didn't really do anything all that wrong. I just had a lot on my mind, and sex wasn't at the top of the list," I lied. "Why don't we start over like nothing happened." I couldn't tell him how I really felt. He'd just think I was a big prude, which I wasn't. Not really. It had to be more than the right time and place for me, and it had to be more than just a roll in the hay. I'd made mistakes in the past and I didn't want to repeat them. I'd know when it was right this time, or die an old maid. I honestly felt that strongly about it.

"You've got a deal," he said. "Now. Would you like to go out to dinner with me tonight?"

"Oh, Richard. I'd really like to but I can't. I've got quite a bit of work to do."

He looked disbelieving so I tried to explain.

"You have to understand. Since I got into this business I've done very little dating. I haven't had the time. Going out with you last night was a real treat for me."

"I'm glad to hear that, anyway. Maybe you should start making time for a social life," he suggested.

"I will, but not tonight. Could we make it for another time?"

"Tell you what," Richard said. "I'll give you a call in a couple of days and we'll set something definite up."

"Thank you," I said.

"For what?"

"For understanding that right now my business has top priority in my life."

We arrived at Richard's house, talked for a few minutes longer and I left. I was anxious to find Pete and tell him about the drugs. I wanted to see if his reaction would be similar to mine.

Men! Richard was just as hard to figure out as Pete. Was Richard aggressive or not? I was so confused. I fleetingly thought of calling my mother. That says just how confused I was. Wouldn't she love this whole situation. It would make her whole day if I called and shared my dilemma with her.

CHAPTER 9

I drove straight to the office, hoping to catch Pete. No luck. The office was locked and his car was nowhere in sight. I drove by the front of the office as I left and noticed that a new window was in place.

Next I drove to my apartment where I sat down and tried to call him. I would have stopped by his place, but I didn't know where he lived and his address was back at the office. The office that I couldn't get into because the locks had been changed and I didn't have a new key.

I dialed Pete's number and when I heard his voice at the other end of the line I said, "Pete, this is Sandi. I've got to tell you…", and I heard his unmistakable baritone saying, "…at the sound of the beep." Great! The stupid answering machine. I hate those things.

I waited impatiently for the beep and said, "Pete, this is Sandi. Please call me right away. Better yet, come over if you can. Be sure to bring my new office key with you. By the way, I hate these stupid machines, even if I do have one at the office."

After I hung up I started a pot of coffee and headed to my bedroom to change my clothes. It had warmed up considerably, so I put on shorts and a different tank top.

By that time it was five-thirty. The day had flown by. I poured myself a cup of coffee and sat down on the couch with my backpack. I was alarmed when I searched through it and couldn't find the plastic bag with the drugs in it. I wanted to show it to Pete. He'd know more about that sort of thing than I did.

I leaned forward and dumped the contents of the backpack onto the coffee table. Wallet, checkbook, address book, tissues, lipstick, sunglasses, antacid, aspirin, matches, bills and everything else you could possibly imagine but no plastic bag. I did find a telephone number I'd been looking for, but no plastic bag.

I leaned back and mentally retraced my steps, relieved when I finally remembered that I'd put the bag in the pocket of my Levi's.

I ran to my room and pulled the pants out of the laundry hamper. As I reached into the pocket to remove the bag I felt something else. Reaching deeper, I pulled out the button I'd picked up in the parking area at the dig.

The doorbell rang. I carried the bag and button with me and let Pete in.

"Hi," he said. "Here's your key. I had them put good locks on this time, although you realize that if someone really wants in the locks aren't going to stop them. I think you ought to consider doing something about a burglar alarm too. Maybe some stripping around the windows or something."

"Good idea. Thanks for taking care of everything for me."

"Got any coffee?" he asked.

"I just made some." I looked at my mug. "Since it's so hot I think I'll switch to iced tea. Which do you want?" I asked impatiently. I didn't want to talk about coffee or tea. I was anxious to show him what I'd found.

"Hot or not, I'll have the coffee. Last night's sleep-over in the car is catching up with me. I need an eye opener," he said.

"Yeah? Well, I've got an eye-opener for you. I've got to show you what I found out at the dig. I want your reaction to this," I said as I handed him the plastic bag.

While he was examining it I glanced at the button I'd found. It was silver with an anchor embossed on it. The kind of button you'd find on beachwear or sailing sportswear. I looked at the back of it and noticed that the shank had broken off. It didn't mean anything to me. I wasn't even sure why I picked it up. I tossed it on the coffee table as I waited to hear what Pete had to say.

"Where did you get this stuff?" Pete asked.

"I found it at the dig, like I said. It was in an envelope with the name Robert printed on it. The envelope is still in my backpack."

"Robert?"

"Not only that, but I found it in the area where Robert had been working. What do you think?"

"I think we'd better talk to Jessica Cushing. This doesn't fit the profile we've been building on Robert."

"I'm relieved to hear you say that because I felt the same way. I'm wondering if this could be what Robert and Samuels argued about. Peterson did say that Robert took an envelope away from Samuels. By the way, what is that stuff?" I asked.

"Cocaine," he answered. "Okay, let's look at the facts for a minute. A kid with a special group of friends, all very scholarly and not my idea of druggies, a straight A student whom everyone seems to like, no past record of drug use. In fact, I get the feeling that the kid is kind of naive."

"Me too," I assured him. "Why don't we call Jessica right now."

"Won't do any good. I called earlier to see if she was up to talking yet and her friend said that after they made the funeral arrangements for her husband, they drove home and she took a sleeping pill. She's going to be out for awhile. We might try tomorrow."

"Oh. You know, I'm beginning to feel very impatient about all of this. I've got a hundred questions, and I can't seem to get the answer to any of them. I wish we could find Samuels. I have a feeling he could clear up a few things for us."

"Can I have that coffee now?" Pete asked pathetically.

"I'm sorry, I'll go get it. Black, right?"

"Yeah."

When I returned with the coffee and my iced tea I noticed dark circles under his eyes. He was exhausted. He couldn't have had much sleep.

"Thanks," he said as he took the mug. "Listen, I'll treat you to dinner if you'll do the driving. Deal?"

"Deal. We can discuss this further while we eat. Are you sure you trust my car?"

"Oh! That reminds me. The garage called the office and said your car will be ready on Monday."

"Terrific! I'll be glad to get rid of that klunker they stuck me with. It sounds like a tank coming down the street. You know it's bad when the teenagers around here laugh at it."

"Yeah, well, it's only temporary. As far as dinner, you can drive my car tonight," Pete said.

"How much sleep have you had?" I asked as he yawned.

"About two hours, and that was in my car," he replied.

"Didn't you have a chance to lie down and rest this afternoon?" I asked.

"No, I didn't. I followed Sands again, but it still didn't pan out. I'll wait 'til Monday and try again."

"I must say, I'm getting my money's worth out of you. But honestly, Pete, you're not going to be of much help to me if you're falling asleep."

"Forget it. Let's go eat. I know a great pizza joint not far from here, and you always seem to be ready for food."

"Do I need to change clothes or can I go in these shorts?" I asked.

"You can go like you are. It's not a fancy place, but they've got great food."

Half an hour later we found ourselves sitting in the midst of chaos, eating a pizza. The chaos was being created by several kids hanging out around some computerized games, the result being lots of noise and plenty of screaming and yelling. The "beep beep" of the games was driving me crazy.

We ordered a large pizza with everything, and Pete managed to eat all but two slices of it. He would have eaten those too, but they were mine.

With two pieces of pizza and a salad, I was full. He was welcome to the rest. I just couldn't believe he could put away so much food.

However, eating seemed to give Pete a second wind. With all the noise we had trouble hearing each other, so we decided to go back to my place to talk about the Cushing case.

I was anxious to leave anyway. I didn't think the two women who had stopped to talk to Pete had anything to do with the fact that I wanted to get out of there, but after they left our table I looked Pete right in the eye.

"Don't tell me," I said, "you used to work this beat too."

"No," he said tiredly.

"Hmph. Let's go," I said, picking up my backpack. I threw the two straps over my left shoulder and headed for the door.

Knowing how tired he was, as soon as we got back to my place I excused myself and headed to the kitchen to warm up the coffee. I knew he needed caffeine to keep going.

"I'll be out in a minute," I called from the kitchen.

While I waited for the coffee to heat I thought about Richard. I could have been out with him, probably at some nice restaurant where I could have my choice of gourmet foods, but instead I was at my apartment with Pete, full of pizza. But, of course, Pete was business and Richard wasn't. Well, Richard was business, but there was more to it than that. But then, wasn't it the same thing with Pete?

I had a brief mental skirmish with myself about whether or not Pete was business or social, finally deciding that maybe he was a little of both. I enjoyed his company, even though we tended to spar frequently, but he wasn't a date. And I didn't really know him any better than I knew Richard. I had to keep reminding myself of that little fact because I felt like I'd known him forever. As far as Richard and Pete were concerned, things were becoming too confusing, too fast.

Every time Pete and I went somewhere together it was on business, including when we went out to eat. Besides, from what I'd observed so far, I wasn't too thrilled about him and his women. He seemed to have too many, and they managed to turn up everywhere.

I poured two cups of coffee and carried them out to the living room, where I found Pete sound asleep on the couch. I didn't have the heart to wake him up so I got out a light-weight blanket and covered him up. It was beginning to cool off and I knew it would turn chilly during the night.

"You sure are a cute little guy," I said quietly. "When you're asleep that is."

I returned to the kitchen and sat down with the newspaper and my coffee. I read all the articles that caught my attention, then rinsed out the cups and went to bed.

I slept well that night. In the back of my mind I knew that I didn't have to worry about anything, like being shot at, because Pete was in the other room sleeping.

*   *   *

I awoke early on Sunday morning, put on my robe and walked out to the living room. I didn't see Pete so I walked on into the kitchen. He was sitting at the table with the newspaper spread out in front of him. He looked up and grinned.

"Thanks for letting me sleep last night."

"I doubt if an earthquake could have gotten you off that couch, but that's okay. Sleep well?" I asked.

"Yeah. Especially after hearing what a cute little guy you think I am."

"Pete! You were awake?"

"I was just dozing off," he said, "but I heard what you said."

"If you think back," I reminded him, "you'll remember that I added something about being cute when you're asleep. Don't let your head swell, huh? You're not always so cute when you're awake."

"You're cute too," he said, making a silly face at me.

"Uh huh. Now that we both know how cute we are, let's get back to business."

In our own screwy way we were sparring again. I figured we probably shouldn't get too close in our personal relationship or it would ruin our working relationship. I also figured he probably felt the same way. Oh well...

"I wonder what the professor would think if he knew I spent the night here," Pete mused. I was wrong, this was more than a business relationship. There was definitely a friendship brewing here too, or he wouldn't tease so much.

"Nothing. Nothing happened, so why would he think anything?"

"He wouldn't know that nothing happened, now would he?"

"Knock it off," I said irritably. If you can't get irritable with your friends, who can you get irritable with? Besides, he made a good point and I didn't like it. "You know, knowing how you are with women, nothing will ever happen between us anyway."

"Knowing *you* nothing will ever happen," Pete said as he turned his attention back to the paper.

I sighed. "Let's just change the subject, okay?"

"Okay. I guess we had Robert pegged all wrong, didn't we. But," he said thoughtfully, "I still find it hard to believe he's involved with drugs. It just doesn't feel right."

"I know what you mean. It's frustrating that the puzzle keeps changing shape and we can't fit the pieces together."

"Yeah, well we don't have too many pieces to work with yet," he commented. "I'll call Jessica this morning and sound her out."

"No, Pete. I know that I wanted to call her yesterday, but I was wrong. Her husband's funeral is tomorrow so let's wait until after that to talk to her."

"Why?" he asked.

"Why?" I repeated. "Don't be so insensitive. Because she's got enough on her mind without us asking her if her brother-in-law was a druggie. *That's* why."

"That's exactly why we should ask her now. She's held things back already, we know that. We're better off talking to her while she's vulnerable," he insisted.

"But Pete…"

"No buts. Now is the best time. If you want to be a good detective you're going to have to toughen up. You take care of business when the time is right for you, not the other guy."

"Hey! I'm tough. Trust me on this, I'm as tough as anyone else when I need to be."

He smirked. "You're about as tough as my grandmother," he said.

"Grandma's a mean old broad, huh?"

"You're weird," he said, laughing.

"Ha!" I retorted.

"Why don't I go home and get cleaned up," he said sobering up. "I'll come back and pick you up and we'll go see Jessica. I think we'd get a lot farther if we talked to her face to face instead of over the phone. We need to get something accomplished."

"You're right," I said after a pause. "You go get cleaned up and I'll be ready by the time you get back. Besides the fact that she'll be vulnerable, there's also the fact that we shouldn't put this off. You know, anything could have happened to Robert. I've got a niggling feeling that maybe we'd better find him soon, or we might not find him at all."

"You may be right. With John's death and Robert's disappearance, things aren't looking too good," Pete said. "We could be working against the clock now. We're going to need all the cooperation we can get from Jessica, so work yourself into your tough mode and we'll get some information. Don't sit and feel sorry for her. If she really wants to find Robert, she's going to have to level with us for a change. No more beating around the bush."

"Pete? You're starting to feel stressed about this aren't you. I mean, it feels like we're running out of time, doesn't it."

"Yeah. That's what I just said."

"Hmmm. Are you thinking what I'm thinking? That John's death is somehow related to Robert's disappearance?"

"There could be a connection," he replied.

He stood up and walked to the kitchen sink, gazing out the window with a faraway look in his eyes.

"You know," he said thoughtfully, "it just could all go back to…" He hesitated, then muttered, "Hey! What the…" Turning away from he window, he raced past me and out the front door.

"Pete!" I yelled after him. "What's wrong?"

Not getting an answer, I ran to my room, threw on my Levi's and shirt, then ran out the front door after him.

I stopped short and looked on in amazement as Pete and some stranger scuffled on the ground. For some unknown reason, I found myself focusing in on how much hair the stranger had. He was a big man and he was wearing a short-sleeved shirt. The shirt had already ripped open and I had a good view of his chest and arms. He was absolutely *covered* with hair. I'd never seen so much hair on one person.

Before I got much further in my observations I saw another man get out of a nearby car and run toward the fight. As he ran I saw him reach into his pocket and pull something out. I saw a flash as the light bounced off the blade of a knife.

Without giving it a second thought, I grabbed a potted plant from beside the door to my apartment and took off running, taking the stairs two at a time, my heart pounding and my breathing hard and rapid.

I was barefooted so the man with the knife didn't hear me coming. Just as he raised his hand to slash at Pete, I raised the pot over my head and hit him with as much force as I could. The jolt made him drop the knife and I saw blood trickle down the back of his neck from the wound to his scalp. He turned toward me with a glazed look in his eyes, but I knew he'd recover soon enough.

Pete and his opponent looked up when they realized something was going on besides their fight. They both stood up, and Pete, recovering first, threw a right that knocked the guy off his feet. Pete turned quickly and yanked open the door of his car. In one swift movement he reached in, opened the glove compartment and turned around with a gun in his hand. Hairy had just pulled himself up and was reaching for Pete when he saw the gun. His eyes sort of screwed up and he dropped his hands and held them out from his sides, backing away.

I saw the other guy slowly inching his way toward the knife. I literally leaped forward and kicked it out of his reach. He looked from me to Pete and began backing away with his crony. There was a hammer lying by the car and I picked it up and waved it at them threateningly. Hairy flinched.

"Hold it right there!" Pete ordered.

Pete's voice seemed to spur the men into action. They both turned as one and ran as fast as they could to their car, jumping in and screeching out of the parking lot.

"Pete! What happened? Why were you fighting with that guy? And why didn't you stop them?" I asked.

"What did you want me to do? Shoot them in the back?"

He put the gun away and walked over to me. Looking into my eyes, he started to laugh. It seemed like this guy was always laughing at me and it was beginning to get on my nerves. I looked at him questioningly.

"What's wrong with you?" I demanded. "What are you laughing at? This isn't funny, Pete. You carry a gun in your glove compartment?" I added as an afterthought.

"Yes, I carry a gun, but it usually isn't in the glove compartment, and the glove compartment is normally locked if it is in there. I'm not sure why I left it unlocked this time, but I sure am glad I did. I must have been in a hurry. And yes, this is funny." He looked so calm and amused. "You're a real terror, aren't you. I think that by the time they left, those guys were more afraid of you than of me and my gun. You told me you were tough. I guess I underestimated you."

"But what was that all about? What's going on?" I asked.

"Let's go up to your apartment and I'll fill you in. Believe me, it's a short story." He took hold of my arm to lead me upstairs.

CHAPTER 10

As we walked I noticed a slight tremor in the hand that was on my arm. He was more shook up than he wanted to admit.

"Now tell me," I said as we settled down on the couch, "who were those two? Ol' Hairy was something, wasn't he?"

"I have no idea who in the hell they were. But it's all very simple really. When I looked out the window I saw Hairy, as you call him, trying to slide under my car. I could see what looked like tools in his hand."

"And that's when you ran out?"

"Well, it was obvious he was up to something," Pete replied. "When I got down there I grabbed his legs and pulled him out from under the car. I saw the hammer in his hand, stomped on his arm and he dropped it. He kicked me, knocking me off balance, and that's probably about the time you came out."

"When I came out," I said, picking up the story, "I couldn't figure out what was going on. There you were, rolling around on the ground with Hairy. I was about to run down the stairs when I saw the second guy heading toward you with a knife in his hand.

"I guess my instincts took over," I continued, "because I never even thought about it. I grabbed the potted plant and ran down the stairs to hit him with it. I gotta tell you, one more second and you'd have looked like Swiss cheese." The thought sent a shiver down my spine.

"That close, huh?"

"That close," I confirmed.

"Thanks, Sandi," he said quietly. "I owe you."

"You bet you do! But I can't help wondering what all of this means. First my car is wrecked and the office is trashed, then someone uses me for target practice, and now Hairy tries to monkey with your car. You know it's all got to be related, right?"

"Probably, but who knows for sure," Pete replied. "I tried to get the license number off the car when those furballs laid rubber out of here, but it was covered with mud or something. Now *that* surprises me. They seemed pretty inept at what they were trying to do, during the daylight and all, but they had enough smarts to cover up the license plate.

"Well," he said before I could reply, "I'm going home to get cleaned up. I'll be back in about an hour or so." He stretched, then worked his back muscles, which were probably tightening up.

"Don't you think you'd better take a look under your car to see if he did any damage?" I asked.

"I'm way ahead of you, although I don't think he had time to do much."

"Good. At this point I think we'd both better start being more careful," I said, concerned. "After all, you're the best operative I've got."

"Your *only* operative, you mean. By the way, can't you find some other word besides operative? It really sounds lame."

"Thanks a lot," I said feeling slightly hurt. I don't like being told I'm lame. By anyone. "I thought it sounded professional. What would you *like* me to call you?" I asked defensively.

"I don't care, but that's so, I don't know. Just lame."

"Fine," I said. "I won't call you anything. How's that?"

"Childish actually, but just call me Pete, and I'll call you Sandi. How's that?"

"Fine!"

"Fine!" he replied.

I'm a little slow on the uptake sometimes, and I belatedly realized that his mood had probably deteriorated after the skirmish. I guess I could have been more gracious under the circumstances.

I watched Pete from the window while he checked out his car. He finally stood up and held his thumb up to let me know everything was in one piece. I waved and smiled at him, hoping to make amends.

After Pete left I changed my clothes and sat down at the kitchen table to eat some toast. As I glanced through the Sunday paper, the phone rang.

"Hello?" I answered.

"Hello!" said a familiar voice.

"Richard?"

"Yes. I was wondering if you have any plans for today?" He sounded awfully chipper.

"Oh. I'm sorry, but actually I do," I apologized. "Pete and I have to see Mrs. Cushing about Robert."

"Pete again. Can't you get rid of that guy?" He was beginning to sound a lot like Pete.

"Richard, it's business. I'm sure by now you realize that business comes first with me." Now why was I so busy trying to explain myself. I didn't owe him any explanation. Pete and Richard were both starting to get on my nerves. They sure knew how to make life complicated.

"What about tonight?" he persisted. "Let's go to a movie or something."

"Well, I am free tonight, and I'd enjoy a movie. Sounds good." So what. Complications can make life pretty interesting sometimes.

"Fine," he said. "I'll pick you up at six o'clock and we'll go get something to eat first."

"Okay. See you at six."

                    *   *   *

About an hour later I heard a horn honking in the parking lot. I knew it would be Pete so I grabbed my backpack and ran down to meet him.

"Hi there," I said as I climbed into the car.

"Hi. I called to let Jessica know we're on our way over," he said.

"Did she try to put you off?" I asked.

"She started to, but when I pushed the issue she gave in. I guess she figured she might as well get it over with. Actually, I interrupted her and told her if she wanted to find her brother-in-law she'd have to cooperate or we were off the case." He looked at me to see what my reaction would be. Had he overstepped his bounds?

"Good," I replied. "I think at this point I would have said the same thing. She can't put us off forever, or we can't help her." I'd pretty much swung around to his way of thinking after considering the facts.

"Yeah. I think she's resigned herself to the fact that she can't keep holding out on us. She must realize her husband's death could have something to do with Robert's disappearance. We might be about to get some of the answers we need."

"I sure would like to know who put Hairy up to working on your car," I commented. "The things that have been happening *must* have something to do with Robert. It makes sense, don't you think?"

"That's an understatement. By the way," he said, "I talked to a friend of mine at the department and he said that John Cushing's death was definitely no accident. This is strictly between you and me because, of course, he's not supposed to be giving out any information on an open murder case, but he said there were signs of a struggle, bruises that couldn't be attributed to the fall, and he was pushed so hard that he had trauma to his neck. Also not from the fall."

"Does Jessica know about this?" I asked.

"She knows it was murder, but she doesn't know any of the details. My contact at the department said that Cushing had been working on some handwritten notes. His secretary walked in and saw the notes and said something to him about typing them up after lunch. He turned the pages over and told her that it wouldn't be necessary because he was working on something personal. Oddly enough, the note pad she saw seems to have disappeared," he said facetiously.

"This is interesting. Did she have any ideas about what he was working on?"

"No. She said he very pointedly turned the pages over so she couldn't see them," he replied.

"I sure would like to know if there's any possibility that the papers had something to do with Robert," I commented. I didn't know why they should, but I couldn't help wondering.

"That makes two of us."

We spent the rest of the drive discussing the new information we had and how it would apply to the questions we wanted to ask Jessica.

I was duly impressed as we pulled into the circular drive at our destination, the Cushing home. The house was quite large, but not really pretentious. It was a modern two-story house with a slightly rustic appearance. The surrounding yard had been tastefully landscaped, with the protective six foot fence being lined with tall hedges and trees. There were colorful gardens with paths running through them and benches strategically placed, a lovely place for a casual stroll. There was even a clump of trees off to one side with an artificial waterfall in the center, spilling into a small pond. It didn't look out of place at all, but added a sense of peace to the overall picture. I had a feeling that if I walked to the rear of the house I'd find a modern Olympic-size swimming pool just waiting for someone to dive in.

Pete and I approached the front door, but before we could ring the bell Jessica opened it.

"I've been waiting for you," she said as she invited us in. She looked pale and was wearing no make-up, but she managed to remain as beautiful as ever. I knew after one look that she was truly grieving for her husband. I couldn't help but feel relieved to find that she really had cared for the man. I'd mistakenly assumed she was just another gold-digger. I was ashamed of myself for having made that snap judgment after only talking to her a few times.

"Mrs. Cushing," I said in all sincerity, "I'm so sorry about your husband's death, and I'd like to apologize for intruding on you right now, but there are a few questions we've got to ask about your brother-in-law. Especially in light of what's happened."

"Yes, I understand. Please come in and sit down," she invited as she led us into the living room.

"I'd like to add my condolences," Pete said. "I know you're having a rough time right now." I looked at him in surprise. Maybe he was more sensitive than I gave him credit for.

I sensed a new maturity in Jessica. Sometimes maturity can be forced on us through circumstances, whether we want it or not. In the past she'd held things back from us, making me feel like she was playing games. However, now she seemed ready to face the situation and help out without the games. I hoped my conclusions were right. I didn't want to find myself making snap judgments again, but there you go.

"Mrs. Cushing," Pete said gently, "we really need to get right down to business. We may ask you some questions that you won't like, but they've got to be asked."

"Don't worry," she replied. "My brother-in-law is missing and my husband has been murdered." She choked on the last word and I could see her eyes tear up. She took a deep breath and pulled herself together.

"I don't know if the two incidents are related or not, but I've got to get to the bottom of this. No matter what comes out," she said.

"Good," Pete said. "You wanted us to help you and that's exactly what we're going to do. Now," he continued, gentleness gone and all business again. "What can you tell us about Robert's involvement with drugs." Right for the jugular. So much for sensitivity.

"Mrs. Cushing," I said gently and with a great deal more sensitivity than my counter-part, "there is an indication that Robert may have been involved with drugs. Can you shed any light on that information for us?"

"Robert has never been involved with drugs!" she said adamantly. "I can guarantee that."

"What makes you so sure?" Pete asked.

"Drugs are one of the reasons John and Robert didn't get along. Look," she said, "it's no secret that John was involved in the underworld and drug trafficking. Well Robert hated the whole thing. He and John had a big argument because Robert told John he disgusted him. He really lit into John about kids and drugs, and even told John he was nothing but a money hungry child killer. He ranted and raved at him about addiction and children being born addicted to drugs. It was awful. I've never seen either John or Robert so angry before. I thought they were going to hit each other, but surprisingly it never came to that.

"You see," she continued, "an old friend of Robert's got involved with drugs shortly after they graduated from high school. The boy took an overdose and died. After that Robert became a real crusader against drugs. He and the other boy had been friends since grammar school, and his friend's death just crushed him. He's a real straight kid, and when he feels strongly about something, he goes all out. To have part of the problem originate in his own family was more than he could handle."

"Was there just the one argument?" I asked.

"Oh, no. They hardly ever spoke to one another because when they did, well, it always ended up in another argument. John would never admit it, but he adored Robert. It really hurt him when they argued, but he wasn't about to change any of his so-called business practices. For anyone." What a discreet way of putting it, "business practices".

"What would you think if you went into Robert's bedroom right now and found some dope?" Pete asked.

"I'd say it couldn't happen," she said with no hesitation and a lot of venom.

"You're that sure he doesn't do drugs?" I asked.

"Yes!" she said coldly and emphatically. We seemed to be hitting a raw nerve on the drug issue. I believed her. I glanced at Pete and knew that he did too.

"Have you ever heard of a boy named Frank Samuels?" I asked.

"No. Does he have something to do with this?"

"I don't know," I replied. "It's just a name which came up that I'm trying to follow up on."

"Do you have any theories about your husband?" I asked. "What I mean is, do you think his death could have any bearing on Robert's disappearance, or vice versa?"

"I don't know," she answered thoughtfully. "When you consider the things John was involved with, it could have been…I just don't know. I've had the same thought, and I'm not keeping anything from you this time. I suppose any or all of it could have been mob-related, but I just don't see it that way. John wasn't having any trouble with anyone, at least not that he mentioned. He never really talked about his activities with me, but I couldn't help overhearing things from time to time." She looked nervous. "I really shouldn't talk about John and his business at all."

She paused, looking reflective. "In some ways John was acting differently, but I honestly don't think it had anything to do with business. He got a couple of late night calls. He said they were wrong numbers, but later, when he thought I was asleep, he went downstairs and used the phone.

"One night I snuck down and tried to listen, but I couldn't hear much." She looked at her hands instead of us. "I heard him mention Robert's name and I heard the word 'brother'. He sounded angry. He said, 'Nobody'd better lay a finger on him', but I couldn't hear much else. I can't explain it. I just know that Robert was in some kind of trouble, and my instincts tell me it had nothing to do with John and his business, or drugs. Something about John's tone of voice. It wasn't the way he talked to his business associates. When it came to business, he never let his anger show. Being calm when he should be angry made his business associates nervous."

"Okay, now we're getting somewhere," Pete said. "So you really don't think your husband was having any business problems, but you know there was a problem of some sort. Right?"

"Yes. As a matter of fact, as far as business, he mentioned that things were never better. He knew that the local police and other agencies were investigating him, but that was nothing new, and he said they weren't even close. I guess John trusted me more than I realized, now that I think about it. He'd never tell me anything very important, but he would open up a little from time to time.

"You see, I loved my husband very much, but I didn't like the way he made the majority of his money anymore than Robert did. So John and I had a sort of unspoken agreement. He gave me the legitimate money from the import/export business and I invested it. Investment is my forte. I seem to have a flare for it. Anyway, he figured that way I'd always be taken care of. He said 'just in case.'" She started to cry. "I didn't think anything like this would ever actually happen. It just doesn't seem real. I feel like I'm in the middle of a nightmare that I can't wake up from."

"I'm sorry we have to dredge all this up, Mrs. Cushing," I said, "but we're almost done. Did your husband ever say anything at all that might give us a clue as to what happened to Robert? Even the most off-handed remark could mean something."

"There were just those calls. I know there was more to it than he was telling me, but I never got the chance to ask him about it. I kept putting it off. I didn't want him to know I'd been eavesdropping." The tears were streaming down her face in torrents by this time.

"Mrs. Cushing?" I asked hesitantly. "Can I get you a glass of water or something?" What I really wanted to do was put my arms around her and comfort her. I knew what it was like to lose someone you loved. Maybe not a husband, but I still remembered the pain of my father's death. Considering the circumstances surrounding John Cushing's death, I really ached for her at that moment. The matter of Robert made things just that much worse for her.

"I'll be all right," she said, shaking her head. "Just give me a minute." She pulled a tissue out of a box she had placed on the coffee table and dabbed at her eyes, taking long, shaky breaths. She sat up straighter.

"Let's just get this over with," she pleaded.

"Did Robert ever talk about any problems he might have had with anyone in one of his classes?" I was thinking of the fact that we found the bag at the site of the dig. Who knew? Maybe someone had it in for him and was trying to get him into trouble. Like Frank Samuels? No, he wasn't part of the class.

"No. Actually, he made a lot of friends through his classes. He liked the other kids, and he thought very highly of his professors, especially the one he had for archaeology. That was a good class all the way around, according to Robert."

I'd have to let Richard know how Robert felt about him. It's always nice to know you're appreciated.

"One last thing," Pete said. "Do you know if your husband was working on anything here at home? Something he might have been keeping notes on?"

"I think he'd been making notes about those phone calls, but I can't be sure. After he talked on the phone he'd disappear into his den for awhile. I know I sound like a snoop, but I peeked through the door and saw him writing something. I looked around later but I couldn't find anything. He always carried a briefcase, so there may have been papers in that. I just don't know for sure."

"Well," I said as I stood up, "thank you for your help. We'll be in touch with you if we need anything else."

As we were leaving, a pool maintenance truck pulled in the driveway. I'd been right about the pool at the rear of the house.

*   *   *

"Pete," I said as we drove back to my apartment, "I'm glad we were right about Robert being such a good kid."

"We could still be wrong," he reminded me. "I hope not, but there's always that possibility."

"I know. It's just that I'd like to think he really was a nice, innocent young man. I can't help it." I groaned. "I'm starting to refer to him in the past tense."

"I know what you mean on both counts. I'm starting to think of him in the past tense too. Things aren't looking good. Too much time has gone by."

"By the way," he said, changing the subject, "you sure misjudged Jessica Cushing, didn't you."

"Yeah, I guess I did," I admitted reluctantly. "I thought she was just your plain old run-of-the-mill, drop dead gorgeous gold-digger, but it turns out she's a gorgeous, sensitive, intelligent woman. She's actually pretty nice."

"She's got nothing on you, kid," Pete said.

"Why you sweet talker, you," I replied. I didn't know what else to say. I was getting too used to his smart cracks about me, and this was probably another one. But, inside, I couldn't help smiling. Glancing out of the corner of my eye I could see that Pete was trying to see what my reaction to his comment was. The invisible smile grew wider.

We pulled into a parking slot at my apartment and Pete turned off the engine.

"Oh. Are you coming up?" I asked innocently.

"No," he replied after a brief pause. "Force of habit, I guess. Turning off the engine I mean."

Now that was lame.

"Whatever," I said as he restarted the engine. "You're welcome to come up if you want to."

"No thanks," he said gruffly. "I've got things to do."

"Well then, I'll see you tomorrow."

"Uh, I'm going to check out a few things. If I come up with anything I'll call you," he said.

"I won't be home tonight, so if anything comes up, save it for tomorrow. Okay? I have a date tonight," I said sweetly. I had to throw that in. He loved giving me a bad time about my dating or not dating, and I felt a need to let him know I wasn't sitting home anymore.

"Oh."

"I'm going to a movie with Richard," I added. "And out to…"

"You don't need to give me your itinerary," he said flatly. "I'll see you later."

I heard him back the car out and leave as I climbed the stairs.

The lock didn't look like it had been tampered with, so I unlocked the door and entered the apartment, throwing my backpack onto a chair as I turned on the television. I decided to lie down on the couch and watch an old movie until time to get ready for my date with Richard.

Things had been busy and I guess it all caught up with me. I watched about fifteen minutes worth of the movie and fell asleep.

The insistent ringing of the telephone woke me up.

"Hello?" I said, still half asleep.

"Thought I told you to mind your own business and back off, bitch," growled a muffled voice. There was no doubting the intent of the call this time.

Sleep was gone, and I knew it would be a while before I slept soundly again.

CHAPTER 11

"Who is this!" I demanded, knowing how ridiculous it was to ask even as I did so.

"Your office and car were warnings. Next time it'll be more than a warning, I promise you. Back off or pay the price." This guy was out for blood. No more playing games and making idle threats, if you can call what happened to my car and office idle.

"Yeah? Well, well…Oh, go suck an egg!" I slammed the phone down and decided that I'd just outdone myself in the ridiculous department. I couldn't believe that someone was apparently threatening my life, and the only thing I could think of was to tell him to go suck an egg. I might as well have recited Sticks and Stones to him. Maybe not. I wouldn't want to give him any ideas about breaking my bones.

"Argh!" I moaned aloud. He was probably sitting there laughing his head off and thinking how easy it would be to take care of me.

Well, so he was through playing games. So was I, and I was ready for the fight, in fact, I was looking forward to it. That is, I would be as soon as I had Pete for back-up. I wasn't going to fight this one alone. The more I thought about it, the angrier I became. No one was going to scare *me* away from a case, especially this one. This one had become personal. The Cushing case had to be the reason this guy was after me. None of my other cases were heavy duty. A little insulting though, I mean, I did have more than one case. Did this guy think he didn't need to make reference because I wasn't working on anything else? Just who did he think he was?

Stupid, stupid, stupid! I thought. I should have tried to keep him on the phone. Anyone else would have kept him on the phone. But no, I had to hang up on him. I should have tried to wheedle some information out of him. I was sure he'd call again, and hopefully I'd handle things the right way next time.

I'd have to talk to Pete as soon as possible. I called his number and left a message on his machine asking him to call me, then told him not to bother. I realized I wouldn't be home when he called anyway.

My thoughts were whirling. Each thought jumped from one place to another before I could get a grip on the first one. I had to do something to calm myself down. For lack of anything better to do, I poured myself some iced tea and sat down at the kitchen table, thumping my foot on the floor. This whole thing was nuts.

The phone rang again and I sort of twitched. Then I thought, "Okay, now's my chance. That flea bag is calling me back because I hung up on him."

"What do you want now!" I demanded as I answered the phone. I heard a familiar voice and cringed.

"Oh, hi Mom."

"You sound like you're angry with me," she said accusingly. "What's the matter with you?"

"Mother, I just thought you were someone else."

"Do you talk like that to everyone who calls you? No wonder you never have a date," she said.

Thanks a lot, I thought.

"Mom, I do have dates. And I answered like that because I thought you were someone else, obviously. Actually, I'm glad it's you. I haven't heard from you in at least two days."

"Don't get smart with me, young lady." Mom was in a mood. A bad mood coupled with a "you're still my daughter and don't forget it" mood. I'd have to handle her carefully, especially since I was in a mood too.

"Besides, why would you answer like that, even if you did think it was someone else?" she asked.

"I've been getting some crank calls the past couple of days, probably just some kids fooling around, but it's getting real annoying. You know?" Fast thinking on my part. I couldn't let her know that someone was threatening me.

"Anyway, how are you? You don't sound like you're in the best of spirits today. Something wrong?" Turn the tables.

"Oh, I'm sorry. I just wanted to hear your voice, honey. The plumbing is acting up in the bathroom, the car wouldn't start this morning, your Aunt Martha isn't feeling well and she keeps calling me asking for favors, and I'm just worn out. You know how Aunt Martha is. Demanding would be an understatement," she said.

"Aunt Martha, huh. You know most of her complaints are just hypochondria. If she'd get involved in something she'd feel a lot better, I guarantee it. She's going to complain once too often, and unfortunately, when something really is wrong no one is going to listen to her."

"As a matter of fact," Mom said, "I was saying almost the same thing about you the other day."

"I may be a lot of things, but I'm not a hypochondriac," I stated emphatically.

"I mean about getting involved in things. If you'd get involved in something besides that business of yours, you'd be happier too."

"Let's not get into this again, okay? Actually, I am dating someone now. No," I corrected, "I'm dating two men right now." So I exaggerated, but it sure would get her off my back. I had to say two, or she'd zero in on the one guy I was dating. With one guy, she'd try to have me married by the end of the year.

"Are you okay?" she asked. "Your mood doesn't sound much better than mine. *Two* men?" she added cheerfully.

"I'm fine. You happened to call right after I got one of those crank calls I was telling you about. And yes, you heard right, two guys."

We gabbed for a few more minutes, both having calmed down. She wanted to know all about the two men I was dating, so I described Richard and Pete. Pete was the only other man I could think of to tell her about. I made a point of exaggerating a bit about both men. It makes her happy, so what the heck. She was thrilled with the idea that I was dating a college professor. I finally wound up the conversation when I told her I had to get ready for a date and I knew her phone bill was going to be sky high from calling me. I promised her I'd call her next time, and that I'd make it soon.

"I love you, Mom," I said as I hung up.

I poured myself some more iced tea and sat down on the couch for a few minutes. Talking to my mother had helped clear my head and I felt better about the threatening call I'd received. My mother was the one who struck terror in my heart, not the other caller. In a way, I felt the other call really had been just a crank call, at least until I remembered the bullet hole in my wall. Even though I hadn't told mother what was going on, talking to her always brought me back down to earth. Yes, even with the hole in the wall.

After I rinsed out my glass and put it in the sink, I decided it was time to start getting ready. I grabbed a fresh towel and washcloth out of the linen closet on my way to the bathroom, then took a quick shower. As I dried my hair and put on fresh make-up, I couldn't get Robert out of my mind. I thought about the threatening call and knew, with certainty now, that it had to be about the situation with Robert.

I walked into my bedroom and tried to decide what to wear. There was so much on my mind that even picking out an outfit seemed like a major undertaking. After a lot of frustration, I finally decided that since we were going to a movie I'd wear something casual. That should have narrowed things down. It didn't.

"This is absolutely ridiculous," I said to myself as I stood, staring dumbly at my closet. "I've never been an indecisive person."

I grabbed a pair of white Levi's and a blue shirt. The shirt was cropped and left the midriff bare. I added Mexican weaved sandals, grabbed a sweater for later in the evening and was ready to go. If nothing else, at least I was comfortable.

It was still early, so I called Pete again. He answered on the first ring.

"What is it!" he demanded before he even heard my voice.

"My, my. Aren't we in a testy mood," I said.

"Oh. It's you." Now I knew how my mother had felt when I answered the phone.

"Disappointed?" I asked.

"The phone has been ringing off the hook since I got home, and it's pissing me off," he said, sighing.

"It ought to make you feel good to know you're so popular," I said facetiously.

"Popular my butt! Someone's harassing me. One call tells me to mind my own business, the next one threatens me, the next one says I'll be sorry, and then you called. I'll tell you one thing though. Each call is the same person. And if I get my hands on him…"

"I see," I interrupted. "I guess I could have saved my breath then."

"What do you mean?" he asked.

"I was calling to warn you to be careful because I got one of those calls too. But I guess you don't need to be warned, do you."

"You got a call too?" he asked. "I wonder why you only got one."

"Because my mother called, so he couldn't get through. I guess he decided he'd pick on you instead."

"Well, it's a pain in the…"

"Now, now," I interrupted again. "My guess is that this means we're getting somewhere and someone doesn't like it. Or at least someone *thinks* we're getting too close."

"I had the same thought," Pete said. "We're going to have to sit down and go over everything one more time. How about if I come over right now?"

"Sorry, but I'm going out in half an hour," I replied.

"Well, if you're going out to eat, I'll come pick you up and we'll go together."

"I don't think that would be very comfortable. I'm going out with Richard, remember?" I knew very well he remembered.

"I'll see you at the office tomorrow morning," he said after a brief pause. He hung up before I could say anything else.

"There must be a full moon," I said to myself. I wondered why he didn't take the phone off the hook or let the answering machine take the calls. Sometimes men can be so dense.

Richard arrived promptly at six o'clock.

"You look wonderful," he said after I invited him in.

"Me?" I glanced down at my Levi's and shirt. "You've got to be kidding."

"I don't give compliments lightly," he assured me.

"Thanks," I said. I was surprised at the compliment, and I'm not gracious about accepting them. Compliments always make me feel uncomfortable. I don't know why exactly. Besides, I'd been thinking of comfort instead of appearance when I dressed.

"You're welcome," he said. "But you always look great. You're an attractive woman."

"You're just full of compliments tonight," I said, embarrassed.

"Shall we go?" he suggested. I looked up at him and saw that he was grinning. My embarrassment must have been showing.

"Just let me get my purse." I walked to the kitchen where I'd left my purse lying on the counter. I paused for a moment and ran some water into the glass I'd left in the sink, then gulped it down.

When I returned to the living room, Richard was sitting on the edge of the couch, deep in thought as he stared at the coffee table.

"What's wrong?" I asked.

"Huh?" He looked up quickly and smiled. "Oh. Nothing. Nothing at all. I was just thinking about Robert. His disappearance is quite distressing, especially after hearing about his brother's death. Robert is a fine young man." His facial expression was that of a worried man. He must have the same feeling as Pete and I, that things weren't looking too good.

"Pete and I talked to Robert's sister-in-law today. It seems that Robert felt the same about you. He told her that he thought you were a great professor."

"I'm delighted to hear that," Richard said.

I noticed that sometimes when Richard spoke he sounded very formal, but at other times he sounded down to earth. It must have been hard for him to pull his three worlds together. Wealthy family, teaching career and trying to be an ordinary guy. I remembered the day we were out at the site of the dig. When he came on to me, the ordinary guy had been trying to come out, but the straight man had been mixed in there too. He was almost poetic, then tried to make love to me, and finally seemed angry. After that he'd apologized. It made me feel almost sorry for him, watching him struggle with his different worlds. I had a feeling that the down-to-earth part of him would win out. I hoped so, because I liked that guy very much. Even if I hadn't been ready for him to come on to me.

"Why are you so quiet, Sandi?" he asked, breaking into my thoughts.

"I was thinking about what an intricate man you are. The many sides of Richard Smythe."

"That sounds like the title of a book," he said, laughing. "I only hope you like all sides."

"Oh, I do. Believe me, I do," I said thoughtfully.

The evening didn't turn out quite the way I expected. We stopped and had a bite to eat, then went to the movies. The movie turned out to be an archeological documentary being shown at the college. It was too technical for me to grasp more than a little of what it was about.

We were strolling out to the car after the documentary, and Richard was extolling the virtues of a new technique displayed in the film.

"Wasn't it marvelous?" he asked.

"Oh, yes," I lied. I didn't want to burst his bubble where I was concerned. I could probably develop a liking for his interests with time. At least I wanted the chance to try. Archaeology was interesting, or at least I thought it would be if I understood it better.

We decided to stop for a nightcap on the way home, and I suggested a place I'd been to near Stanley Hawks' apartment. Even when relaxing I couldn't get the two cases out of my head. Richard talked nonstop about the film.

"Richard, slow down," I said, after the cocktail waitress took our orders and brought the drinks. "You're wearing me out. You have to remember that you're an expert in the field, and I'm just getting started."

"I'm sorry. I do get carried way, don't I," he said.

"Don't apologize. Just slow down. You have to take into consideration that this is like Greek to me. Try to talk in layman's terms until I can figure out what you're talking about."

I knew I'd hurt his feelings when he changed the subject and seemed to sort of withdraw into himself. I felt like a heel. He had been so excited until I threw water in his face, figuratively speaking.

"I didn't mean to hurt your feelings," I said. "I just wanted you to remember that I don't have the schooling you do."

"You didn't hurt my feelings. Not really. I do tend to forget that there are other things in life besides my work. You're a good reminder for me. Actually, I think you're good for me in a lot of ways. You've been drawing me out of my work. I was reaching a point where nothing else mattered to me until I met you."

What a charmer, I thought.

"Well," I said, "I'm glad you feel I'm having a good effect on you."

He reached across the table and took hold of my hand, smiling. His touch gave me a warm, fuzzy feeling.

"Sandi, these last couple of days have meant an awful lot to me. Something important is happening between us. Can't you feel it?"

I felt the warm, fuzzy feeling fizzle out and I was suddenly uncomfortable. He was trying to make things move too fast. Just like that other guy, years ago.

"I'm afraid we'd better be going, Richard. I've got to get to the office early tomorrow. Things are picking up at work."

"You can change the subject, Sandi, but I'm not through talking about it. I'll bide my time for now though."

"Now," he said. "What do you mean, that things are picking up?"

"We must be getting close to something. Pete and I have both been receiving threatening phone calls. And, after thinking about it, I honestly don't think that envelope belonged to Robert."

"Envelope?"

"You know, the one I found at the dig. It doesn't fit in with anything we've learned about Robert. I think maybe someone was trying to set him up."

"Oh, that envelope. If I gave it more thought, I guess I'd have to agree with you. But what's this about the calls?" he asked, concern in his voice.

"Oh, I'm sure it's nothing to worry about. It's just someone trying to scare us off. I don't think it really amounts to anything." I was trying to convince him so he wouldn't worry about me. I could see it wasn't working.

"I wouldn't take this so lightly if I were you," he said. "Maybe I should come stay with you for awhile. Or you could stay at my place. Don't forget that someone shot at you the other night. I do worry about you, you know," he said, looking me in the eyes.

"Hey, I'm okay. Really. And, believe me, I certainly can't forget that someone took a pot shot at me." I was beginning to feel smothered. I wasn't about to go through that again. I liked him a lot, but whether it would grow into anything else, only time would tell. I knew I had to keep him at a distance for my sake, as well as for his. If he pushed too hard, I'd end up hurting him, and I didn't want to do that. He gave me the impression that he was probably a very sensitive person inside. Maybe if I explained about the other guy he'd understand and quit pushing me.

Just about then I glanced over Richard's shoulder and saw Mr. Stanley Hawks planting himself at the bar across the room.

Richard began to say something, but I hushed him. Mr. Hawks looked scared spitless.

"Sandi,…" Richard persisted.

"Shhh."

"What…"

"Wait a minute," I ordered, thankfully changing to business.

Richard turned his head to see what I was studying so intently.

"Who's that?" he asked.

"One of my clients. It doesn't have anything to do with Robert," I said quietly.

I knew that something was up by the expression on Hawks' face, and I wanted to know what it was. I didn't have long to wait for the answer.

Al Sands walked through the door and blatantly seated himself next to Stanley. I could see the poor little guy flinch. Sands placed a large, skinny hand on Stanley's shoulder. Was it time for a showdown?

I stood up and told Richard I'd be back in a minute. I casually sauntered over to the bar where the two men were sitting and ordered a drink from the bartender, trying to get close enough to hear them.

"Hey, fella," Sands said. "Got a light?" He stuck a cigarette in his mouth.

"No. I don't smoke," Hawks said softly, his voice a notch higher than usual. He was visibly shaking.

"I got a message for you," Sands said quietly, leaning closer to Hawks. "Beck ain't gonna give you much more time."

I could see Sands' knuckles turn white as he placed his hand on Hawks' shoulder and squeezed.

"Got that?" he asked.

"Who's…who's Beck?" Stanley asked timidly. There was pain on his face as Sands applied more pressure to his shoulder.

"Don't try to be cute, sucker. It don't suit you," Sands said.

Poor Stanley was blinking rapidly and looked terribly close to tears. He tried to pick up the drink he'd ordered, but knocked it over.

Enough was enough.

Chapter 12

"Stanley," I said loudly. "Stanley Hawks! How are you? I haven't seen you in ages. Mom was just asking about you the other day."

"Get lost bitch," Sands snarled at me.

"That's no way to talk to a lady," I said to Sands. "Didn't anyone ever teach you any manners?"

"Who is this creep?" I said to Hawks.

"Bartender," I said. "You got a bouncer in this place?"

The bartender looked at me like I'd lost my marbles. This was just a quiet neighborhood bar.

Sands withdrew his hand from Hawks' shoulder, obviously having second thoughts about me. Maybe he remembered the fiasco with the waitress and decided I could be more trouble than he wanted. Stanley looked relieved. He caught on immediately and played along with me.

"It's so good to see you," he said. "Really, *really* good to see you. How's your mother? Sit down and talk to me. Tell me what's new. Oh, it's so *good* to see you!"

"Don't overdo it," I whispered, but I knew he meant what he was saying. He'd never been so glad to see anyone in his life.

"Excuse me," I said as rudely as possible. "Could you move down a seat so I can visit with my old friend?"

"I was just leaving," Sands mumbled. "I'll see *you* later," he said as he poked Stanley's chest.

It wasn't until Sands was out the door that Stanley began to breathe normally again.

"Thank you," he said gratefully.

"What happened?" I asked.

"Just a minute." He ordered another drink and took a big gulp, choking as it went down.

"I was walking home from the market and that man was following me, as usual. Only this time he started to catch up to me. He never actually tried to catch up before, so I came in here, thinking that if there were people around me then maybe he wouldn't bother me. I'm so thankful you were here."

"So am I," came Pete's voice from behind me.

"Pete!" I exclaimed, whirling around.

"Hi! I got tired of the phone ringing, so after I talked to you I drove over to Stanley's place to see if anything was going on. I followed him to the store with Sands between us all the way. I saw you at your table when we all came in here, so I sat down at the end of the bar to see what would happen."

I glared at him.

"You handled that very well." He was grinning.

"For crying out loud! Why didn't you step in and help me?" I asked disgustedly.

"You seemed to be doing fine on your own. You didn't need my help," he replied.

Richard walked over and put his hand on my shoulder.

"Oh! Richard, I'm sorry. With everything that was going on, I forgot about you for a minute." Wrong thing to say. Again. "I didn't mean that the way it sounded."

"No problem. I didn't want to intrude," he said.

"Uh, could you wait at our table for a few minutes? I'd like to talk to Mr. Hawks privately."

"Sure. I just wanted to be sure everything was okay," he said as he glanced at Pete.

"Richard, this is my partner, Pete Goldberg," I said, taking the hint. "Pete, this is Richard Smythe."

They acknowledged each other but didn't shake hands. I wondered if I should tell them to go to neutral corners. Men can be such children sometimes. I shook my head in resignation over the situation, although in a way I was enjoying it.

"Nice to meet you," Richard said half-heartedly as he turned and walked away.

"Yeah," Pete said.

"Pete," I whispered, "there's no reason for you to act that way."

"Yeah? What about him? He wasn't exactly Mr. Congeniality himself," he retorted.

Ignoring him, I turned my attention to Stanley.

"Who's this Beck person Sands referred to?" I asked.

"I honestly don't have any idea. I'm as much in the dark about this as you are," he replied.

"Now wait a minute. Take your time and think about it for a second. Isn't there someone you've dealt with at some time or other by the name of Beck?" I persisted.

He was quiet, looking thoughtful.

"I don't know anyone by that name," he said, slumping over.

"Okay. But if you think of anything, let us know. In the meantime, I'm sure Pete would be happy to see you home."

I glanced at Pete and he rolled his eyes at me.

"Sure, Stanley. Come on and I'll give you a lift. You don't want to walk home alone tonight.

"On second thought, why don't you finish your drink first," Pete said as he looked at Richard. "Maybe it will help settle your nerves."

"Righto," Stanley said as he turned and knocked over his second drink. He ordered another one, a double this time.

As I returned to the table, I could feel Pete's eyes boring into my back. "Richard, let's go. I've still got that early morning tomorrow."

"So that's Pete," he said, ignoring my plea. Would anyone ever listen to me again?

"Come on." I picked up my purse. "Forget about Pete," I said impatiently. "We'll go to my place and have coffee before you go home."

He laughed, relaxing. "You had to throw in the part about me going home, huh?"

"Absolutely. This has been quite an evening."

I waved to Pete as we left.

"See you tomorrow," I called out.

He nodded and held up his glass as though making a toast to Richard and me.

Richard drove us back to my apartment where we settled down with our coffee. Everything was fine as long as the conversation consisted of small talk, but eventually he brought the subject of us up again.

"Sandi, I really mean it. I care for you a lot. I know this is happening too fast, but…"

"Richard, please listen to me," I interrupted. "I like you too, but I want to keep things light for right now. I don't want to get involved with anyone. You sound like you're getting serious, and I'm not ready for that. We barely know each other. Please give it some time."

"It's that Pete, isn't it," he said petulantly.

"Pete? Pete works for me. And I've only known him about a day longer than I've known you. Pete is an employee, pure and simple."

Richard sat back and stared at the ceiling.

"Look Sandi, I know we've only just met each other, but sometimes that's the way it happens. I feel very strongly about you. I can't help myself."

"I like you Richard, I really do. But you're coming on too strong, and that's the fastest way to get rid of me. Another guy came on too fast once before, and it was a disaster. You've got to take your time and let me take mine. Okay? Can we just let it go for now and enjoy each other's company?"

"You're right," he said, taking a deep breath. "I'm moving too fast for both of us. I'll let it go for now, but that doesn't change how I feel about you."

"I almost hate to bring this up after the conversation we just had, but I think you'd better leave now. I've really got to get some sleep."

"What do you mean that you hate to bring it up?" he asked.

"I didn't want you to take my asking you to leave the wrong way. I'm not asking because of anything that was said, but I do need some sleep."

"Hey," he said. "I'm not that sensitive. I know you have to get up early. Can I call you?"

"Of course you can," I replied. "I didn't say I don't want to see you again. I only said to take things slower."

"Understood!" he said, smiling.

I walked him to the door where he kissed me good-night. It was a gentle kiss, but there was a subtle demand behind it.

"Good-night, Richard," I said.

"Good-night, Love," he replied. He brushed my cheek with the back of his hand, then ran his fingertip along my lower lip. It caused a good kind of chill, and I knew instinctively that there was more to this man than met the eye.

He had been making me feel smothered, but I felt my willpower slip away ever so slightly as he left. Sometimes a kiss can do that.

*　　　　　*　　　　　*

The next morning, Monday, I arrived at the office earlier than usual. Pete was already there.

"Good morning," I said cheerfully, testing the waters.

"Good morning," he mumbled.

"What's the matter with you?" I asked, noting circles under his eyes. "You and ol' Stanley have a late night?"

"Very funny," he said.

"Well, you do look awfully tired again," I observed.

"Got home late. And no, I didn't spend the evening with Hawks."

I decided the wisest thing to do was not to push the issue. He'd probably been out with one of his girlfriends, and that was his business, not mine.

I stored my backpack in the desk drawer and got myself my first cup of coffee. I'd overslept and had to rush to get to work as early as I wanted to. That first taste of coffee was wonderful.

"What do you think?" I asked.

"About what? Am I a mind reader now?" he snarled.

"About the calls," I replied, ignoring his mood.

"He's a real jerk, you know." A statement right out of the blue. We weren't getting off to a very good start.

"What on earth are you talking about, Pete?"

"Professor Smythe," he replied. "I don't like him. I sure as hell don't know what you see in him."

"Ask me if I care," I snarled back.

"Well you should care. Last night I was there and ready to jump in if anything happened. Your professor just sat and watched. He seemed to think the whole thing was pretty comical, judging by his expression. I almost felt like he was hoping something would happen."

"Oh, come on Pete. That's ridiculous. He would have helped me if I needed it."

"You didn't see his face," Pete said. "He looked anxious, but not ready for action. Then he almost looked like he was going to laugh. I don't know, maybe he's just a pansy, the kind who doesn't like violence." His lips tightened up as he spoke, leaving the skin sort of white around his mouth. "But I still think he was looking at Sands like he wanted something to happen. If he's not a chicken, maybe he gets his kicks out of other people's problems, and your situation was definitely uncomfortable for a few minutes."

"You're imagining things," I said angrily. "You saw what you wanted to see and that's all. Richard was very concerned about the whole thing. As a matter of fact, on the way home he told me he was worried about the kind of work I do. He doesn't like it. He'd like to see me get into something else. In fact, he wanted to stay at my place to be sure I'd be safe."

"Safe? Sure! And what did you say to that?"

"Drop it Pete," I said, sighing in exasperation. "It's none of your business what I said to him, but he didn't stay. I don't know what's bugging you, but I want it to stop. You and Richard don't know each other, so there's just no reason for all of this. You're both being jerks about the whole thing."

"Can I assume from what you're saying that he feels the same way about me?" he asked.

Refusing to answer him, I walked over and turned on the radio.

The phone rang and Pete answered it. I could only hear his end of the conversation but he was upset. Something was wrong.

"What?!" he said incredulously. "When?" He listened intently.

"Right. We'll be right over." He was already out of his chair as he hung up the phone.

"Come on," he said. "That was my friend from the department. They think they've found Robert's body. They're taking Jessica to make a positive ID and she asked that we meet her at the morgue."

I stood there with my mouth hanging open. I just couldn't believe that our worst fears had come true.

"Sandi! Come on," he said, pulling on my arm.

"Let me get my backpack," I said, pulling away from him. I grabbed it out of the drawer and ran out the door after Pete.

"We both knew he wouldn't be found alive," I said. I felt defeated. "I couldn't help hoping, but you and I both knew, didn't we."

"Yeah. He's been missing for too long. I guess I knew for sure after what happened to John Cushing. I know there's some kind of connection between the two deaths, but I can't put it together." He was as frustrated as I was. He slammed his hand against the steering wheel. "We should have moved faster on this, damn it."

"I don't think it would have done any good," I said. "I have a feeling he's probably been dead all along. Besides, we didn't have enough information to work with."

"You're right," he said. "Rick, my friend, said it appears he's been dead for a number of days, and it's only been a few days since Jessica first came to see us. I feel like we should have been able to do something, even though I know there's nothing we could have done. In some ways, being a cop was easier. I didn't get so personally involved in the cases I worked on."

"Yes you did," I said quietly. "I'm getting to know you real fast. You're the type who always gets personally involved. Only you try not to let anyone know how you feel."

"What are you, some kind of psychiatrist now?"

I didn't answer him, and during the rest of the ride we were both caught up in our individual thoughts.

Rick Mason and Jessica were waiting by the front entrance when we arrived at the morgue. Jessica looked like she'd aged ten years since the day before. She looked haggard and whipped.

Rick left her side and came over to meet us as we walked up from the parking lot.

"She refused to view the body until you got here," he said to Pete. "She tried to call a friend, but the woman wasn't home, so she asked for you. She was adamant about not wanting to see the body unless you were here."

"Okay," Pete replied. "Let's go."

Pete introduced me to Rick as we walked toward Jessica.

"A pleasure to meet you," I said. "I just wish it was under different circumstances."

"Yeah, I know what you mean," he replied.

"You didn't tell me what a babe your new partner is," he said, thinking I was out of ear shot as I approached Jessica. I couldn't hear Pete's reply, but wished I could.

As I got closer to Jessica, I noted that the change in her was even more obvious than I'd seen from a distance.

"I'm so sorry," I said to her.

Her face crumbled and she began to cry. I put my arm around her waist and she turned and cried on my shoulder, heaving painful sobs. My heart broke for her. Maybe I was in the wrong line of business after all. I was trying to be tough, like Pete had suggested, but I couldn't do it. Instead, I cried with her. I pulled some tissues out of my backpack and handed a few to her as I wiped my own eyes. There was always the possibility that the body wouldn't be Robert's, but I knew in my heart that it was.

"I'm ready," she said, pulling herself together. "Let's get this over with."

She let go of me and took hold of Pete's arm. Rick led us inside, and we walked down long echoing corridors. I felt like we were on the way to the gallows. The closer we got, the shakier she was. It took both Pete and Rick to steady her. She kept glancing at me, and then at the floor. At one point I thought her knees were going to buckle, but she caught herself.

It was just like I'd seen in the movies. A man in a white coat came out and showed us into a small, clinically white room with a lot of drawers. It was cold, making me shiver in spite of myself. The man in the white coat checked a log on a clipboard that he held in his hand, then walked over and opened a drawer. He pulled out a shelf.

Jessica stood and stared, unable to take her eyes off the body. Her mouth drooped and her lip quivered. There was a slight tic in her left eyelid. We all waited on her.

"Mrs. Cushing?" Rick said. "Can you identify the body?"

"Yes," she said flatly, no emotion in her voice anymore. She slowly turned away. "That's my brother-in-law, Robert Cushing."

The man in the white coat pushed the shelf back in and closed the door with a final clank. Pete ushered Jessica out of the room quickly, Rick and I at their heels.

We stood in the hallway for a moment while Rick asked her a few questions.

"Would you mind excusing me for a minute?" she asked. "I think I'm going to be sick."

Rick pointed to the restroom and she ran down the hall as fast as she could, holding her hand over her mouth.

"Rick, what was the cause of death?" Pete asked.

"They haven't done the autopsy yet, but it looks like strangulation. There were marks on the body that indicate he put up quite a struggle, too."

"Anything else we should know?" I asked.

"Not much. There's a scratch on the inside of his hand with tiny particles of silver paint, and a very small piece of white thread. Those are being analyzed now. I'll let you know if we can determine what they're from.

"By the way," Rick continued, "we've been trying to reach his friend, Ray Peterson, but he's been avoiding us like the plague. Have you had any contact with him?"

"Yeah," Pete answered. "He was cooperative when I talked to him. I don't know why he'd be avoiding you. He was concerned about Robert and wanted to help if he could."

"I wonder what scared him off," Rick said.

"I don't know, but he did give me another name you might check on. Ray said Robert got into an argument with a kid named Frank Samuels the night he disappeared, and I can't locate this guy. Maybe you'll have better luck. There's at least a possibility that he's involved, but he seems to have disappeared too."

"Where was the body found?" I asked. "And if he's been dead for a number of days, shouldn't the body be more decomposed than it is?"

"Some hikers found the body in an old cave in the hills. The body held up pretty well because it was so cool in the cave."

Rick and Pete discussed things further while I went to the restroom to see if I could help Jessica. When I walked in, she was leaning against the wall, holding a wet paper towel to her forehead.

"Are you going to be okay?" I asked.

"I'll be fine," she replied. "There isn't anything else that can happen to me now. It's all happened. I'm not sure I've even got any tears left." She was extremely pale. "John's gone, Robert's gone, nothing else can hurt me now. I have no family of my own, you know. They were my only family. Nothing else can hurt me. All the hurt that could have been done has been done. I wonder what I did to bring all this on."

"You didn't do anything," I said softly.

Now I know what "haunted eyes" look like.

"Please! I don't want you off the case." She grabbed my hand, squeezing hard. "Find out who did this for me. Please," she said.

"We'll do everything we can to find out who killed Robert," I assured her.

"Do that," she said, "and I'm sure you'll find John's murderer too."

"You may be right," I said.

"I don't have anyone else to turn to," she said forlornly.

"Did you drive yourself down here?" I asked.

"No. Detective Mason drove me," she answered.

"Do you want Pete and I to drive you home?"

"Not really. I'd prefer you do whatever's necessary to get to the bottom of this, as soon as possible. I feel like there's a ten ton weight on my shoulders, and it won't go away until this is settled."

We returned to the two men and I saw a genuine look of concern on Rick's face. He took her arm and led her out of the building, saying he'd talk to us later.

"Jessica impressed Rick," Pete told me as we drove back to the office. "He knows about John's business connections, but he was surprised to find out how different Jessica is from her husband. I think maybe he's more interested than he should be."

"Well, what do you know," I said. "I just hope he realizes that she's not going to be ready to get involved with anyone for quite some time. Right now what she really needs is a friend with a big shoulder to lean on. I didn't care for her at first, but my opinion has changed drastically. She sort of grows on you if you give her half a chance. She's a lot stronger than I gave her credit for."

"Why didn't you like her?" Pete asked.

"It's like I said before. She struck me as being shallow, a user. I don't know. Maybe the way she dresses, and the fact that she married a man with lots of money. I guess I'm the shallow one. She's actually pretty nice. Like I said one time, I shouldn't make snap judgments."

"No, you shouldn't," Pete admonished. "Since we're on the subject, why don't you give me a break."

"What do you mean?" I asked. What had I done?

"You're constantly bugging me about my so-called girlfriends. There's nothing wrong with a man having female friends."

"But so many?" I teased.

"You're becoming the proverbial thorn in my side," he said.

"Good. You need someone to keep you in line," I said.

"Bull!"

We arrived at the office and checked the messages on the recorder. One of the insurance companies had called about another suspected fraud, and Stanley Hawks had called. He left his business number with a request that one of us call him.

"I'll call the insurance company and you call Stanley," I suggested. "I hope he didn't have any more trouble last night."

"I doubt it. When I left him he was locked up tighter than the mint. I went in with him for a minute and I swear, he must have a dozen locks on his door."

"Now why doesn't that surprise me," I said.

I turned and picked up the phone, dialing the number of the insurance company. After some discussion and obtaining the needed details, I informed them I'd get busy and dig up what I could. Things were busy, even though there were two of us now. If it stayed this way I'd have to hire another employee. This was a good thing.

The mail had come in and when I hung up Pete was sorting through it.

"Payday," he told me.

"Huh?"

"Jessica's first check is here. There are two nice-sized checks from a couple of insurance companies. And Hawks, bless his pea picking' little heart, sent us a payment with a thank you note."

"A thank you note. What a sweet man." I chuckled.

We looked through the rest of the mail, but there were just a couple of bills. Things I'd rather put off until later.

"Okay," I said decisively. "We've done enough fooling around. Let's get hot on these two cases. We'll work together from now on instead of going in opposite directions."

"Where do you want to start?" Pete asked.

"Let's start with Hawks. I think his will be the easiest, taking everything into consideration. Then we can really concentrate on the Cushing murders. We'll follow Sands and see where he leads us. If push comes to shove, we'll corner him and pound him with questions until he can't stand it anymore. Let's get some answers for a change."

"This is more like it," Pete said, grinning. "I've got an address on Sands. Want to start there?"

"Yes. But first I've got to take care of some business for this insurance company. That will take most of the afternoon. While I'm doing that, why don't you follow up on Ray Peterson and see what the story is there.

By the time we both get back, we should be able to devote all of our time to Hawks and Sands."

"I'm on my way," Pete said. "I'll see you back here in a couple of hours." He pulled a notebook out of his drawer and left the office.

CHAPTER 13

I made some calls and ran a few errands, getting the fraud case underway. There wouldn't be too much to do on this one.

Pete and I returned to the office within a few minutes of each other.

"Did you find Ray?" I asked.

"I did, but he wouldn't talk to me," Pete replied. "Something's wrong. He knows something, I'm positive. He tried to act like nothing was wrong, but he couldn't wait to get rid of me."

"Forget it for now. Starting tomorrow we'll concentrate on the Hawks case. Once we get that out of the way, we can get back to Cushing."

"Sandi, we can't let things get too cold or the Cushing murders are going to get away from us," Pete warned me.

"I know that. But there's nothing we can do for Robert now, and I think we may be able to get Hawks out of the way real quick with the two of us working together. Hawks is still alive, and I'd like to keep it that way."

"It would help if we could figure out who Beck is," Pete said.

"I think we ought to search Sands'…By the way, where is Sands living? In an apartment or a house? Where?"

"He's living in a cheap hotel," Pete answered.

"Figures. Okay, then I think we ought to search his room. I get the feeling he's not a very careful person. Maybe he left something incriminating lying around for us to find. It's worth a try."

"I've been thinking about Sands and this Beck," Pete said thoughtfully. "I think the only reason Sands has been following Hawks is to scare him. I don't think he's as careless as I had him pegged for. I think he *wants* Hawks to know he's being followed. He's trying to intimidate him."

"You're right," I said with sudden insight. "You're absolutely right. It's been a warning and scare tactic all along. This Beck, whoever he is, has been deliberately trying to harass and scare Stanley."

"Now if we could just figure out why, we'd have the whole thing solved," Pete said.

"Brilliant," I applauded.

"Don't try to be cute," Pete said.

"You know what?" I said excitedly. "I don't want to wait. Let's check out Sands' room tonight. We'll just make sure he's out first."

"Okay." Pete smiled indulgently. "If we leave now, we'll be able to get in while Sands is following Hawks, assuming he keeps it up after last night."

"Are you any good at picking locks? Whoops! That's illegal, isn't it," I said innocently.

"My credit card and I have opened more than one lock in our time," he said, ignoring my remark about the legality of the thing.

"Before we go, would you take me to pick up my car? It's supposed to be ready today," I reminded him.

"Sure. But let's hurry."

I picked up my car and met Pete back at the office. We took his car, deciding to grab something to eat on the way to Sands' place. We stopped at an In-N-Out® where we got the best hamburger in Southern California. We sat in the car and ate, discussing our strategy for the evening. We wanted to get in and out of Sands' room as fast as possible. Neither one of us knew if he could actually be dangerous or not, but we didn't want to take the chance. If he found us in his room there was a distinct possibility he wouldn't like it. Duh!

We finished eating, after Pete went back for another burger, and drove to the hotel, parking a block away. It was corny, I knew, but I brought a large floppy hat along that I kept at the office. Sands had seen me the night before, so I pulled the hat forward to shadow my face, just in case we ran into him. I didn't want to be recognized. Pete shook his head when I put the hat on.

"Well, at least I didn't bring a fake nose and mustache," I commented.

"Thank heaven for small favors," Pete mumbled.

We weren't sure if Sands would recognize Pete or not, but Pete wouldn't have lowered himself to wear a hat anyway.

We entered the hotel and nonchalantly strolled to the elevator.

"Let's take the stairs," I suggested strongly after one look at the dilapidated elevator. "They've got to be safer than that thing."

Pete grabbed hold of my wrist and pulled me through the elevator doors without a word. We rode up to the third floor and walked down the hallway, looking for Room 311.

Pete knocked on the door when we found it, while I stood to the side. There was no answer, so he knocked again, a little louder. Still no answer.

"I knew he wouldn't be here," Pete assured me. "You can bet he's out chasing Hawks around."

"What would you have done if he'd answered the door?" I asked in a whisper, as I looked over my shoulder to be sure no one was watching us.

"Never mind," he said as he pulled his credit card out of his pocket. He slipped it into the door jam by the lock, fiddled around a bit, and voila. The door opened to his touch.

"You've got to teach me how to do that," I whispered.

"Later," he replied.

"I didn't mean right this minute, for Pete's sake."

He gave me a look, sort of curling his lip at me.

With one last look over our shoulders, we entered Sands' room. It was dusk by then and the room was filled with long, dark shadows. There was a gaudy sport jacket lying on the bed, a sort of red and black plaid thing, but nothing else was lying around. I hoped he wasn't tidy about everything. We needed a lead, and we needed it fast. I had a feeling this was going to take some major searching on our parts.

"He's tidy," I commented, voicing my thoughts.

"Yeah. This isn't the type of place that provides maid service, is it."

The old double bed was in the far corner with a night stand by its side. At the foot of the bed, against the other wall, there was a straight-backed wooden chair. It looked terribly uncomfortable. There was a round table under the window with a hot plate placed right in the middle.

Across the small room from the bed there was a beat up, aging desk, criss-crossed with scratches and gouges, with another chair shoved against it. There were paper, pens and pencils neatly placed at the right corner. It appeared that Sands had been doing some writing. Next to the desk was a small chest of drawers.

The walls were devoid of any type of decoration. In fact, the only decoration in the whole room was a large framed photo of an elderly woman, probably Sands' mother, placed on the night stand. There was a minor resemblance between the two. Poor lady, she had the same eyebrow.

All in all, the tiny room was overcrowded with furniture. It looked like someone felt they had to fill every inch of the confined space with something. Every inch except the walls, that is. You'd think they'd at least have put up a couple of cheap pictures. Oh well…

There was a narrow door between the bed and the wooden chair. I walked over and opened it, finding the bathroom. It was extremely small, containing only a shower stall, toilet and sink. I closed the door after a brief look around. The sink and toilet were stained a disgusting rust color, not something I wanted to spend much time investigating. I'd actually never been in a seedy hotel before, and I didn't like what I'd seen so far.

There was another door located a short distance from the entrance to the room. Upon opening that one I found a closet, surprisingly large compared to everything else in the room. I closed the door, deciding we'd get to that after we searched the rest of the room.

Pete was already going through the desk, so I began checking out the dresser. As with the room, the items in the drawers were neatly arranged. I tried to be careful, not wanting Sands to know that anyone had been in his room. The only thing out of the ordinary that I found was, believe it or not, a ragged old Teddy bear. I picked it up and held it out towards Pete.

"Pete! Check this out," I said, giggling. "Can't you just see Sands cuddled up with this in his arms?"

"Shh," he hushed me as he looked up.

Pete had finished with the desk and was looking through a drawer in the night stand. I noticed that he wasn't being quite as careful as I was.

"Pete, slow down," I whispered. "The idea is not to let him know we've been here. Remember?"

"Yeah, yeah," he said impatiently, but I did notice that he replaced things more carefully after that.

"Well? Shall we tackle the closet?" I asked. "I noticed a suitcase and all kinds of boxes in there."

"Let's get to it," Pete said, sighing.

I opened the door of the closet and Pete was reaching toward the suitcase when we heard whistling outside the door of the room. We both stood quite still, until we heard someone fumbling with the lock.

Pete shoved me into the closet, into the corner, and followed behind, pulling the door shut behind him. We huddled in the corner, waiting.

"Get that hat out of my way," he whispered as it poked him in the eye.

I pulled it off and shoved it behind me, leaning on it.

We heard the door open, then Sands mumbling to himself. Pete gently moved some clothes on the rod so they'd hide us. At least they'd hide us as long as Sands didn't look too closely.

He started whistling again. We could hear his footsteps as he approached the closet. The door opened and some light shown in. We shrank back into the corner even farther.

Sands took a hanger off the rod and hung a jacket up, closing the door as he turned away.

I let out the breath I'd been holding. We were blanketed in blissful darkness again.

"Sandi, you're cutting off the circulation in my fingers," Pete whispered.

I loosened the fearful grip I had on his hand. I didn't even realize I'd taken hold of it.

We heard Sands walk across the room and a door opened. Then we heard water running.

"Come on," Pete whispered. "We'll try to get out while he's in the bathroom."

He stepped forward and opened the door a crack, looking out. Closing the door quietly, he stepped back into the corner and onto my foot. I grimaced, but kept my mouth closed.

"Forget it," he whispered. "He's got the water running, but he's standing by the bed taking a gun out of his shoulder holster."

"Wonderful," I whispered. "I sure hope he's going out again. We could be stuck here all night unless he finds us and decides to use us for target practice. I don't think I want out of here that way."

"I could live with being stuck in here all night," Pete chuckled.

I pinched his arm.

"Ouch!" he moaned quietly.

Before I knew what was happening, Pete took me by the shoulders and turned me toward him. He held me tightly and kissed me. I started to push him away, thinking how lousy his timing was, but he tightened his grip. I didn't fight him too hard, I have to admit. It was a long, lingering kiss, or at least it felt that way. But all too soon we heard footsteps coming toward the closet and we both froze. Pete didn't even move his lips from mine.

The door opened and between us we didn't move a muscle.

Sands shuffled through the clothes. Fortunately for us he was looking through the opposite side of the closet, and withdrew a hangar with slacks and a jacket on it. After what seemed an eternity, he closed the closet door again.

I pulled away from Pete and tried to catch my breath. I wasn't sure if it was because of the kiss or because of half smothering while we waited for Sands to close the door. We couldn't see each other in the dark and neither of us said a word.

We could hear Sands moving around, apparently changing his clothes and finishing whatever else he might be doing.

"Who could resist a dude as hot as you, ol' buddy," Sands said to himself. I choked back a laugh, just barely. He left the room as soon as he was through complimenting himself.

"Whew!" Pete said as he threw open the closet door. "Glad he's gone. That was no pea shooter he had in his holster."

"I'm glad I didn't see it," I said.

Both of us pointedly avoided mentioning the kiss. It had been spontaneous and hadn't meant anything anyway.

"I think maybe I'd better start carrying my gun again," Pete commented.

"Pete, please don't carry a gun unless you absolutely have to," I begged.

"I think I have to," he said as he started rummaging through the closet.

We searched every nook and cranny, but didn't come up with a single thing.

Pete walked over to the desk and leaned on it, his eyes looking far away and pensive. He reached into his pocket and pulled out a cigarette, then fished for his lighter. His eyes began to clear as he dug deeper and couldn't find it.

"I didn't know you smoke," I said.

"You don't know a lot of things about me," he replied. "I'm trying to quit."

"Not going too well, huh?"

He finally shrugged and opened one of the desk drawers, pulling out a book of matches.

"I saw these when I was searching the desk," he said by way of explanation.

"Okay."

He opened the book, tore out a match and lit it. He just stood there, the flame burning closer and closer to his fingers.

"Ouch!" he yelped, shaking it out. He looked up and grinned at me.

"What?" I asked.

He took his sweet time and lit another match, puffing on his cigarette to get it started, and took a long, slow drag off it. He blew a smoke ring and watched it rise in the air.

"What is it, Pete?" I asked impatiently. "What did you find? Don't play games with me."

His smile widened, spreading across his face, and he replaced the matchbook in the drawer. He was going to drive me crazy if I gave him half a chance.

I walked to the desk and reached for the drawer handle. He put his hand over mine and stopped me from opening the drawer.

"I just found Mr. Beck," he said, gloating.

"WHAT!" I yelled. I clamped my hand over my mouth. "Excuse me," I whispered. "What?"

"Yep. This good ol' boy did it again. I found our man."

I shrugged his hand off mine and opened the drawer. Removing the matchbook, I opened it up, expecting to find something written inside, but it was only gray cardboard. Nothing noted inside or out.

"What do you mean you found Mr. Beck? Where?" I asked, my frustration building by leaps and bounds.

"Close the book" he ordered.

"What the…"

"*Close* it," he repeated.

I closed it, light dawning on me finally. I turned the book over and looked at the advertisement on the back. In block letters it said, "Becker Loan Co.—$1,000.00 or More".

"I don't know why I didn't think of him before," Pete said. "I've heard of this guy. I guess it threw me because we thought Sands said Beck, not Becker. He makes legitimate loans all right, but he also makes loan shark type loans. Loan sharks need collectors. Sands is probably one of his so-called collection agents."

"Oh fine. Just what we need. A run in with a loan shark. What do we do now?" I asked.

"You're the boss," he replied.

"You're right. Let's go talk to Becker," I said.

"After we talk to him," Pete said, "I'm going to talk to Rick to see what they've got on Becker. Maybe we can do something about getting him off the streets."

"Maybe we should talk to Rick first," I said hopefully. "Besides, I can't imagine Mr. Hawks going to a loan shark. He's not the type."

"There isn't a special type that goes to a loan shark," Pete replied. "Besides, if we're going to help Hawks, we need to talk to Becker before Rick does. He's not going to say anything to us if he knows the cops are involved. Let's talk to Hawks before we go see this guy. Maybe he can shed a little light on this. I want to keep Hawks out of it if we can. I sort of like the little guy."

We left the room, but this time I took the stairs while Pete rode down in the elevator. I met him on the first floor.

"I forgot my hat," I said when Pete tried to lead me out of the hotel.

"It doesn't matter anymore if he knows we were there. We found what we needed. Your hat's all crumpled up in the corner anyway."

We drove straight from the hotel to Stanley's apartment, hoping he was home. We pulled up at the curb in front of the building and Pete took a good look around before we got out of the car.

"Looks like Sands took the night off. I don't see him anywhere."

"Maybe he had a hot date," I suggested. "After all, he did take pains to get cleaned up, more or less, and he was certainly in a good mood when he left."

"Hawks' lights are on, so he's probably home," Pete said. He pointed to an apartment at the end of the building. "That's his place over there."

We got out of the car and I followed him to the last apartment. He knocked gently on the door.

I glanced at him, wondering why he didn't just pound on the door, which seemed to be more his style.

"Hawks is pretty skittish," Pete explained. "He told me last night that lately loud noises make him jumpy."

I nodded in understanding.

"Who's there?" came a timid voice from inside the apartment.

"Pete and Sandi," Pete replied.

I heard various noises, Hawks was apparently undoing all of his locks, and the door opened a crack. I could see that a chain lock was still in place. When he confirmed that it was actually Pete and me, he closed the door and removed the chain, reopened it and invited us in.

Once inside, I turned to examine all the locks on the door.

"Mr. Hawks, you might save yourself some grief if you were to install a peep hole in the door," I suggested.

"You're right. Wonderful idea. I'll have it done tomorrow," he replied gratefully. "I'd never thought about a peep hole."

"We'd like to ask you a few questions about this Mr. Becker," Pete said. "By the way, it's Becker, not Beck."

"Please come in and sit down. I'll answer anything I can, but I doubt if I know enough to help you," he replied.

Mr. Hawks led us into a small living room, tripping on the edge of a braided rug on his way into the room. Pete caught his arm just in time to keep him from falling flat on his face. Pete and I sat on the couch in the tiny living room, with Hawks taking a chair across from us.

From what I could see, Stanley's apartment was just as I'd imagined it would be. The furnishings were somewhat old-fashioned, and it was very crowded. There was an overabundance of knick knacks, and there were books everywhere. Still, he managed to keep it looking fairly neat, and it almost had a comfortable feel to it. Everything seemed to have its own special place.

"I'm ready," he said, sitting very stiffly on the edge of his seat. "Ask away." He sounded like he thought we were really going to grill him. I noticed the muscles in his jaw flexing.

"Stanley," I said quietly, "sit back and relax. We work for you, remember? We only have a few questions and we won't take up much of your time. We need to get a couple of things straight."

He seemed to think about that for a minute, and then relaxed only very slightly, still sitting on the edge of his seat.

"Now," Pete proceeded. "First of all, the man's name is Becker, not Beck, like I said. Does that ring a bell?"

"No," Hawks replied promptly.

"Becker makes loans, both legitimate and under the table," Pete prompted impatiently.

Poor Stanley looked more confused than ever.

"Under the table means he's a loan shark. He loans money and charges extremely high interest on the loans," Pete explained. "It's all done very quietly, and the loans aren't legal."

"I see," Hawks replied. Aghast was the only word I could think of to describe the look on his face.

"Well?" I said.

"Well what?" Hawks asked.

"Have you taken out any loans lately? From Becker maybe?" I asked.

He looked at me questioningly.

"I've never heard of this Becker before in my life, and that's the truth." He sounded both confused and offended. I studied his face while he chewed on his thumbnail, deciding that he was telling the truth.

"Let me explain," I said. "When someone borrows money from the loan shark, and they don't make their payments on time, he sends someone out to collect. These so-called collectors usually aren't too pleasant to deal with, using force if they think it'll get the point across. I would guess the amount of money involved here isn't too much since Sands has only been following you around and trying to scare you. But now that he's made contact, I think things will probably escalate."

"Are you telling me that Mr. Sands wants to do bodily harm?" Hawks asked, his voice shrill and squeaky.

"Exactly," Pete replied. "I don't want to scare you, but up until now he's just been playing with you. Count your blessings that we figured this out before he actually did anything. They've been known to shoot off a guy's kneecaps, things like that. It can get pretty ugly."

Stanley blanched and his eye began to twitch at that tidbit of information. His face was turning red.

"Pete!" I said sharply.

"Sorry," he said.

"We're going to have a little chat with Becker and find out what's going on. We may be able to clear this up real soon," I assured Hawks. "I'll give you a call tomorrow to let you know what we find out."

Pete and I stood up, ready to leave, and Hawks stood up with us. He reached out to shake Pete's hand, then mine.

"You folks are just fine. I really appreciate all your hard work. Please call me at your earliest convenience tomorrow."

"We will," I replied.

After we got back in the car I jumped all over Pete.

"If you were trying to scare ten years off his life, I think you did it quite well. What's the matter with you, anyway. Kneecaps of all things. Couldn't you think of anything else to say?"

"Hey!" he said, defensively. "I just figured if he was lying, that would scare him into leveling with us."

"I think he was telling the truth. I don't think he has the foggiest idea of what's going on."

"Yeah, I shouldn't have scared him like that. But if he's telling the truth, that just clouds the issue even more. Why would Becker be after Hawks if he didn't borrow money. It doesn't make sense," he said, scratching his jaw. "Becker isn't into anything else that I know of. Well, maybe drugs, but I don't think Hawks would be involved in anything like that."

"Not Hawks. He wouldn't know anything about drugs, I'm sure. Hopefully we'll find out what it's all about tomorrow morning. At least we know Hawks is okay for tonight. I mean with Sands out for the evening."

"Yeah, but let's make a point of getting to Becker's place early," Pete said. "We don't know how long Hawks will stay safe. I'd hate to see anything happen to the little guy. He sort of grows on you, you know?"

"I know what you mean. How about if we meet at the office at seven-thirty or so, and we'll drive to his office together," I suggested.

"I have a better idea. Let's meet at the office at six-thirty and drive to his house together. He wouldn't be expecting anyone to show up there."

"Good idea," I said. "We'll get him where he's more vulnerable."

"Maybe we can get him without his goons around."

"Lord, I hope so," I said.

Pete drove me back to the office to get my car. I felt measurably relieved to find my car still in one piece.

CHAPTER 14

The next morning I arrived at the office at six-fifteen and started the coffee while I waited for Pete.

I'd had another call from my mother after I got home the night before. She wanted to know how things had gone on my date. I told her everything was just fine. She brought up my job again, lamenting that she just knew at the very *least* I'd eventually get shot and maimed for life. She didn't use those words, but the meaning was unmistakably clear. I intentionally talked about the insurance cases and didn't mention Hawks or Cushing. I didn't want to fuel the fire.

Mom said that Aunt Martha was feeling better, and added that she'd feel better too when I got married and settled down. She can be so frustrating sometimes. I told her she was beginning to sound like a broken record. She just "humphed" at me. Actually, my mother and I get along quite well. She simply thinks a woman my age should be married with a house full of kids, not running around chasing bad guys. I know her intentions are good though.

I was thinking about that conversation when Pete walked in. I tapped my watch with my finger, noting the time as a quarter to seven.

"You're late," I said.

"Overslept," he replied.

"You're the one who said we should get there early," I pushed.

"Chill," he said as he poured himself some coffee. "Come on, let's get moving before we miss him." He had his cup in his hand, ready to take it with him.

"Do you know where we're going?" I asked. "I checked the phone book, but I didn't see him listed."

"This is not a man who would want his address and phone number listed in the phone book. I know where he lives. I called Rick and he got the information for me."

"You're gonna be lost if Rick ever leaves the department," I said.

"Nah. I've still got other connections."

"Yeah? Well, treat them nice. These guys are proving to be invaluable." At that point I didn't know what I'd do without Pete and his so-called connections.

We got in the car and Pete headed for one of the nicer parts of town. The section we were looking for loomed into view after about a twenty minute drive. As we pulled up to a rather large and pretentious house, I looked at Pete and saw that the coffee had finally taken effect. He looked alert, his eyes brighter and clearer.

"Okay," Pete said as he pointed to a car in the driveway. "We'll wait until he comes out to get in his car, then we'll approach him and play it by ear."

"I'll follow your lead," I said. "I don't think we're going to have to wait long. Is that him coming out the front door?"

The man was tall and lean, athletic looking. Actually, he looked quite respectable, proving that appearances can be deceiving. He had thick steel-gray hair and a neatly trimmed mustache, and he was wearing a very expensive suit. Definitely not something off the rack.

"Are you sure this is the right place?" I asked. "He doesn't look like a loan shark."

"And just what does a loan shark look like?" Pete asked sarcastically. "When are you going to quit judging people by the way they look? Or by their name, for that matter."

"Point well taken," I said sheepishly. I'd only recently learned the true meaning of not judging someone by their appearance. Jessica Cushing immediately came to mind.

"Okay, time to attack," Pete said as he got out of the car and started up the driveway. I followed behind him.

"Mr. Becker?" Pete called out.

Becker was putting a briefcase in the back seat of his car. He stopped with a jerk and turned to look at us. He hadn't heard us coming and we'd obviously startled him. He scowled as his gaze zeroed in on Pete.

"Who wants to know?" he asked.

"Pete Goldberg, Webster Detective Agency. Can we speak to you for a moment?"

"I don't think I have any business with you," Becker said as he turned back to his car.

"Oh, yes you do," Pete said sharply.

I could see Becker's face hardening as he turned to face us again, and I didn't want to lose him. I put a restraining hand on Pete's arm. Maybe a woman's touch would work this time.

"Excuse me, Mr. Becker," I said as pleasantly as possible. "We have a problem, and I believe you may be the only person who can help us. It's really important, and I'm sure you can spare just a minute or two for us. Please?"

He shifted his gaze from Pete to me as I spoke, his expression softening almost imperceptibly.

"What is it you need, young lady?" he asked.

"Young lady?" I said, breaking the ice. "I wish Pete would talk to me that way once in awhile." I gave Pete a meaningful look which told him to keep his big mouth shut.

"Okay," he said chuckling, "what can I do for you? But make it fast, I'm running late."

"Thank you," I said. "It's like this. We have a client who's being followed by a man named Al Sands."

His face began to harden again.

"Now wait a second," I said in a soothing tone of voice. "Please let me finish before you close me out."

His eyes were narrow slits clouded with suspicion.

"Our client is a Mr. Stanley Hawks. He's a pale, meek little man who wouldn't hurt a fly. Why, he even works for a greeting card company of all things. And he *swears* he's never heard of you. I believe him.

"This is strictly off the record," I continued, "so I'm not going to play games with you. I know about your, shall we say, sideline, and he says he's never borrowed any money from you."

I saw Pete grimace out of the corner of my eye.

Becker visibly stiffened, and I knew I'd hit a nerve. I hoped he wouldn't hit back. I didn't want the situation to turn ugly.

"I don't have the vaguest idea of what you mean by sideline," he said coldly.

"Look. All I want to know is, do you know Stanley Hawks or not? The man is scared out of his mind and he doesn't know why he's being followed."

Becker stared at me for a few seconds. He glanced at Pete and back to me. He seemed to reach a decision.

"Wait here," he said shortly. He returned to his house and left us standing by the car.

"I'm tempted to grab that briefcase he put in the back seat," Pete said. "Can you even guess how much valuable information is in there?"

"Forget the briefcase. I just hope he's not going in for reinforcements. Right at the moment I'm a little worried about my kneecaps."

"Hell," Pete said, looking at the briefcase longingly, "he probably doesn't have anything incriminating in it anyway. He's not that stupid."

We waited for quite some time for Becker to return. I was beginning to worry that he wouldn't be back when he finally opened the front door and stepped out. His face was deep red, and he was as angry as anyone I'd ever seen.

"I hope that anger isn't directed at us," I said, nudging Pete.

"I don't know, but it doesn't look good."

Becker was in a hurry. He pushed past us, opened the car door and slid in, starting the engine in a hurry. He wasn't even going to give us any answers.

"Hey!" I said angrily, all pretense of pleasantness gone. "What's the story here?"

"The story?" he repeated. "The story is that I've got a jack ass working for me. Don't worry about your client. He won't be bothered anymore. I promise you that."

"That's not good enough," Pete said. He sounded like he thought he finally had the upper hand, and he probably did. "Why has Sands been harassing him?"

Pete sounded angrier than Becker by that time. Becker looked surprised that Pete would stand up to him, something he probably wasn't used to. Suddenly he slammed his fist against the steering wheel of his brand new Jaguar. He stopped himself and rubbed it like he was sorry he'd hurt his nice car.

"A case of mistaken identity," he said, sighing. "I'm looking for a *Samuel* Hawks, and he's a large black man, not a timid little white guy."

Pete didn't say a word as he turned and walked back to his car.

I stepped up to the side of the Jaguar and smiled at Becker.

"Mr. Becker, you'd better reach Sands real quick. I like Mr. Hawks, and if anything happens to him I'll make *sure* you pay for it. Trust me," I said, wiping the smile from my face.

"You'd better do some growing before you run around making threats, little lady," he said menacingly, "or you might find yourself in some big trouble. Don't say things you can't back up."

"Oh, I'll back it up, I promise you," I said vehemently.

His facial expression changed and he looked at me long and hard.

"You know? I almost believe you."

Not wanting to push the issue, I turned on my heel indignantly and stalked back to Pete's car.

Becker stared at us as we pulled away from the curb. After we were out of sight, Pete laughed.

"What's your problem?" I asked.

"You."

"Oh. You heard what I said to Becker?"

"The whole neighborhood probably heard you. You weren't nearly as quiet as you thought. But you sure made it worth getting out of bed this morning."

"I have my moments," I said smugly.

"You really had that guy going," he said, slapping my knee. "It was great!"

"Are you still going to call Rick?" I asked.

"You bet. That's a bunch of crap about mistaken identify. Becker made one big mistake though. He told us the name of the guy he's really after. Samuel Hawks is going to get a visit from the police real soon, and I have a feeling that he'll be only too happy to cooperate. Becker made another mistake, too, when he left us and went into his house. He's got records in there somewhere or he couldn't have answered our question. Rick ought to be real interested in knowing that the guy keeps stuff at home."

"He's probably got a computer inside the house. I hope you're right about all of this. I'd sure like to see Becker off the streets. For good. Will they be able to get into his house to look for the records?" I asked.

"I'm sure Rick will find a way."

"Let's go see Stanley instead of calling him," Pete suggested. "We'll catch him when he goes to lunch."

"I like that idea, Pete. I want to see his face when we give him the good news. Can you imagine how relieved he's going to be?"

We drove back to the office where I made a few phone calls regarding my insurance cases. Since insurance fraud was one area where I had more expertise, Pete sat down and let me give him some pointers. He proved to be a good listener with an ability to grasp facts quickly, and he didn't act like he thought the fraud cases were too piddly for his attention. He asked questions, then took a couple of files to his desk to look over and begin working on.

The phone rang and I answered it. It was a wrong number. It rang again and I scheduled an appointment with a Mr. Frederick Frye who wanted to locate a long lost relative. When the phone rang for the third time I thought to myself that business was good.

"Webster Detective Agency," I answered.

"This is Ray Peterson," came shaky voice at the other end of the line. "Is Mr. Goldberg there?"

"Hold on just a second," I replied.

"Pete," I said as I covered the mouthpiece. "It's Ray Peterson. He sounds kind of upset."

"Thanks," Pete said.

I returned to my work while Pete talked to Ray. He only talked for a minute before he hung up.

"He wants me to meet him tomorrow morning," he said.

"Did he say what it was about?" I asked.

"No, he just said that he had some information for me. Important information, but he can't see me until tomorrow."

The phone rang again.

"Busy place this morning," Pete commented.

"I love it," I replied.

Coincidentally, it was another long lost relative problem.

While I was on the phone, Pete answered a call on the other line. He put the call on hold and waved the receiver at me to indicate it was for me. I could tell by the disgusted look on his face that it was Richard. I completed my call and switched to the other line to talk with him.

"Hi there!" I said delightedly, somewhat for Pete's benefit.

"Hi yourself," he replied. "Are you busy?"

"Always, but I can take time for you." I could see that Pete was pointedly ignoring my conversation. Or at least trying to.

"Can you talk?" Richard asked.

"Huh?"

"Pete answered the phone," he said.

"Oh, come on. You guys are being ridiculous. Hold on for a second," I said as I stood up. I put him on hold.

I walked over and turned the radio up a little louder so I could talk more freely, without Pete being able to hear me. The radio was directly behind his desk.

"I'm back," I said, picking up the phone. "So what's up?"

"Not much. I thought, if you aren't busy, that you might like to drive out to my place for dinner tonight."

"I'm really sorry, Richard. I won't be able to make any plans for the next couple of nights. I have some work to catch up on. Could we make it another night?" I asked hopefully. I honestly had to get caught up on the insurance cases or I'd end up losing business.

"How about Friday night? I've got a seminar to attend on Thursday evening."

"Friday is fine. What time?" I asked.

"Come on out as soon as you leave work. I'll barbecue some steaks."

"Sounds great," I replied.

"Good. I've got to get to my next class now. Talk to you later."

"Bye Richard."

Pete walked over to my desk as I hung up, tapping his watch, no doubt trying to give me a dose of my own medicine.

"We'd better go. It's just about time for Hawks to leave for lunch."

"Okay," I said, pulling my backpack out of the desk drawer.

The drive to the greeting card company where Hawks worked was relatively quiet, the camaraderie of earlier that morning seemingly gone. We parked the car across the street from the building, and as we started across the street Hawks came out of the door. He saw us and waved. As he reached the bottom of the steps we saw Sands come out of nowhere. He grabbed Hawks, pushing him toward a car parked in the adjoining alley.

"Hey!" Pete yelled. He took off running toward the alley.

Sands looked over his shoulder, shoved Hawks into the car on the driver's side and jumped in behind him.

Pete almost made it. In fact, he was close enough to slam his hand on the trunk lid just as Sands took off. Pete never slowed for a second as he turned and ran back to the car.

I was way ahead of him. I jumped into the car, planning to drive over and pick him up, only to realize that he had the car keys. I slid over and put on my seat belt, contemplating a wild ride ahead of us. Pete had reached the car and was starting the engine as I fastened the belt.

With tires screeching, he turned left into the alley in pursuit of Sands. When he reached the other end of the alley, he looked first right, then left. Looking right again, we could see the tail end of Sands' car just going around the corner to our right. More screeching tires as Pete pulled out of the alley.

I covered my eyes as I saw a huge garbage truck pulling out from the curb. Pete flew around him, on two wheels it felt like, barely missing a bus coming at us from the other direction. He turned the corner, back wheels fishtailing, and picked up speed.

"Have you ever thought about driving for the NASCAR races?" I asked. He didn't answer me.

We could see Sands' car about a block ahead of us. Pete swung to the left to avoid hitting a car that was in the process of parallel parking.

"Do you believe this? Look at him. He looks like he's out for a Sunday drive. I don't think he realizes we're behind him," I said incredulously. "How could he think we wouldn't chase him?"

Pete slowed down, keeping Sands in sight.

"He probably figured we couldn't get back to the car in time to catch him," Pete said. "Let's just hang back and let him believe that."

"Yeah, he probably doesn't realize just what a maniac you are behind the wheel," I said.

Pete bared his teeth at me.

"Vicious, too," I mumbled.

"We'll leave two cars between us and them," Pete informed me. "We're going to have to wait it out until we can get to him. Becker must not have been able to reach him."

I didn't take my eyes off Sands' brown Chevy again, afraid of losing him.

"Pete, he's turning right at the next corner."

Fortunately, one of the two cars between us was too.

"I see him," Pete replied.

Sands seemed to be heading toward the outskirts of town. I tried to imagine where he might be taking Hawks and decided it was probably too awful to contemplate.

"He's probably taking him to some isolated area to try to make his point," Pete said, as though reading my mind. "We're going to be in big trouble if we run out of traffic to hide us. No telling what he'll do to Stanley."

The car between us suddenly turned right without signaling, leaving us in plain view. We ran out of luck when I saw Sands look in his rearview mirror. I knew he recognized us when he tromped on the gas pedal and his car lurched forward.

"This is it!" Pete said loudly as he stepped on the gas. "Hold on!"

Within seconds the two cars were flying down the streets of Los Angeles at outrageous speeds, dodging traffic like it was an obstacle course.

"Where are the cops when you need them?" I asked weakly.

"On the other side of town," Pete replied.

"Pete!" I yelled as we turned a corner a little too fast for my comfort.

I glanced at him and knew he was enjoying the chase. He probably felt like he was back in a patrol car again, and totally in control.

"You're going to kill us," I howled.

"Don't be a wimp," he snapped at me. "I know what I'm doing. You'd better worry about Sands and Hawks, not us."

We passed a street, I couldn't read the name, barely getting through a signal before it turned red, and kept going. As we passed the street I noticed a police car waiting for the light to change. He was behind us in a split second, siren wailing and lights revolving.

"All right!" Pete yelled over the whine of the laboring engine. "He'll call for a back-up unit and we'll get Sands."

"Whooppee," I whispered as my stomach lurched for the umpteenth time.

I fleetingly thought of Hawks. If I was scared, he had to be out of his mind with fear. I hoped he had a good, strong heart.

We passed another street and a second police car joined the parade.

I closed my eyes and started saying a silent prayer. Mom had been right. I would be shot by the police, and instead of being maimed, I'd die. I knew I should have listened to my mother.

I opened my eyes in time to see what I thought might be Sixth Street, I couldn't be sure, go whizzing by.

"Oh Lord," I prayed.

Sands made a sharp right turn and we followed right along.

"This is it!" Pete yelled.

"Oh no!" I yelled back.

"He's going to hit a dead end and go right into that field," Pete said, ignoring me.

Pete began to slow down, much to my relief, while one of the police cars pulled up behind us, honking his horn. Why on earth was he honking his horn?

I said a silent thank you.

The second police car followed Sands to the end of the street. He'd slowed down too, because he knew Sands had nowhere to go.

Before I realized what was happening, there was a cop with a gun drawn standing by my door ordering me to get out. I obliged willingly, even though my legs would barely hold me up. I looked at Pete and he was being ordered out of the car too.

"Put your gun away, Hank," the cop on Pete's side of the car said. "You won't need it."

"What are you talking about," came an agitated voice from behind me.

"You won't need your gun. This is Goldberg, the guy I told you about that…"

"Never mind," the cop said as he glanced across the car at me. "I'll tell you later. Put your gun away."

Good ol' Hank put his gun away, grudgingly. I could see he wanted some action, and I was glad I wouldn't be involved. For a minute, I'd felt like he was almost willing me to make a break for it. He was young, probably a rookie, but that was no excuse in my opinion. What did they call the new, overly anxious guys? Hot dogs. That was it.

We met at the front of the car with cops number one and two to talk. I looked up to see cops three and four walking our way, being none too gentle with Sands and Hawks.

"Pete," I said, pointing their way.

"The little guy with the glasses is the victim," Pete hollered at the approaching policemen. "Take it easy, huh?"

"Hey, Goldberg," one of them yelled back. "What're you doing out here?"

I felt like I was in the locker room when the approaching cops began banging and slapping Pete on the back, saying sweet things like "How's it hangin'?"

"What's going on," asked cop number one.

"Got a good story for you," Pete replied.

CHAPTER 15

Pete and I gave them a brief account of what had happened. They all stood around shaking their heads when he explained about the mistaken identity. Sands turned pale. Obviously, Becker hadn't reached him in time, just like I thought. He knew they were going to nail him, and if they didn't, Becker would. He didn't have a snowball's chance, no matter what he did.

Pete agreed to drive to the station so we could give our statements. Hawks wanted to ride with us, which the police gratefully consented to. Hawks was so shaken and nervous, we had to turn our backs while he got sick. The cops were more than happy to let someone else take care of him. They didn't want him tossing his cookies in their unit, but they sure wanted him to get to the station safely to give his statement and fill out some forms regarding Sands.

On the way in I tried to make small talk to calm Hawks down. He kept saying he was okay, but I knew better. I was still terrified after the wild ride, so I had some idea of how he must have felt.

"You're not really all right, are you?" I asked.

"No," he replied, as a smile crossed his face, "but I'm getting there. I have to admit that after the initial shock, I find this was the most excitement I've ever had in my entire life. In fact, in a way, it was exhilarating."

"Now don't get carried way," Pete said over his shoulder. "You were in a pretty tight spot."

"Oh, I know, I know. He had a gun pointed at me until the chase began. Can you believe it? A gun. It's just that, well, my life is so *boring*. I'm going to have quite a tale for the fellows at work."

I could see him forming the story in his mind even as we talked. I knew he'd embellish the story, even though he wouldn't need to. Actually, his attitude seemed to calm me down. It was all in the way you looked at things. It could be construed as frightening, or it could be construed as an exciting adventure. I guess that was pushing it, but it helped.

"That kind of excitement I can do without," I said to Hawks.

We arrived at the police station and I accompanied Hawks while he gave his statement.

"I'll catch up with you in a few minutes," Pete said. "I want to see if Rick is here."

"Okay," I said, nodding.

"Becker will probably be in custody by tonight," Pete said when he finally joined us. "Sands is spilling his guts. They can hardly shut him up. He's even waived his right to an attorney. Apparently, he's more afraid of what Becker could do to him than the law. He wants to be sure Becker is locked up. He keeps asking if they'll promise he and Becker won't be anywhere near each other."

"He's not too bright, is he," I commented.

"All the better for us," Pete replied. "He's spilling things that will really nail Becker to the wall. I'd hate to be in his shoes if Becker does get hold of him."

"Mr. Hawks," I said, turning to Stanley, "can we give you a lift home?"

"No," he replied, "but you may drive me back to work. I've got to retrieve my vehicle. And, to be frank, I can't wait to tell everyone about today's escapade. The fellows at work will never believe it. Me. In a high speed car chase with a gun pointed at me, just like on television."

Stanley had a war story, probably the first one in his life, and he couldn't wait to share it with a captive audience.

"Tell you what," I said. "Pete will make sure a police unit drives you back to work instead of us, and that they escort you into the building, just to be on the safe side." It would add a little credence to his story.

Pete nudged me in the back, but I ignored him. He tried putting his hand on my arm, but I gently peeled it off. With a roll of the eyes, he left us alone while he made arrangements for Stanley's transportation.

By the time everything had been taken care of it was after four-thirty.

"Are you hungry?" Pete asked as we drove back to the office.

"Starved," I replied. "Where shall we eat?"

"I don't know. What are you in the mood for?"

"I know exactly what I want," I said without hesitating. "Let's make this a business dinner and I'll treat. I want lobster. I've got to have lobster tonight."

"Expensive taste," Pete said.

"Think of it as a celebration in honor of solving the Hawks case," I said. "The first one that we've solved together. We'll discuss the Cushing case briefly just to make it a real business dinner."

"We might as well celebrate. I have a feeling that starting tomorrow we aren't going to be in the mood."

"What do you mean?" I asked. He sounded pessimistic, a role reversal since pessimism was usually my role.

"I mean that I think this thing with Robert Cushing is going to get pretty ugly. Even if we see a light at the end of the tunnel, it could turn out to be a freight train. I don't think we're going to be in the mood to celebrate again for awhile."

"You're probably right," I said. It depressed me to think we'd never had a chance to find Robert. He'd been dead even before Jessica Cushing had come to see us. I frowned, deep in thought.

"But for tonight," Pete said, brightening, "let's forget everything but that precious lobster you want so much. You're right, we should be celebrating."

My mood didn't lift until we were seated and talking at the restaurant. Our business dinner turned out to be more pleasure than business. We didn't do much sparring, but instead had a pleasant social evening. We opened up and told each other about our two very different backgrounds.

"I come from a large family," Pete said. "I've got three sisters and four brothers, and we grew up in New York." That explained why he seemed street-wise, in conjunction with his years as a cop.

"We didn't have a lot of money growing up, but then Pop developed a new aquarium filter."

"Aquarium filter?" I asked. "You mean like for fish aquariums?"

"Yes. It was revolutionary to fish lovers, and that was only the start. That went over so well that he began looking at other things. You know, trying to figure out what might make life a little easier. He came up with some pretty good ideas, and was inventive enough to follow up on them. It turned out my mother was good at marketing, so they made a great team. Actually, he ended up being pretty well off financially. He was able to put the kids left at home through college, and now he's retired."

"It's nice to hear a success story like that. I grew up right here in Southern California. I'm afraid my story isn't quite so nice though. Don't get me wrong, I loved my father very much, but he sure screwed things up. He made some drastic business errors, at least that's the way I like to put it. He made a few business deals that weren't quite legal. He eventually died of a heart attack, a broken man, and left my mother with all kinds of debts. It wasn't until he died that we found out what was going on and why his life fell apart. I was still at home at the time, so I got a part-time job at a department store and helped my mother to start paying things off. It wasn't enough though, and Mom had to file for bankruptcy, much to her embarrassment. I tried to reassure her, but she couldn't help how she felt. She didn't have any other choices.

"She loved my father deeply," I continued, "and she never voiced any blame about the mess he'd left her in. I was only a teenager at the time, but I still wished I could have helped more. Eventually mother inherited some money from an aunt, which she invested wisely, and she's pretty comfortable now. Not rich by any means, but comfortable. Now she spends all her time trying to get me married off."

"She never remarried?" Pete asked.

"No. I don't think she wanted anyone in her life other than my father. I wish her Mr. Right would come along though. You know, to distract her so she won't worry so much about me."

Pete finally got around to the subject of Richard. It didn't surprise me, and he was about as subtle as a bull in a china shop.

"What about this Richard character?" he asked. "Do you really like this guy?" I noted a look of disdain on his face.

"Well, yeah. He's a nice person. I enjoy his company." I hesitated a second too long with my answer and Pete picked up on that.

"Is there something wrong with him?" he asked.

"No, not really. It's just…hmm. I don't know, he seems to have a battle going on inside. It's a little disconcerting sometimes."

"What do you mean by a battle?"

"Richard is from an extremely wealthy family. He's also a college professor, very involved in his work. He's really trying to be down-to-earth where I'm concerned, but it's coming across as pushy. I can see all of his worlds colliding. Rich man and professor trying to act like a regular guy. He can't seem to quite pull it all together."

"What do you mean?" Pete asked. "How are his so-called worlds colliding?"

"What is this? Twenty Questions?"

Pete raised his eyebrows and looked at me questioningly.

"Okay. He tries to act like every other guy I've ever dated, then apologizes. I don't think he really knows how to act around a woman. Sometimes when he talks to me he's quite formal, and then he catches himself and tries to sound more casual. And he becomes extremely quiet sometimes, like he doesn't know what to say. It's hard to explain, but I see him as trying to balance all the facets that make him up at once. And it's not an easy trick to pull off. I don't think he's comfortable with himself. I'd like to see him find a happy medium," I said. "All of his different sides have good points."

"Sounds like a flake to me," Pete observed.

"Come on, Pete, give it a rest. At least give the guy a chance. I mean, he is trying, and he is a nice guy. Kind of sexy, too. The one thing that bugs me is that he's as hardheaded as you. He doesn't like you either, and I think the whole thing is ridiculous."

"How about if I just stay away from him," Pete said.

"Good idea. But why don't you like him?" I asked, frustrated.

He shrugged evasively.

So, as I found myself doing more and more often, I tactfully changed the subject. We talked about general subjects, keeping the mood light.

"We should probably head over to the office so I can get my car," I said when we'd finished an after dinner cup of coffee.

"I suppose so," he replied.

After the short drive back to the office, he turned off the engine and came around to open my door for me. He walked me to my car and we stood and talked for a few more minutes.

"Well," Pete said, "I'd better get going. I'm supposed to meet Ray Peterson at seven o'clock in the morning, before his first class."

This is it, I thought to myself. This is where he kisses me again. Surprisingly, I was looking forward to it, and that made me feel like a traitor to Richard. Dumb, huh? I wasn't tied to Richard in any way. I was a free agent.

Needless to say, I was quite surprised when Pete looked me in the eye, took hold of my hand and shook it, and walked back to his car without even trying to kiss me. He'd done that on purpose, just to get my goat. I could feel it in my bones.

I couldn't help feeling disappointed though, as I drove home.

"Don't be a jerk, Sandi," I said aloud. "You know he loves all the women, and you know it's only a physical attraction you're feeling. Get a grip. He's nothing but trouble."

After a few more words to myself on the subject I finally halfway convinced myself that I wasn't really disappointed and that I was better off for not getting involved with him. I tried thinking about Richard, but my mind kept slipping back to Pete.

I turned on the television when I got home and saw that *The African Queen* was on. I tuned it in, sat back and lost myself in the movie, temporarily forgetting about everything else. When the movie ended I turned off the TV, sighed and went to bed. I was almost asleep before my head hit the pillow.

That night I had an odd dream. The entire dream took place in a grocery store with me standing in front of the vegetable counter. I spent hours, in the dream, agonizing over which melon to buy. There were only three left, but I couldn't make up my mind. I'd pick one up, and put it down. Then I'd pick up another one, sniff it, and put it down. I even juggled them for a minute, but stopped because I was afraid I'd drop one and it would break open. Then I just stood and stared at them.

Frustrated, I decided not to buy any melon. When I woke up, I wondered if the three melons represented Richard, Pete and the unknown. Stupid dream!

As I got ready to go to work that morning, I found myself taking more time than usual with my make-up and hair, and I hummed. I never hum, but that morning I hummed.

"Pete's right, I am getting weird," I said, looking at myself in the mirror.

I arrived at the office at seven-thirty. Pete wasn't there yet, which didn't surprise me. I pulled an insurance file out of the drawer and started making notes as to how I wanted to proceed with the matter. I had a court appearance on another case coming up, so I pulled the file on that one to double check the date and time.

I heard a car pull up outside, and thinking it was Pete I got up and looked out the window.

Instead of Pete, I saw the two men who'd tried to rearrange his car. As I backed away from the window I saw them looking around, like they wanted to be sure no one was watching them. Fortunately, they hadn't seen me.

Taking quick action, I grabbed my backpack and ran into the small bathroom, locking the door behind me.

I climbed up and balanced myself on the toilet seat, quietly trying to unlatch the hook-type lock on the window. I could hear them entering the office.

"Her car's here," I heard one of them say. "She's got to be around somewhere."

"She could be out with the geek," the other one said.

"Nah, they wouldn't have left the door unlocked."

I knew it wouldn't be long before they found me, but the stupid lock was stuck. I couldn't get out! It was a hook and eye type lock. When the window had been replaced, they must have bent something. I looked around, searching for something to force the hook with. Nothing. I heard the supply closet door open and close. The bathroom would be next. There was nowhere else for them to look.

My hair brush! I pulled it out of the backpack and began beating it against the hook. By that time they'd discovered that the door was locked and they were trying to break in, so the noise I was making didn't matter.

Suddenly the hook gave way and slipped neatly to the side. I pulled myself up, and climbed out the window.

"Get outside in case there's a window," I heard one of them yell.

Talk about timing. I lowered myself as far as I could and dropped the extra couple of feet to the ground. I knew one of them would come around from the front, so I ran around to the other side of the building, into the alley. Just as I rounded the corner, I heard heavy footsteps.

I waited for a moment, then peeked around the corner. The hairy guy was looking up at the window, shaking his head. He started looking around for something to climb up on, so I ducked back out of sight and took off running. It would only be a matter of seconds before they realized I'd gotten away, and then they'd come looking for me.

My heart was pounding and my legs were beginning to shake, but I ran as fast as I could. I wished I'd been more involved in physical fitness throughout my life. Maybe I'd better take up jogging, assuming I got the chance.

I ran to the front of the building and turned in the opposite direction from my office, passing the shop across the alley. I passed one more building and turned up another alley, ran up the alley to the next street and stopped, out of breath.

I glanced up in time to see their car coming around the corner. I ran back into the alley and kept going until I was back by my own office. My heart felt like it was ready to burst. I looked back around the corner, but their car was nowhere in sight. I ran back to the main street, hoping someone would be around to help me. There wasn't a soul in sight, because it was too early and nothing else was open yet.

Carefully, I made my way back to the parking lot. I didn't see their car, so I ran the last bit and jumped into my car. It was hard to get the key in the ignition because I was shaking so hard, but I finally got it started and backed out of my parking space as fast as possible..

My luck ran out as I tried to pull out of the parking lot. They were coming around the corner, saw me, and sped up in order to force me over to the curb.

I knew I was in big trouble. I stepped on the gas pedal, hoping to at least give them a run for their money, and barely made it past them as I pulled out into the street.

I'd driven about a block when I saw Pete's car coming toward me. I felt a surge of relief as I waved at him, frantically trying to flag him down. Unfortunately for me, he seemed to think I was merely being social, so he waved back and drove merrily on his way. I made a mental note to punch his lights out if I got out of the situation alive, which was questionable.

I made a sharp right turn at the next corner, laying rubber all over the street, then made another sharp right, trying to work myself back to the office where I knew Pete would be trying to figure out what had happened. He knew I never left the door unlocked when I went out.

I finally worked my way back to the street the office was on, and as I approached the office I leaned on the horn. After a split second I saw Pete pop his head out the front door to see what all the commotion was about. I pointed at the car chasing me and zipped into the parking lot. Pete came flying out the door and ran to my car, pulling a gun out from under his coat as he moved.

"Hit the ground!" he yelled at me as he hid himself behind my car. When the two goons pulled in behind me, Pete jumped up and fired a single shot, hitting their front fender.

I never knew a car could be thrown into reverse and backed out of a parking lot that fast until that fateful day.

Pete ran out to the street. He jumped back as one of them stuck his head out the window and pointed a gun at him. His partner turned the corner before he could shoot. Pete had taken them by surprise and scared them off.

"Damn it!" he said. "I missed their license number again."

"I didn't," I said cheerily as I handed him a piece of paper. "While you were busy shooting, I got the number. Sorry about the handwriting, but I was shaking pretty hard when I wrote that."

"Good work," he said as he took the paper. "I'll call the department and have them run the number. Don't be surprised if it turns out to be a stolen car though."

"Well, it's worth a shot. Sorry, no pun intended."

We returned to the office where Pete called another friend of his. He gave him the necessary information and turned to me after being put on hold.

"Things are never dull around here, are they," he said.

"Oddly enough, they were until about the time you started working for me. I guess it's a good thing I hired you when I did."

"Yeah. Two car chases in two days. Working for you is worse than being back with the department," he joked.

I started to say something smart, but he held his hand up to silence me because his friend was back on the line.

"It was a stolen car, just like I thought," he said as he hung up. "I don't think that will cause much of a problem though. If those guys didn't ditch it after the episode at your apartment, then they probably won't ditch it now. They're really not very bright, but they are getting on my nerves."

"If you say so," I said agreeably. "It seems that a lot of people we're running into aren't too swift. First Sands, now these guys." I was feeling better now that Pete was there to protect me. Uh oh, did I say that? Fortunately, I only thought it, and I'd never admit to him that I was glad he'd been carrying his gun.

"I wonder why they came after you," Pete said thoughtfully. "After the incident with my car, I thought they were after me."

"I have to admit, I'm beginning to feel just a tiny bit scared now. And maybe a little paranoid. I find I keep looking over my shoulder lately. They came in broad daylight, and they obviously weren't just going to leave a warning this time. I'm sure of that, because I heard them and they were specifically looking for me. And I'll tell you what else, I think you're next. I think you may get another visit from them real soon. Next time they'll be more careful since they now know you're carrying a gun. In fact, I think the situation is becoming more and more dangerous all the time."

"I've thought about that too. But you know, this is a real easy town to get lost in. I think we ought to get a motel room and stay away from home, at least for tonight. They'll never find us unless we stay here or go home. It's time for us to do a disappearing act."

"Maybe you're right. I'll call and reserve rooms for both of us across town," I said. "With any luck, maybe the police will track that car down within the next couple of days."

"Don't hold your breath. They're hiding that car somewhere or they wouldn't hang onto it."

CHAPTER 16

"So tell me," I said, changing the subject. "What happened with Ray Peterson this morning?"

Pete searched my face before he answered, obviously realizing I sounded too nonchalant after what had just happened. I knew those two goons had to have something to do with Robert, and the only way we'd be safe would be to solve the case. Ray seemed to be a link in the chain.

"Not too much. He said he's been receiving threatening calls similar to what we've been getting. The difference is that in his case the caller seems to think that Robert told him something which could cause trouble. He said at first he couldn't think of anything Robert ever told him that might be important.

"But he kept thinking about it," Pete continued. "He finally thought of something, but he wasn't sure if it would help us or not. Robert used to talk about his brother and the fact that his line of business upset him. Mind you, Ray doesn't know what Cushing was really into because Robert told him he was better off not knowing. It sounds like although Robert talked to Ray, he was pretty evasive about his brother's business, just letting him know it was shady. Anyway, Robert told Ray that he had some information that would stop his brother. Ray didn't pay much attention because he had no idea what Robert was talking about. He tried to pump me to find out what's going on, but I told him I also thought he was better off not knowing. He did say he thought Frank

Samuels might have something to do with it. I tried to pin him down on that, but he said it was just a gut feeling, that there was nothing specific he could put his finger on.

"Anyway, the calls were really spooking Ray. Then he found a nasty note spray-painted on the side of his car, like you found on yours. Since he's young and he has no idea what's going on, it's harder for him to handle."

That's what you think, I thought to myself. Maybe I didn't show how nervous I was, but I was pretty freaked out. I'd learned how to hide what I was feeling when we'd gone through the "family scandal" with my father. Mom and I didn't want everyone to know what was going on, and I learned my lesson well.

"He's leaving for Nebraska tonight," Pete continued. "He'll stay with relatives for awhile. I told him I thought that was a good idea. He left me a phone number in case we need to get in touch with him."

"I can't say I blame him for leaving," I said. "This whole thing is getting pretty sticky. I wonder what Robert got on John. I'd be willing to bet that the envelope I found has something to do with it."

"Okay, here's what we've got so far," Pete said. "Robert starts acting weird, and even weirder the last time he was at the dig. He tells Ray he's got information that would cut off his brother's activities, which just happen to include drug trafficking. Then he disappears.

"We get involved in the case and almost immediately start receiving threats, we're both attacked in one way or another, with you even being shot at, and you find an envelope with coke in it and Robert's name on the outside. And right after that John Cushing is murdered. We don't have any motive or suspects, except that in his line of work, well, who knows what went down. We don't know if his death had anything to do with Robert or not, and there's no way of knowing for sure, but the odds are there's some connection..

"The threats to us continue, even though John is dead, and Ray starts receiving similar calls. I have a feeling that Ray's only problem is that he was Robert's closest friend. Someone must be assuming that he knows more than he does.

"Then the hikers find Robert's body," Pete concluded.

"Wow! You sure know how to brighten a person's day," I said, feeling creepy. I'd been downplaying all the things that were happening to Pete and me in my mind, but when he laid it all out for me, I realized what a precarious situation we were in. I felt a chill run down my spine.

"I guess that sums it up pretty well," I said. "There aren't a whole lot of clues to go on. Drugs, drug trafficking, I just don't know. It sort of points to the underworld, but that almost seems too pat. And what could possibly have happened at the dig? That doesn't fit in with the rest of what we know."

"What else have we got?" Pete thought aloud.

Something was nagging at me, but I couldn't quite put my finger on it. Then it struck me.

"One very small thing," I said. "I don't now if this is anything or not, but do you remember Rick saying that Robert had silver paint and a scratch on the inside of his hand?"

"Yeah, so what?"

"Well, it's a minor thing, but I found a silver button lying by the spot where Robert had gone to get some supplies for Richard. It was after Robert went out to the car to get some brushes that his behavior changed more drastically. Maybe someone stopped him out there. Maybe it got a little rough and Robert pulled a button off someone's shirt. Richard and Ray both said Robert was pretty shook up when he returned to the site."

"That's a stretch, but we'll keep it in mind," Pete replied. "At this point *anything* could turn out to be important. We've got so little to go on."

"I'd sure like to get my hands on the two idiots who took a shot at me though," he added. "I don't think we'd have too much trouble getting them to open up, because they backed off so easily. Whoever hired them doesn't seem to realize just how useless they are. It's like dealing with two more Sands types."

"They didn't shoot at you," I reminded him. "The one guy only aimed his gun at you. Besides, when did you start carrying your gun?"

"It was close enough to be a shot for me. And I started carrying it this morning, fortunately for you."

"Yeah, well, I wouldn't exactly call them useless. They could be the ones who killed Robert and John. Other than some damage to my car and office, they haven't really gotten to us yet. That doesn't mean they didn't get to Robert and John. I hate guns, you know."

"I sort of got that impression."

"Something just occurred to me," I said thoughtfully. "If these two are like Sands, you don't think…no. I guess not."

"What?" Pete asked.

"You don't suppose Becker is behind this, too, do you? I mean, you did mention that he's also involved in drugs. I know this might be a stretch too, but stranger things have happened."

"I think it's too much of a coincidence," Pete replied. "I don't think Becker would dirty his hands like this. It's gotten too messy. Although, he did hire Sands, which was a bad move."

"Yeah. Maybe we should dig a little deeper."

We discussed it some more, coming to no conclusions, other than drugs and maybe the underworld seemed to be involved. It was frustrating because we had so little information. Pete finally agreed that maybe we should take a closer look at Becker. And, of course, we were still looking for Samuels. It was like he'd just disappeared off the face of the planet. It was too much of a coincidence that Samuels disappeared at the same time as Robert. I knew there had to be a connection.

Poor Robert appeared to have walked into a situation that was out of his element.

We cleaned up some business at the office and then spent the day running errands to keep busy. I wanted to stay away from the office in case those two creeps came back. Pete wanted to wait and stomp on them if they came back, but I said no. I wanted to stick to the original plan and stay out of sight for awhile. Besides, I honestly didn't think they'd be back any time soon. I finally got to the shopping mall and picked up a couple of cell phones.

After checking out the area and finding no one suspicious lurking around, we did stop back at the office to pick up a few things.

I'd never met Robert, but I felt a heavy weight on my heart for him. I sat at my desk and thought about him. He was only nineteen years old when he died, barely out into the world yet. He'd never have a chance to find out what life was all about, to love and be loved, to experience all the things that most of us take for granted. I wanted to find his killer and make him pay for the life he'd so easily cut short. I wanted to face this man and tell him what an awesome void he'd left in Jessica Cushing's life by taking both Robert and John. I wanted to tell him what scum he was, even knowing that it wouldn't phase him. But it would make me feel better.

My eyes filled with tears. I poured myself a drink of water and gulped it down to stop myself from crying.

"What's wrong with you?" Pete asked.

"Nothing."

"Come on, Sandi. You look like you're ready to start bawling. Your face is turning red. What's the matter?" he persisted.

"It's just not fair," I said tearfully. He'd gotten the tears started, so now he'd have to finish it out with me. "Robert was so young. He didn't even have a chance to find out what the world is all about," I said, all the vehemence of my feelings gushing out.

"The Cushings, all of them, have been cheated and violated, especially Jessica, who's been left to try to deal with all of it. Can you imagine how lost she must feel? I'm so very angry and I don't know what to do about it."

Before long I was rambling about it, almost irrationally. Pete sat there quietly, letting me talk it all out and letting me cry.

"Do you feel better now?" he asked when I finally quieted down.

"No," I replied. "I won't feel better until we catch whoever did this. Like I told you once before, sometimes crying can be a sort of release, so maybe I can get back to work on this. We've been down this tearful road before, remember? When my car was ruined."

"How could I forget," Pete replied. "But your car is fine now, so take it easy, huh? Besides, Sandi, I've watched you try to be hard-nosed and tough, but there's a soft heart in there. Go ahead and act as hard as you want to, but don't stop caring. I sort of like the soft side of you."

I didn't know what to say, so I didn't respond. Pete looked a little embarrassed, like he wasn't used to saying such personal things. He turned back to his desk and began searching for something, anything would do as long as he wasn't looking at me.

The phone rang and I grabbed for it, not wanting our conversation to go any further for the moment.

"Sandra," came my mother's familiar voice, "where have you been? I've been trying to call you for a couple of days."

"Hi, Mom. Why didn't you just leave a message on the answering machine. I would have called you back."

"I don't want to spend my money on a machine. I know it picks up on the fourth ring, so I hang up after the third. Now where have you been?"

"I've been working, like always," I replied.

"Well, where have you been that could keep you away from the phone so much?"

"I'm an investigator, remember? I work out in the field a lot." Unfortunately, my tone of voice was pretty sarcastic.

"I'm not being nosey, honey, I was beginning to worry."

"Well, you don't have to worry. I told you I hired someone to work with me, and he's with me a good deal of the time."

Pete glanced over at me. I couldn't tell whether he was ready to laugh or not, but I got the feeling he was close.

"Anyway, I'm fine Mom, so don't worry needlessly. What did you want, by the way."

"Nothing in particular. I was just checking in with you to make sure everything was okay."

I knew I was still snapping at her, but I didn't want to explain why. She'd worry all the more.

"I'm a little tired, but like I said, I'm fine. How's Aunt Martha doing?" I asked.

"She's better," Mother replied. "What's this guy like? The one you hired."

"Can we talk about that later? My partner and I were going over a case here, and I need to get back to work," I said, letting her know I wasn't alone.

Pete was leaning back in his chair, listening, with his arms folded across his chest. He was getting quite a kick out of hearing me sidestep my mother's questions, and I was feeling uncomfortable. I didn't like being evasive with her, but it was for her own good, after all.

"Oh, I understand," Mom replied. "He's there, isn't he?"

"Yes, you're very understanding. Anyway, I'd better get off the phone and get back to work. Besides, this is costing you money."

That got her attention.

"Call me soon, honey," she said as she hung up.

"I love you," I said.

"You're very good at that," Pete commented after I hung up.

"At what?"

"At avoiding your mother's inquiring mind."

"I've had years of practice, and why don't you mind your own business. Besides, I know she worries about me and my work, and she doesn't even know what's going on. I don't want her to worry any more than necessary.

Can you imagine what she'd be like if she knew any of the details of the case we're working on?"

He turned back to his desk without another word, but I could see the corner of his mouth quiver. I could imagine what he was thinking. How could he understand someone my age still answering to her mother. Well, I wasn't really answering to her, but it sure was hard to ignore her.

"We'd better get moving and get out of here before those guys come back," I said, looking out the window. "We've probably been pushing our luck as it is. Let's pick up a few things at home and get over to the motel, and then maybe we can start thinking about getting something to eat."

"Yeah, there's not much else we can do here," he replied.

"Why don't we leave your car here, and take mine," I suggested. "We might as well stay together."

"Two sets of eyes are better than one?" he said.

"Something like that." Actually, I think he was being agreeable because he felt sorry for me. Between the crying and the call from my mother, *I* felt sorry for me.

"You can follow me and I'll leave my car at home," Pete said. "I'd rather not leave it here. It might get the same treatment your car got."

"I hadn't thought about that," I replied.

We drove to Pete's place first, checking to be sure it wasn't being watched before we pulled into the driveway. I went in with him and waited while he got some of his things together.

"I like your place, Pete," I said, looking around.

"Thanks," he replied as he took off down the hall and opened the bathroom door to get his shaving gear.

His home was neat and clean, the opposite of what I'd expected. He'd told me what a slob he was, joked about it quite a bit actually, but there wasn't a thing out of place. He had nice furniture, traditional in style, and I noticed a large bookcase filled to overflowing with books covering a wide range of subjects. It was a masculine home done mostly in earth tones, with some accenting blues and greens. Before I had a chance to look any further, Pete came out with an overnight bag, ready to go.

"Let's go ahead and take my car," he said. "You can leave yours in my garage. I'll feel more comfortable driving my own vehicle."

"That's fine with me," I replied.

We drove to my apartment, again checking to be sure we weren't being watched or followed. As I ran around stuffing the bare necessities into my overnight bag, Pete watched the parking lot from the window. I watered a few plants, with him hurrying me along, and we left.

We'd driven about half a block when Pete suddenly slammed on the brakes and turned into someone's driveway.

"What are you doing?" I asked as I peeled myself off of the dashboard and remembered to put on my seat belt.

"Hiding," he replied.

"From who?" I asked. I looked over my shoulder just in time to see two familiar faces, one of them hairy, slither by in a stolen car. Fortunately, they were looking straight ahead.

"Oh. Did they see us?"

"I don't think so. Damn! I killed the engine," Pete said, trying to start the car. "We could turn the tables and start following them." The car wouldn't start.

"I sure hope they don't wreck my apartment," I said, thinking of all the destructive things they'd done before.

"Better your apartment than you," Pete mumbled as the engine finally started. "I knew I needed to have the starter looked at. I've been having trouble lately."

"Oh. Well, if things don't quiet down, my landlord is liable to kick me out. He's been giving me some funny looks lately. I don't think I'm quite the kind of tenant he wants anymore. Actually, I think he probably saw your scuffle in the parking lot."

By the time we backed out of the driveway and drove past the apartment, we'd missed those tacky guys, so we turned around and headed for the motel. We checked in and they gave us neighboring rooms, which calmed my nerves. I wanted Pete as close as possible without being in the same room. The thought of sleeping in a room by myself made me feel vulnerable under the circumstances. But with Pete right next door, I knew I'd be okay. I didn't want to let Pete know how I felt though. The tough act was back in place.

We went to an out of the way sandwich shop for dinner. I'd found this tiny place on a back street when I worked for the county. It was run by a young Chinese couple and was called, simply, The Cafe. They made the best sandwiches I'd ever had, including cole slaw and pan fried potatoes that made your taste buds beg for more.

We found we were the only customers in the place.

"You haven't been in for a long time," Mr. Chan scolded. "How have you been?"

"Fine," I replied. "And believe me, I've missed you and your food. I brought my friend along to see just how good a sandwich can be."

Mr. Chan grinned and said something to his wife in Chinese. She beamed at me before turning back to her work.

We took our time eating, enjoying every morsel. Pete felt cheated that he hadn't found the place himself. He thought he knew all the good places to eat.

"I can't believe anyone can make a plain old sandwich taste so good," he said. "I mean, these are great!"

"Now we're on my turf," I joked.

By the time we left, the place had filled up. I felt sorry for the young couple as I watched them trying to handle so many people by themselves, but then I noticed they seemed to be enjoying all the commotion.

"It's still early," Pete said as he glanced at his watch. "Why don't we go hide out in a movie for awhile."

"Why Pete! Is this going to be a date?" I asked, trying to sound demure and failing miserably.

"No."

"Oh. Okay, then let's go."

We both laughed as we got into the car. We drove to a nicer part of town, temporarily ridding ourselves of the problems of the day, and bought tickets for an adventure movie.

Pete said he thought this one would be corny, but ended up enjoying the movie in spite of himself. About midway through the movie, he nonchalantly put his arm around my shoulders, and I nonchalantly leaned toward him, snuggling just a little. It was reminiscent of high school dates in years past.

On the way to the car after the movie, Pete took hold of my hand, gave it a squeeze, and then abruptly let go.

I tried to hide the fact that I was enjoying the evening and the attention. I didn't want to be one of "Pete's girls". Besides, I knew it was only the situation that was creating the feeling of closeness. I'd be seeing Richard the next night, assuming we could come out of hiding, and Pete would be back on the streets with all of his women.

As we drove back to the motel our conversation was quite animated. I supposed that he felt the same way I did, that it was just circumstances creating the mood.

Things would have ended there if Pete hadn't walked me to my room.

"I just want to be sure everything is okay before I leave you alone," he said.

Right. That's why I unlocked the door, we walked in and he immediately pulled me to him and kissed me. I mean *really* kissed me. The feel of his hands on my back was like a tonic. It was wonderful. I couldn't help but respond to his kisses. He moved his hands to my sides and lifted me a little as he kissed me again. I felt one hand move to the back of my head, caressing my hair.

He knew what I was feeling. He stopped and held me at arm's length. We looked into each other's eyes.

"That was just a sample," he said quietly. He patted me on the behind and turned and walked out the door.

"You creep!" I yelled after him. "Male chauvinist pig!" But I was smiling to myself. I couldn't help it.

Trouble sleeping that night? You'd better believe it. I kept picturing Richard and Pete standing side by side. It was like putting one guy in each hand and weighing them. Richard, Pete, Pete, Richard. What did I want, or more importantly, what and *who* did I want. I wasn't the type of person who often had a choice to make in affairs of the heart. Maybe I still didn't have a choice. Maybe Pete was just playing games to kill time. Thoughts like that kept me awake until around three o'clock in the morning. That's when I made up my mind not to worry about making a choice. Things would work themselves out. I decided I'd just sit back and enjoy all the attention. I'd been working so hard, for so long, that I deserved a diversion.

CHAPTER 17

Bright and early Friday morning I awoke to someone pounding on my door. I dragged myself out of bed, opened the door and peeked out, my sleep-robbed eyes seeing nothing but a blur.

"Hurry up," Pete said. "Get ready and I'll take you out to breakfast before we go to work."

"Don't you think this would be a great day for sleeping in and forgetting breakfast?" I asked lamely. "We don't need to start work for at least a couple of hours, right?"

"Wrong. Now pull yourself together and let's get going," he said relentlessly. "How fast can you get ready?"

"Give me half an hour," I said in resignation. Why was Pete so eager all of a sudden. I thought he'd probably sleep late since we were supposedly hiding out. Instead, he was disgustingly bright and cheerful, and very ready to get to work..

Pete strolled back to his room, whistling.

"Go ahead and whistle, you bum. I'll bet you slept like a log," I mumbled to his back.

By the time I showered and dressed I'd perked up enough to focus my eyes, but that was about all. After applying some make-up and brushing my hair I felt halfway human again. Almost, but not quite, ready to face the day.

Exactly half an hour after waking me, Pete came knocking at the door again. This was one morning when I didn't need a punctual partner.

"How are you this morning?" he asked cheerfully as I let him in.

"Miserable," I replied testily. "I hate it when people wake me up cheerfully. My mother used to shake my foot and say 'Wake up, little Mary Sunshine'. I know she did that just to drive me crazy. Let's go eat." Big mistake. Somehow I knew the Mary Sunshine thing would come back to haunt me.

He smiled at me as if I'd said something witty instead of growling at him. I knew what it was though. He was pleased with himself over last night's performance, and it was obvious that I hadn't slept much. He knew the whole thing bothered me. Isn't that just typically male.

We walked next door to another one of the numerous Los Angeles coffee shops where I ordered a light breakfast, food being one of my last priorities. I noticed that Pete ordered enough to feed a small army.

Wouldn't you just know it? A female cop and her partner walked in, saw Pete, and the woman plopped herself down next to him to chat for a few minutes, while sending her partner in search of a vacant table. The male partner obviously didn't know Pete, and he didn't look too happy.

Pete introduced us, but after the introduction I felt like a fly on the wall, something to be put up with but ignored. However, I had a feeling that if she'd had a flyswatter she might not have ignored me so completely. That seemed to happen a lot when women saw Pete. I'll give him this much though, he kept trying to include me in the conversation, but she just kept touching his arm and talking exclusively to him. She *finally* excused herself, after what seemed like an eternity, and joined her partner at another table. I noticed her partner still looked miffed.

"You just drive me crazy, you know?" I said.

"That wasn't my fault. You'll notice that I didn't invite her to sit down," he said defensively. "So lay off. Or do I detect a bit of jealousy here."

"It's a little difficult to conduct business with constant interruptions every time we go anywhere," I growled. Jealous my foot! Pete and his women were beginning to wear thin. Heaven only knew why I let him make me lose sleep.

"I don't seem to remember us discussing any business," Pete observed.

"Then let's discuss it now."

"Sure. It seems to be the only thing we *can* discuss without you jumping all over me." He was beginning to sound a little testy himself, and I silently congratulated myself. If I had to lose sleep, he didn't deserve to be so cheerful. What was it he'd said last night? Something about my just getting a sample. What nerve. What conceit!

We ended up eating in silence, not discussing anything. What a way to start the morning. He finished stuffing himself while I stared at my food and shoved it around my plate, trying to figure out my mood, as if I didn't know what was causing it. I felt like I was on a roller coaster ride and I couldn't get off.

If I was honest with myself, which was difficult at the moment, there was just the tiniest bit of jealousy involved, but I'd never let him know that.

We finally spoke as we left the coffee shop.

"I think we'd better keep the rooms for at least one more night," Pete said.

"So we won't be going to the office today," I said.

"I think we'll be okay at the office," Pete replied. "I have a gut feeling it's when we're home alone and more vulnerable at night that we need to worry."

"But they came to the office yesterday," I argued.

"I don't think they'll try that again. They know we'll be watching for them," he explained.

"I suppose," I said reluctantly. "I guess one more night at the motel would be a good idea."

He spoke to the manager while I returned to my room to get the Cushing file. I was now keeping it with me all the time. After arrangements were made for the rooms, we drove to the office. Pete started the coffee while I turned on the answering machine to listen to messages.

There were a couple of hang ups, and Richard had called, requesting that I return his call.

I dialed his number, hoping he hadn't left for the college already. He answered on the second ring.

"Hi, Richard. I got your message. What's up?" I asked a little louder than necessary.

"I wanted to be sure you're still coming for dinner tonight."

"Of course I'm still coming over tonight." I was fully aware that Pete was taking in every word, which was exactly what I wanted. "I'm looking forward to dinner at your place," I said innocently, glancing at Pete out of the corner of my eye.

Pete turned the radio on, loud, and sat down at his desk, making a great show of ignoring me.

"What's the matter with you?" Richard asked.

"Nothing. Why?"

"You're talking so loud that you sound like you're angry."

"Oh, no. I'm sorry. It's just been one of those mornings. You know, hectic," I lied. It was pretty early for things to have already gotten hectic.

It would be counter-productive to tell him I was having mixed emotions about him and Pete. I had a feeling that once I saw Richard I'd realize how silly I was being and I'd forget all about Pete. Richard was more in line with my taste in men, at least he had some class. And Richard had a way of making me feel good, most of the time, instead of confusing me and making me angry. At least I felt I knew where I stood with him. I wasn't sure Richard knew where he stood with himself though. I'd have to work on helping him build his self-confidence.

"Okay then, I'll see you tonight," Richard said.

"I'll be over as soon as I'm through here at the office," I assured him.

"About what time do you think that will be?"

"Oh, probably around six-thirty or so. Is that okay?"

"Perfect," he said, sounding pleased.

We hung up and I turned to Pete.

"Would you mind turning down that radio?" I asked. "A person can't hear themselves think around here."

He reached over and turned down the volume without saying a word.

"Some people can be so rude," I mumbled.

He ignored me and went back to his work.

"I'm going out to pick up some information on one of the insurance cases," I said, picking up my backpack. "Be back later."

"Yeah."

I'd gotten a lead on a pawnshop across town where an insured might have pawned some jewelry that she'd reported as stolen. It had been an anonymous call, someone who sounded bitter. She'd confided in someone apparently, and that someone didn't want to see her get away with the fraud. Maybe it was a poor relation or something.

I confirmed with the pawnshop owner, after fluttering my eyelashes a lot, that she had indeed pawned some jewelry. Chalk up another one. No insurance claim would be paid. I got copies of receipts and signatures, after a lot more flirting, then headed back to the office. Men can be so easy sometimes.

It seemed like some of the cases were almost too easy to solve, and it was becoming tedious. Hawks and Cushing, regardless of the circumstances, were a good change for me. They were more along the lines of what I'd hoped to be doing, cases I could sink my teeth into. But the insurance cases were bread and butter on the table, so I couldn't complain too loudly.

As I drove back to the office, I thought about Pete some more. Things were getting sticky. I'd have to talk to him. He'd have to be more businesslike and keep his kisses to himself. I didn't want to be another name for him to add to his apparently long list. Besides, I was getting too old for playing games. I preferred the stability that Richard represented. Even if he lacked self-confidence, he still represented that precious stability I wanted.

As I pulled into the parking lot beside the office, I saw the tail end of a tan Ford sticking out from behind the building. So much for Pete thinking we wouldn't be seeing Hairy and his friend around the office.

"Oh, no," I said aloud. Big trouble!

I ran over to Pete's car with one thought racing through my mind. The door on the passenger side was locked, so I ran to the other side. The driver's side door was unlocked. Would he have left the car unlocked with the gun still in the glove compartment? Would he have even left the gun in the car again?

I heard the sound of a crash come from the office. Then another. It sounded like a real free-for-all.

I clambered into Pete's car and ripped the glove compartment open. I started pulling things out, looking for the gun.

"Where is it?" I muttered distractedly. Why would anyone want to put such a large glove compartment in a car. Pete had everything but the kitchen sink in it. I could hear all the noise in the office and it was scaring me. I reached in to pull out whatever was left and felt the cold metal of the revolver. He'd hidden it underneath all the junk. Relief washed over me, even as I thought how much I hated guns, but I had to help Pete. I swallowed hard and got a grip on the gun.

Pete's car was parked right under a window. I heard him groan as I climbed back out of the car, which spurred me along.

I ran to the rear of the building where I found the car parked under the bathroom window, as I had suspected. I climbed up on the hood of the car and quietly pulled the window open. I imagined they had snuck up on Pete, entering through the bathroom just as I was doing. I was surprised he hadn't heard them until I remembered that he tended to turn the radio fairly loud when I wasn't there. I was always asking him to turn it down when I walked in.

I slid through the window, balanced myself on the toilet seat and lowered myself to the floor. The door was ajar and I could see into the office. Fortunately, the goons had their backs to me. Pete was sprawled in a chair, blood running down his face from a cut over his eye. His nose was bleeding and his lip was split.

I stood in the doorway and aimed the gun at the hairy guy's head.

"What a mess!" I said disgustedly. "I already cleaned this office up once because of you jerks. I'm *not* doing it again. You should be ashamed of yourselves. Are you guys listening to me?"

You never saw two such startled faces in your life. I lowered the gun, only slightly.

"What the…," began the hairy one. Then he noticed the gun. "Hold it, lady. Now just take it easy."

"Easy? The way you guys took it easy on my office? The way you took it easy on Pete?" I said, more to the point. I aimed the gun menacingly.

"Is that thing loaded?" Hairy asked.

"You bet," I bluffed. I didn't have the faintest idea. I'd never thought to look.

Out of the corner of my eye I saw the second goon edging toward the desk corner, ever so slowly. I felt a strange sense of amusement, having the upper hand and wondering what he was up to. What a rush! He slid his hand in the direction of the stapler.

"Don't even think about it," I said, leveling the gun in his direction. I knew he meant to throw it at me.

To my amazement, his face turned red. He was embarrassed. I started to laugh, unable to contain myself. These guys were bozos.

"Are you okay, Pete?" I asked.

He was attempting to stand up, without much success. His eye was already changing colors, and he looked pale. He moved like he was dizzy.

"Oh, I'm just fine," he said as he winced in pain.

I groaned involuntarily. Seeing him in pain made me hurt too. The fun and games were over.

"Okay you guys," I said angrily. "On the floor and spread 'em. And don't move a muscle or you'll find out just how angry I really am."

Apparently they believed me, because they threw themselves on the floor and didn't move, although I heard a lot of grumbling.

"Shut up!" I ordered.

"You really have a way with words," Pete commented. "I think you may be watching too much television. 'On the floor and spread 'em?'"

He dragged himself out of the chair, some of his color returning, and searched the two men for weapons. He came away with two guns and a knife.

"I guess they decided it would be best to come prepared," Pete said.

"Nice guys," I said. "Call the police so we can get rid of this garbage. Then I'm taking you to the hospital."

"I'm okay. I don't need to go to the hospital," he insisted.

"Bet me."

He picked up the phone to call the department, and I noticed he was holding his stomach.

"Are you sure you're okay?" I asked.

"Yeah," he groaned.

The police arrived about ten minutes later. After the formalities, they took the two men away in handcuffs while I loaded Pete in the car and left for the hospital.

"I really don't want to go," Pete said.

"You're going," I said, accepting no arguments. He was too weak to put up much of a fight anyway.

*   *   *

After an unbelievably long wait, Pete was examined in the Emergency Room and it was determined that he was pretty much just a mass of cuts and bruises. There were no broken ribs or anything, but he did have to have a couple of stitches over his eye. The doctor warned him that his stomach would be sore for a few days and suggested he take it easy.

We got in the car to leave, and as I turned to look at Pete, all the remaining animosity I'd felt that morning melted away.

"Oh, Pete," I cried sympathetically as I reached toward his split lip. I stopped short of touching it because I was afraid I'd hurt him. He looked like a whipped puppy and I figured he would play it up for all it was worth. I didn't care though. I was glad he was in one piece.

"I'm taking you home so you can lie down for awhile," I told him. "You really need to take care of yourself."

"No. Take me back to the office. I'll be bored stiff at home."

"But you're hurt," I protested. "You should take a hot bath and lie down."

"Only if you'll stay with me." His grin turned to a grimace as his lip started to bleed again.

"Serves you right," I said sharply. "Now I mean it, as your boss. I want you to go home and get some rest."

"Come off it. You were more worried about your precious office being busted up than you were about me."

"Not really. I was just trying to get your goat."

"You have lousy timing. By the way, Rick is going to call me as soon as they get something out of those two guys," he said, changing the subject. "I don't think they're going to be that easy to crack though. They're stupid, but they know they're in a lot of trouble with whoever hired them for getting caught. They're the opposite of Sands. They're more scared of whoever hired them than the law, and they *don't* want to snitch on him."

"But not talking will get them a lot of trouble, like jail time," I said.

"They'd rather do jail time than answer to whoever pays them. I don't know though, Rick is pretty good at getting information. We could have this thing wrapped up before long. I just can't say for sure."

"I hope so," I said. "I want to know what's behind this whole mess. I want to know why Robert was killed. Obviously these guys are tied to Robert in one way or another."

I finally talked Pete into going home. By that time it was late in the day anyway. I told him I'd pick up our things at the motel and cancel the rooms. So I took him back to the office—he insisted on picking up some files—and he left.

I decided to stay at the office to try to clean up some of the mess before taking care of things at the motel and driving out to Richard's house. The guys had wrecked the office. Again. Things were knocked over and broken, and I almost shed a tear when I saw Pete's blood on the floor. I felt my anger building again, but I was relieved that he was okay and they were finally in jail.

I did a perfunctory job of cleaning, then walked into the bathroom to freshen up. I rinsed my face with cool water, applied some lipstick, a little mascara and blush, and ran a brush through my hair. I knew I didn't have time to run home and change clothes. I splashed on a little cologne, checked my watch, and thought I'd better get going before it got any later. Richard would have to accept me the way I was. It was supposed to be a casual evening anyway.

I drove over to the motel and settled things there, then drove to Pete's place to return his overnight bag.

When I knocked on the door I could hear Pete moving around, but it took him a few seconds to open the door. He looked tired as he motioned for me to enter. He was wearing a raggedy old bathrobe and his face looked like he'd probably been sleeping. He was slightly bent over and holding his stomach.

"I'm sorry, Pete. I didn't mean to wake you up," I apologized.

"Don't worry about it. I was only dozing. Actually, I was beginning to think about fixing myself something to eat."

"Is there anything I can do to help before I leave?" I asked as I set his bag on the couch.

"You could stay and eat with me," he replied. "I could use some company tonight."

"Come on, Pete. You know I've already got plans for tonight. I will get something started for you if you want me to though."

"Never mind," he said sullenly. "I forgot about your barbecue. You just go and have a good time. I'll be fine by myself as long as I keep an ice pack handy." It seemed like he bent over just a tad farther.

He was trying to play on my sympathies again, but it wouldn't work this time.

"I offered to help you get some dinner together. Beyond that, you're on your own for tonight. Do you want help or not?"

"No. Just go away and leave me alone for awhile."

He sounded like a kid. Funny how men can be so childlike when they don't feel well. Women seem to go and go, never letting anything stop them, short of childbirth, but men just curl up in a little ball and usually become petulant. If man and woman are sick at the same time, woman takes care of man and he pretends not to notice that she's pale and feverish too.

"If you don't feel well tomorrow, don't worry about coming into the office. I can take care of things," I said.

"I'll be in tomorrow. Don't you worry about that."

"Whatever," I said, shrugging. "I'm going to be late if I don't hurry, so I'll see you later."

As I opened the door to leave I couldn't help softening a little.

"Take care of yourself, Pete. Okay? And if you *really* need anything later tonight, give me a call on the cell phone. By the way, in case you've forgotten, tomorrow is Saturday, so you honestly don't have to come in if you don't want to. Oh, and forget the cell phone. I left it at the office."

"Fat lot of good the cell phone is going to do," he said.

"I still haven't gotten used to carrying it," I said. "I'm trying to change things, but it takes a real effort."

I left and closed the door quietly behind me.

This man, Peter Goldberg, confused the daylights out of me. What was it about him? I couldn't figure it out.

I headed toward the freeway, dreading the traffic I'd hit on the way to Richard's house, but looking forward to a relaxing evening. At least I wouldn't have to hide out for another night, and that thought lightened my mood.

CHAPTER 18

It turned out to be a pleasant and fairly leisurely drive out to Richard's house. The traffic was extremely light for a Friday night. I briefly wondered if there had been an accident somewhere, which would tie up traffic and clear the way for me, but hoped I was wrong. That was usually the only reason traffic lightened up on the Los Angeles freeways. I counted my blessings that I hadn't had an accident on the freeway.

The wind had been blowing since morning and in its wake it left blue, mostly smogless skies. A rare treat. I could see purple mountains with wisps of white clouds creeping over the tops. The wind picked up, and as I left the freeway I noticed that trees lining the off ramp were gently swaying, the bushes rustling.

It struck me how quiet it was. I'd hit a brief moment in time when there were no cars anywhere near me, no horns honking or brakes screeching, no traffic noises at all, and I'd actually been able to hear the bushes rustling when I stopped at a signal. It was so seldom that peaceful moments like that occurred. I hoped this was an indication of what the evening would be like.

A horn finally honked and it brought me out of my reverie. I sighed and turned the corner, heading for Richard's house. He lived in a quiet area and the further I drove the more I looked forward to a peaceful evening.

That horn honking made me suddenly and acutely aware of how I had become used to the everyday clamor. I wanted, no needed, to get away from it, even if it was only for a couple of hours. At that moment Richard's house represented an oasis in the desert, a place to hide away from the outside world.

I wasn't exactly sure what I wanted to hide from, but I knew it was more than general clamor. Maybe it was the dirty feeling I got when I thought about Robert's untimely death. Drugs, murder, violence—it did seem dirty. It *was* dirty. It violated all the values I'd grown up with. I read about violence in the papers every day, but this was hitting closer to home since I was actually involved in looking for his killer.

Or maybe I just wanted to hide from all the confusion I'd been feeling about Pete and Richard, but if that was the case, I wouldn't be going to Richard's house. I'd probably drive down to the beach and go for a long walk. I'd always had things pretty much together, but these two men were making a sham of all my clear-headed thinking. I had a plan for my life, but this situation wasn't a part of it. Nothing had ever confused me like this. I always knew where I was going and how I felt, about everything.

I was sure going through a lot of mood swings. I decided I must be more tired than I realized. I shook my head to get rid of the cobwebs and turned on the radio. I found a station playing rock and roll oldies and found myself drifting back to the simple days of football games and school dances. A song came on that reminded me of an old boyfriend and I smiled, my mood elevating again. Good ol' Jimmy Ross. I wondered what ever happened to him.

I pulled up in front of Richard's house just as the tune faded out. Good timing.

Richard walked out the front door to greet me, obviously having watched for my car. He met me in the middle of the driveway and gave me a welcoming hug. Jimmy who? Pete who?

"Hi," he said.

"Hi yourself," I said. "Where's dinner?"

"You do have a way with words."

"I've been told that. I was only kidding though. Look," I said pointing toward the sky. "No smog. We should even see some stars tonight if it doesn't turn cloudy. It's going to be a beautiful evening."

"It sure is," he said as he looked into my eyes.

Feeling unusually shy, I shifted my gaze toward the ground.

"What's this? Sandi's embarrassed? I thought we were past that."

"Awww," I said. I swung my arms by my sides like a child, trying to cover with being silly.

He laughed and we walked to the house.

"How about a drink while I put the steaks on?" Richard offered.

"Sounds good, but would you please make it a mild one? I'd hate to fall asleep on you, and that's just what a drink would probably do to me tonight."

"Rough day, huh?"

"That's an understatement. It looks like we might be onto something concerning Robert's death."

"Oh? Tell me about it while I mix your drink."

"Why don't we talk about it later," I suggested. I didn't want to slip back into the sluggish mood I'd been fighting.

"Okay. Then tell me about your day. What made it so rough?" he asked.

"I'll tell you what," I said. "Why don't you tell me about your day. I'd much rather listen to you than talk right now."

"Sure. You relax and unwind and I'll talk. My day wasn't hectic at all. In fact, I can probably put you to sleep before any drink can. I taught classes, answered questions and graded papers. My job, at least in the classroom, isn't as hectic as yours, and I feel great."

"Good," I said.

"Good," he replied, and we both smiled. I sat down on the couch while he mixed my drink at the bar.

He brought me a mild bourbon and water and sat down next to me. He took me by the shoulders and turned me so I was facing away from him. He began kneading my neck and shoulders and he rubbed my back.

"That feels wonderful," I moaned. "I can't think of anything in the world that you could do that would make me feel any better right now."

"Your muscles are extremely tight," he observed. "You really are wound up."

"I know. I wasn't joking about my hectic day and being tired."

"I thought you were exaggerating, but I guess you weren't," he said apologetically.

"If you were to keep rubbing my back for awhile, I'd be forever in your debt," I said hopefully.

"I can live with that," he replied. "Let's get you relaxed and then I'll go put the steaks on."

He kept working on my back while he talked to me in soft, soothing tones. I couldn't concentrate on what he was saying, so I closed my eyes and let my mind go blank for the first time in days.

"Hey, are you listening to me?" he asked, giving me a gentle nudge.

"Uh, not really, but don't take it personal. I'm sorry, Richard. You just about put me to sleep with all this tender loving care."

"What you need now is food," he said as he squeezed my shoulder and stood up. "I'll go put the steaks on. Be right back, so don't go to sleep on me."

"I won't," I promised.

I heard a lot of noises coming from the kitchen, and then I heard the back door open and close. I was right. I'd found my own peace and quiet at Richard's house. Not only that, but Richard was making Pete slip right out of my mind. Richard was giving me attention instead of asking for it. The feeling didn't last for long though. I kept wondering if Pete was okay. I knew he wasn't hurt badly, but I worried about him. I was turning into my mother, a born worrier.

I glanced at my drink but decided I didn't want it. Since I was already tired, I didn't' want to have a drink and then get into the car to drive home.

"Sandi, come on outside. It's really nice out here," Richard said, sticking his head in the back door.

I pulled myself up and wandered out to the kitchen. As I stepped out the back door I was awed by the sunset. The clouds had rolled in and the sun's reflection created a breathtaking horizon. Gray and white clouds had drifted to the sides, but the clouds in the center of my line of vision were absolutely golden. As I watched, they began to turn pink, and the longer I gazed at them, the darker they became. The gold slowly and gently became the most beautiful dark, dusty rose I'd ever seen. The whole sky was lit up.

"Oh Richard, look at that. I wish I had a camera with me so I could capture this moment and never lose it. I've never seen anything like this before."

"I knew you'd appreciate it," he said as he looked up and over his shoulder at me. He was sitting in a lawn chair and motioned for me to join him in the second chair. I sat down next to him and we were quiet as the colors in the sky began to fade and turn gray again.

"You know," I said quietly, not wanting to break the mood, "you've given me an oasis tonight."

"An oasis?" he said, turning toward me. "I don't know about that, but I'm sure glad you're here. And I'm glad you feel comfortable with me."

"I do, Richard. I really do feel comfortable with you."

I turned my attention from the sunset to Richard, and immediately began to tighten up again. Something was wrong, but I couldn't put my finger on it. There was something that I couldn't quite focus on, and it made me feel uncomfortable. Just a moment after telling him how good I felt. Strange.

"What's the matter?" Richard asked. "You look so serious all of a sudden."

"Nothing," I assured him. I didn't want to tell him that there was something wrong, especially since I didn't know what it was. It would sound silly. It could just be that I was feeling guilty about leaving Pete alone when he felt so miserable. Yeah, that was it. I was probably just feeling guilty. Guilty and exhausted. What a combination. I forced myself to begin to relax again.

"Kind of a lazy night, isn't it," Richard commented. "How do you like your steak?" He stretched as he stood up and wandered over to turn the steaks.

"Medium," I replied.

I watched him as he turned the steaks. Even that simple task made the muscles in his arms and back flex slightly. Apparently, all that digging kept him in pretty good shape. I flashed back to the day I met him and remembered that he was a jogger, too.

A warmth washed over me as I watched him. He moved the coals around to create more heat and he sprinkled spices on the steaks. I noticed he also had potatoes baking on the grill. I was back to feeling comfortable. The scene was sort of domestic. I enjoyed watching him. I wished these mood swings would stop though.

"It smells wonderful," I commented. "The aroma is making me hungry."

He returned and sat in the chair next to me, taking my hand in his. I felt a renewed awareness of his strength when he gently squeezed my hand.

"I like having you here with me, Sandi. You know how I feel about you."

"Richard…"

"Don't worry. I'm not going to push the issue. I only wanted to remind you. Maybe with some time you'll feel the same as I do," he said hopefully.

"Let's enjoy this evening," I suggested, "and forget everything else for awhile. I need a break from the world right now."

"Okay, I'll back off. For now."

Richard lit a cigarette. It was only the second time I'd ever seen him smoke, and he didn't look natural with it in his hand. Considering his personality, I was surprised he'd ever developed the habit.

"I'm surprised you smoke," I said, voicing my thought.

"I very seldom indulge," he replied. "I guess I should quit. I don't really have the habit." He sounded slightly defensive, so I dropped the subject.

When the steaks and potatoes were ready we took them into the house where Richard had the table set and ready for us. He brought out a salad which he'd prepared ahead of time, and he placed a bowl of fresh fruit next to it. One more trip to the kitchen and he added garlic bread. It looked like a feast to me. Lately it seemed like all I'd done was eat in fast food joints or coffee shops.

I didn't realize how hungry I was until I tasted the food. I had to hold back so I wouldn't wolf it down and look like a pig.

"This is delicious," I said between mouthfuls.

"And this time I didn't buy it at the deli," he bragged.

"Will wonders never cease."

I tasted the obviously expensive wine that Richard had placed before me. Only the best for this man. He had class, no doubt about it. He sure seemed a heck of a lot more refined than Pete. But, as with the bourbon and water, I didn't take more than a sip of the wine. I was too tired, and not in the mood for a drink. If the truth be told, I should have called Richard and asked if we could make it another night. I felt I should have been sleeping on Pete's couch, just to be there if he needed anything.

Pete! Why couldn't I stop thinking about Pete. This was getting old real fast.

"So," Richard interrupted my thoughts, "now tell me what was so exhausting about today."

"Well," I began, "I cleaned up an insurance fraud this morning, but that was mostly a lot of footwork.

"And Pete and I have been playing Hide and Seek with a couple of hoods. When I came back from checking out the insurance thing, I found…"

The telephone rang and cut me off. Richard got up to answer it, then turned to me and held out the receiver.

"It's your sidekick," he informed me.

"Pete? I wonder why he'd be calling me here."

I glanced at Richard as I took the phone and immediately got that uncomfortable feeling again. But this time I realized what was causing it. He was wearing the type of shirt you might wear to go sailing, the kind with silver buttons. There were anchors on the buttons and the bottom one was missing. The button was such a small thing, but I felt a wave of heat and nausea roll over me. I turned my attention to the phone quickly because I was afraid my face might give me away.

"Pete," I said as casually as I could. "What's up?"

"I heard his crack about your sidekick. I'll let it pass until I see him face to face."

"Yeah, yeah. What is it? Is there anything wrong? You're not sick are you?"

"No. I just got off the phone from talking with Rick. I wanted to let you know that those two guys are singing at the top of their lungs. They've decided they're not going to face all the heat by themselves. Rick did some fancy talking and convinced them it wasn't worth it."

"And? Don't keep me waiting. What'd they say?"

"Becker hired them." I could tell by his tone of voice that he was waiting for a stunned reaction, and he got one.

"We were right about him? I can hardly believe it. I was just grasping at straws when I mentioned him."

"I'll give you the details when I see you, but for now I just wanted to let you know that Becker killed John Cushing. A couple of the guys are on their way to arrest him right now.

"Murphy and Marlow, the two hoods," he continued, apparently changing his mind about waiting to give me the details, "made an earlier attempt on Cushing but they blew it. Becker went to Cushing's office, they quarreled about Robert, and Becker pushed Cushing out the window when they got into a fight. It seems that Robert had come up with something tying Becker to Cushing and had telephoned Becker about it. It had to do with the drugs. By the way, remember that

Cushing's secretary said he'd been writing something the day he was killed? Turns out he was putting everything in writing in case anything happened to him or Robert. Becker took the notes with him when he left the office. I guess Cushing had been working on his notes at home too. If you remember, Jessica mentioned him writing in his library after the phone calls."

"What about Robert?" I asked. "Did Becker or the hoods get him too?"

"Don't know for sure yet. Murphy swears they don't know what happened to him, but if he or Marlow did the deed, then they wouldn't be admitting to it. He's trying to convince Rick that they were supposed to get rid of Robert, but someone beat them to it."

"Okay, Pete, I'll be at your place in about forty-five minutes."

"Sandi, you don't have to…"

"No, I can't make it in less than forty-five minutes," I said, trying to make it sound like he'd asked me to come over. I had to get away from Richard now that I'd noticed the missing button. I had to do some thinking.

"Okay, but…"

"I'll see you then," I said as I hung up.

"Richard," I said, turning from the phone and trying to appear casual, "something's come up. I'm really sorry, but I've got to go."

"Must you?"

"Yes. It seems that the police are about to arrest someone for the murder of John Cushing, and there's the possibility that the guy may be involved with Robert's death."

Had I said too much on the phone? I thought I detected a change in Richard's expression, but I couldn't be sure, and I couldn't remember exactly what I'd said. Maybe my tone of voice didn't sound convincing. The button really bothered me and I didn't want to give myself away. I didn't want Richard to know anything he didn't have to.

"Any chance you might be able to come back later?" he asked.

Maybe I was mistaken. He didn't sound like anything was wrong.

"I don't think I'll be able to get back. Can I have a rain check and we'll get together another time?"

"Certainly," he said, his voice beginning to cool. I imagined he thought I was putting him off. I guess I was, in a way.

He was standing near me, and as I walked forward to say good-bye I tripped and fell against him, grabbing his shirt to keep from falling any farther. What a stroke of luck. I couldn't have planned it any better.

"I'm sorry," I said as I regained my balance. "Oh dear, it looks like I've torn a button off your shirt."

He looked down and fingered the spot where there should have been a button.

"You didn't do it. I forgot there was a button missing on this shirt. I lost it out at the dig. I guess it came off when I was unloading my car. It's sort of a good luck shirt," he said sheepishly. "Since you were coming over I decided I'd wear it. For luck."

"Oh. Then I guess I don't need to feel guilty," I said, meaning that in more ways than one. Did I ever feel stupid!

If the button had meant anything he wouldn't have explained it away so easily. I'd jumped to conclusions and assumed the button had something to do with Robert. Besides, Becker was probably behind Robert's death.

I gave Richard a hug and kissed his cheek. I didn't feel that after all I'd said I could suddenly change my mind and stay for the evening. I knew I'd have to cut my losses and leave.

"I do feel bad, Richard. Call me tomorrow, will you?"

"Of course." The coolness had turned to formality.

I was sure I'd insulted him by leaving so soon. How could I have ever suspected him, even for a second. But the reality was, I had.

Richard didn't walk with me out to my car. I knew that I had hurt his feelings. As I left I decided to go home instead of stopping at Pete's place. I'd call him from my apartment and let him know that everything was all right. I'd tell him I was tired and had used his call as an excuse to leave. That would probably thrill him. Too bad I'd left the new cell phone at the office, or I'd call him on the way home.

*   *   *

By the time I reached the freeway, the fatigue I'd felt earlier was catching up to me again. Things had been so hectic lately that I wasn't surprised it was finally catching up.

The window was down all the way and I opened the vent, hoping the cool night air would revive me. It was a hopeless cause. The last thing I remember was thinking that I'd better pull the car over and rest for a few minutes before I had an accident.

CHAPTER 19

The next thing I knew, there were voices all around me. I stirred, trying to move, but it seemed all my strength was drained.

I felt a restraining hand on my shoulder as I tried to sit up.

"Don't open your eyes," a faraway voice said. "There was a lot of broken glass, so we've got to be sure you didn't get any in your eyes."

"Can you hear me?" he asked when I didn't respond.

I nodded, trying to say yes, but I wasn't sure if any sound had come out of my mouth or not.

"The paramedics are on their way," said a second voice.

"What happened?" I managed to croak.

"Another driver said it looked like you fell asleep at the wheel," replied the first voice. He patted my hand reassuringly.

"Oh." I remembered telling myself I needed to pull off the road and rest, and vaguely remembered my eyes feeling extremely heavy.

"Here's her ID. Her name is Sandra Webster," a third voice offered.

"Yeah," said the first voice, thoughtfully. "I thought she looked familiar. I think this is the one Pete Goldberg is working with. I met her recently. At least, I'm fairly sure it's her." I sensed he moved closer to me.

"Don't you work with Pete, Miss Webster?"

"Yes."

"I thought so. I was one of the officers in on that chase the other day. Do you want me to call him for you?"

I nodded as I felt tears begin to roll down my face. At least, I hoped it was just tears. I was afraid. I could feel myself trembling. Maybe this was a wake-up call. I'd been taking everything that had happened too lightly. I'd been trying to be tough, like a detective should be, but this felt like it might be my undoing.

"Am I okay?" I asked of anyone who might be within hearing distance.

"You tell us," said the second voice.

"I can't tell," I replied. I felt someone throw a blanket or something over me.

"I think you'll be okay," he said. "You don't look too bad except for a cut over your eye."

"Cut over my eye? Is it big?"

"Calm down. I shouldn't have even mentioned it. It's just a small cut. Nothing to worry about. Honestly."

"Did someone go to call Pete?" I asked. I suddenly wanted him by my side very desperately. I began to shiver a little harder, and I could feel panic rising in my chest.

"My partner is contacting him right now," the voice assured me. I hated not being able to see who I was talking to, but obviously it was another cop.

I didn't hear any sirens when the paramedics pulled up, but in a moment they were there and checking me over. Pretty soon they loaded me onto a stretcher and I was on my way to the hospital. I began to shake violently, practically bouncing. I felt someone tuck the blanket closer around me.

"What's the matter with me?" I asked, the panic more pronounced than ever.

"Shock. You'll be okay," said a new voice, most likely one of the paramedics. "You really will be all right," he reiterated.

"Thank you," I said gratefully, through chattering teeth. He squeezed my hand very gently.

In one sense the ride to the hospital seemed to take forever, and yet in no time at all we were there. Within minutes I was in the emergency room with a doctor by my side. A nurse cleaned me up and the doctor put something in my eyes, checking for glass.

"Okay," he said. "No glass. Do you feel good enough to sit up?"

"Yes," I replied. The shaking was subsiding, but I still felt weak. The nurse helped me up.

The doctor began checking my cuts and there was a lump on the back of my head. He flashed his little light in my eyes and tested my reflexes. He whistled while he worked, a very cheerful type guy, which I wasn't exactly in the mood for. I looked at my arms and noticed several small abrasions.

"No broken bones, and you won't need stitches. That ought to make you happy," he said as he placed a butterfly patch on the cut over my eye.

I glanced down at all the blood on my blouse.

"Cuts near the eye bleed a lot even when they're small," he explained when he saw the direction of my gaze. "It's about an eighth of an inch long. You won't even notice the scar. Actually, from what I hear about the condition of your car, you're a pretty lucky young lady. Sounds like it's totaled. However, you do appear to have a mild concussion. I think we ought to keep you here over night."

Pete walked in the door just in time to hear the doctor's advice. He looked quite pale and drawn. As soon as I saw his face I began to cry. It made my head hurt.

"My car, Pete. It's totaled. Not my car," I cried.

"Better your car than you, damn it!" Pete said.

"Oh, Pete." I held out my arms and he walked over and held me. After a moment he pushed me away and took a good look at me.

"You're a mess," he said.

"Thanks a lot. Just what I needed to hear." But it did make me stop crying.

He didn't laugh, but held me close again.

"Now I know how you felt about me this afternoon," he said.

"You look as bad as she does," the doctor said, glancing at Pete's face. "You've even got matching cuts over your eyes. Walk into a door?"

"Something like that."

"I guess you heard what I said about keeping her over night," the doctor commented to Pete. "She does have a mild concussion."

"Is it mild enough that I can go home if I want to?" I asked.

"I wouldn't recommend it," the doctor replied, "but it's your choice. You're going to have one heck of a headache."

"I've already got one, but I can go home, right?" I persisted.

"Do you have someone who can stay with you?" he asked, sighing.

"Pete'll stay with me," I said, looking expectantly at Pete.

"Sure I will," he said, a look of surprise on his face.

"Okay. We'll take care of some paperwork and then you can leave. Against my better judgment. When was the last time you had a tetanus shot?"

"It's been years," I answered.

"Well, before you leave we're going to give you one, and I have some medication I want you to take for a few days. Be sure to make an appointment with your own doctor for a check-up."

"I will," I promised.

The doctor left the room after giving the nurse instructions about the shot and medication.

"I got a call from the station saying you'd been in an accident, but they didn't have any details," Pete said. "What happened?"

"I'm not really sure. I think I fell asleep at the wheel. I don't really remember anything except thinking that I needed to pull over. I think I was unconscious for a few minutes after the accident. I don't remember anything until people started talking to me by the side of the road."

"Why didn't you pull off the road if you knew you were that tired?" he asked. "You know you should have."

"I was going to, but I guess I fell asleep before I could do it. I just don't know what happened. One minute I was thinking about pulling over, and the next I was lying on the ground with a lot of noise and people standing around me."

A cop stuck his head in the door and called Pete outside. I recognized him from the day of the Hawks chase. I thanked him for all his help before he could get back out the door. He just nodded at me.

The nurse came in and gave me a shot and a prescription that the doctor had written. I signed some forms and she said I could leave as soon as she brought in a wheelchair. I was happy to see that someone had thoughtfully seen to it that my backpack accompanied me to the hospital. I climbed off the table and was picking it up when Pete returned.

"You look awfully white," he said.

"I feel sort of dizzy, and my head is throbbing."

"Sit down for a minute," he instructed. "Are you sure you want to go home?"

"Yes, absolutely." As soon as I sat down my head began to clear.

"It seems you hit the center divider, flipped over and skidded across the freeway, then hit a pole," Pete explained. "You're lucky there was no traffic close enough to add to the situation. If you hadn't been thrown out of the car, you wouldn't be here right now. I guess you didn't have on your seatbelt, huh?"

"I must have been so tired that I forgot to put it on. I *always* wear my seatbelt. I can't believe I forgot to put it on."

"I'd probably bawl you out, but in this case it's a good thing you forgot. Just understand this was an exception. If you hadn't been thrown out, well…"

"I'd rather not think about it. Is the car really shot?"

"I'm afraid so. Hank described it to me, and it's done for. You're going to have to get another one."

"I can't afford another car," I said as I began to cry again.

"You've got insurance."

"That doesn't make me feel any better right now. You know how I loved that car. Besides, now my rates will go up."

Pete shook his head.

The nurse came in with a wheelchair and rolled me out to Pete's car.

"Now you take it easy, dear," she said. "Don't rush things. A concussion is nothing to fool around with."

"Thank you," I said as Pete helped me into his car. "I'll be careful."

Pete pulled out of the parking lot and headed toward my apartment.

"I'm glad I didn't get the same doctor you had today," I said tentatively. Pete had a dark look on his face and didn't answer me. In fact, he hadn't spoken to me since we pulled out of the Emergency Room parking lot.

"He would have had a field day with you this afternoon and me tonight." Still no answer. "I can't believe this happened." Dead silence.

"Would you mind stopping so I can get something cold to drink on the way home?" I asked.

"Yeah." More silence.

I was tired and aching, and I began to cry for the third, or was it fourth, time. I needed Pete to talk to me. I couldn't stand the silent treatment.

"Pete, what's the matter? Why won't you talk to me?"

"Nothing's wrong," Pete said gruffly as he took hold of my hand. "When the department called it scared the shit out of me. I didn't know anything except that you were alive. Now that I know you're okay, I'm trying to pull myself together. I'd just rather not talk right now."

I think maybe it had to do with the shock from the accident, but I couldn't seem to quit crying. I cried and sniffled, lamented the loss of my treasured vehicle, then blubbered and sniffled some more. And, of course, I whined about my insurance rates.

"Look," Pete said, trying to console me. "It's all going to work out. At least you've *got* the insurance, and in the meantime you can get another loaner car."

"Not another loaner," I wailed. "Oh no!"

"Well, maybe a rental car, or I can help you out," he added quickly, knowing he'd added fuel to my already raging fire. "The main thing is that you're okay. I can't believe that with all the excitement we've had lately, chases, thugs, crazy things going on, you never got a scratch. No, *you* had to fall asleep at the wheel."

I thought about it and attempted a chuckle.

"I guess it does seem pretty ridiculous. You're right. I've been shot at, chased, received stupid threatening calls, and everything else, but I had to fall asleep at the wheel before I got hurt. What a dope."

Pete smiled as he pulled into a drive-thru and bought me an iced tea.

"I hate to admit this," I said, "but actually my mood hasn't been as carefree and rosy as I've tried to paint it. I figured that after some of our conversations it would be best if I kept my feelings to myself. You know, I felt I should try to be strong and tough."

"Well, I guess you really are a dope, aren't you," he said.

"Excuse me?" I said, feeling insulted, even though I'd said the same thing about myself.

"You're a dope. There's no reason on earth why you had to try to act tough. If you were scared, then you should have let me know."

"But I'm a detective. I'm not supposed to be scared," I replied. "How many clients would I get if people thought I was scared. Think about it."

"I was a cop. Wasn't I supposed to feel fear? Believe me, there were plenty of times I was afraid of things. It's okay to try to act tough, but you need an outlet. Like a friend you can talk to about what's been going on," Pete said.

"Like you," I replied, letting my head drop.

We arrived at my apartment and Pete pulled into the parking lot, turning off the engine.

"Pete," I said, "you don't really have to stay with me tonight. I just wanted to get out of the hospital, so I said that you'd stay with me for the doctor's benefit. I didn't want him to hassle me."

"Don't worry about it," he replied. "I'm going to drive over to my place and get a few things, then I'll be back."

"Really, Pete, you don't have to stay. I know you feel lousy too."

"So we'll feel lousy together. If you've got a concussion, you shouldn't stay by yourself. In fact, I insist."

"It's about eleven o'clock now," he said, checking his watch, "so I'll be back around midnight. I've got a couple of things to do before I come back."

"Okay. I'll leave the door unlocked in case I fall asleep. As long as Murphy and Marlow are in jail, I won't worry about locking up."

"You must be out of your mind! This is Los Angeles, sweetheart. Why take chances?"

"Trust me, Pete. This isn't a bad neighborhood."

"Yeah, right. At least try not to go to sleep before I get back, huh? I'd hate to have you go into a convulsion or something."

"Thanks a lot! I need that kind of encouragement. Now I'll be afraid to close my eyes."

He helped me up the stairs, saying he was afraid I'd get dizzy and fall. What a cutie.

After I was settled on the couch and he turned on the television for me, he left, assuring me he'd see me in an hour.

"Pete," I said, "I know you don't feel so hot either, so take your time. I'll be okay."

"I'll be back in one hour," he said adamantly.

Pete left and I turned off the television and walked into the bathroom to look at myself in the mirror. After scaring myself half to death I decided to clean up a little. The dizziness seemed to have disappeared, although the headache was getting worse. I turned on the shower and pulled a bottle of shampoo out of the cupboard.

I stepped into the shower and washed myself. The hot water felt good, relaxing. For the first couple of minutes I stood and let the water spray my body. I could feel at least a couple of the aches draining away.

I picked up the shampoo and tilted my head toward the shower head, and immediately felt dizzy again, so I sat down on the floor of the shower. The dizziness passed but I waited for a minute before attempting to stand up. This time I stood directly under the shower head instead of tipping my head. As I washed my hair I found that I had to delicately pick several pieces of glass out of my hair and scalp. Maybe I'd been a lot luckier than I realized. No such thing as luck. The good Lord was watching over me, and it wasn't my time to go yet.

I got out of the shower and dried off, feeling only slightly better. I put on my robe and slippers and combed the snarls out of my hair. I noticed that the headache was throbbing again. I placed a fresh bandage over my eye. I got out the hair dryer and began drying my hair.

I thought I heard something and switched off the dryer. Maybe Pete had come back early. I listened carefully, but didn't hear anything. I was awfully tired again and knew I was probably imagining things.

"Pete?" I called out, just in case. Since there was no answer and no more noise, I decided not to get excited. I was so very tired.

I turned the dryer back on. I wanted to get done and go lie on the couch. I ached all over.

I stopped waving the dryer over my hair and looked into the mirror. I noticed a puzzled and slightly wary look on my face. There was a warning signal going off in my brain and my heart began to race, missing a beat here and there. I knew there was something wrong, but I couldn't figure out what it was. Why would my internal signal go off for no reason.

Oh no! My stomach began to churn. When I turned off the dryer...*when I turned off the dryer I heard the television blaring*. I remembered turning it off before I started my shower! And Pete hadn't answered when I called out. I realized he hadn't had time to get to his place and back.

Becker! I forgot to ask Pete if Becker had been arrested yet or not.

I left the dryer on, laying it down on top of a towel. I crept over to the bathroom door and peeked out toward the living room. I couldn't see a thing. I reached behind me and picked up a decorative glass vase which stood on the end of the sink, thinking it was the only thing in the bathroom that I could use for protection. I should have listened to Pete when he told me to lock the door.

I quietly stepped into the hallway and made my way to the living room. There was no one there and nothing looked out of place. I moved on to the kitchen, looked around the corner and found no one there either. I realized that I was crouching, and that I was too sore for crouching, so I stood up straight. My head immediately began to throb again.

I had a mild concussion. Could I have truly imagined that I turned the television off? I was certain I had, but with the accident and all, maybe I couldn't be sure about anything. I didn't have the slightest idea whether a mild concussion could confuse a person or not.

The bedroom! I hadn't checked the bedroom. Someone could be hiding in there. I ran to the bedroom, which made my head hurt even more, but it was exactly as I'd left it. I briefly thought of going to the manager of the building to get him to help me search instead of doing it by myself, but quickly discarded the idea. He'd think I was being an hysterical woman, and as a private investigator I didn't need that. Always keep your reputation intact.

Returning to the living room, I looked around once more. There wasn't one single thing out of place. The door was closed and still unlocked. I should have listened to Pete. I walked over and locked it, better late than never. If I fell asleep, Pete could knock and wake me up. I felt a lot more secure with the lock in place. I turned off the television and sat down on the couch.

I heard my dryer shut off, but remembered that it automatically shut off when it overheated. It had been on long enough to overheat. I'd have to wait for it to cool off before I could finish drying my hair.

Realizing I was still thirsty, I stood up and walked to the kitchen to get a glass of water. I noticed that I'd left the broom closet door open that morning, so I closed it and got my glass of water.

I reached up and fingered the lump on the back of my head. It was still sore to the touch. Of course it was sore, what did I expect.

Deciding the dryer had probably cooled off, I returned to the bathroom to finish the job. I switched the dryer off, then back on, and it whirred into life. I finished my hair, turned off the dryer, and put everything away.

"You idiot!" I whispered to myself angrily. I hadn't been in the broom closet since the day before and I'd definitely closed it.

I reached for the vase again, but it wasn't there. I'd left it in the kitchen. I began to feel claustrophobic as I stood there in the tiny bathroom trying to decide what to do. The first thing I had to do was get out of that room. I hadn't heard any more noises, so maybe everything was all right.

I stepped out into the hallway and took a deep breath. I decided I didn't want to be in my robe, just in case, so I tiptoed into my bedroom and changed into Levi's and a shirt. Somehow being dressed made me feel less vulnerable. Heaven only knew why being dressed made a difference, but it did.

But what was there to defend myself from? I chuckled. Maybe my concussion was worse than the doctor had thought. I was paranoid now that I was over my claustrophobia.

I put my slippers back on and sat down on the edge of the bed, holding my head. I knew I'd end up waiting up for Pete. Accident or no accident, sleep was a long way off.

I wondered if someone really had been in the apartment and I hoped Pete would be back soon. I couldn't even remember what the noise was like that I'd originally heard, but I still had that funny feeling in the pit of my stomach.

I picked up a magazine which was lying on the night stand by the bed and took it to the living room with me where I curled up on the couch. There were just too many aches and pains to allow for comfort, so I turned and put my feet up on the coffee table and crossed my legs at the ankles.

I glanced at the clock and saw that it was eleven forty-five. Pete should be back any minute. I opened the magazine and tried to read, to no avail. I found myself continually turning to look at the door in the hope that I'd hear Pete's knock, almost willing him to hurry back.

I began to feel more uncomfortable around midnight. It wasn't just that Pete wasn't back, there was more to it than that. I couldn't rid myself of that uncomfortable feeling in my stomach. My own advice had been to trust your gut feeling.

I turned my gaze to the kitchen. The light was on and everything appeared normal. I turned my head to the right to look down the hall. It was dark. I couldn't see a thing. I shouldn't have turned out all the lights in the back of the apartment. Light could be so reassuring.

Where was Pete?

I was turning my head from the hall when something caught my eye. I looked back, straining my eyes. Oh dear God! There was someone in the hallway, hiding in the shadows. My heart dropped to my feet.

CHAPTER 20

"Who's there?" I asked uncertainly, my voice a bit louder than necessary. There was no response. Maybe it was my imagination. I mean it was a hallway, with shadows and all.

"Who's there?" I repeated, jumping up from the couch.

I knew I saw something. I sat down quickly as the dizziness overtook me again. I thought I might pass out.

"What happened to you?" came a voice from the dark shadows.

I just about jumped out of my skin. I didn't honestly expect anyone to answer me.

"Richard? Is that you?" I said in disbelief.

He stepped out into the light. His face looked strained and flushed. He walked closer and I saw that his eyes were tired and glassy looking.

"Richard, why are you here? Why were you standing in the hallway like that? What's going on?"

His upper lip sort of twitched. My stomach was churning, which didn't go well with my aching head. He looked so odd.

"Richard, you're scaring me. Will you please answer me?" I pleaded.

He smiled and his face relaxed ever so slightly.

"Scaring you? You shouldn't be afraid of me. I'm the one who loves you, remember?" His smile disappeared.

"I remember. But if you love me, then why are you here scaring me? Why were you hiding in the hallway? Where were you before? I thought I heard a noise and I searched the whole apartment."

I stood up slowly, trying to avoid any further bouts of dizziness. Could he have been watching the apartment and seen Pete bring me home? Could he be jealous? Of course, that was it, he was jealous. Something was terribly wrong with this picture. He must have been in the broom closet. The idea of Richard hiding in the broom closet would have made me laugh under other circumstances, but I knew this wasn't a time for laughter.

"Don't play games, Sandi. You know exactly why I'm here." He sounded so calm, but the tension showing on his face belied his tone of voice.

I knew I'd better humor him and be careful. Gut instinct told me that much. He'd sneaked into my apartment and hidden in the broom closet. It was the one place I hadn't checked. Even when I realized the door should have been closed I didn't check. He must have crept behind me and into the hallway while I was browsing through the magazine.

"Richard, I really don't know what you're talking about, but I'm glad to see you." I had an uncontrollable urge to talk fast and long, like that would stave off something I wouldn't want to deal with.

"Don't I look awful? I was in an accident on my way home from your house. My car is totaled, but I was thrown clear. Fortunately, all I got out of it was a mild concussion and a few cuts and bruises. I fell asleep…"

"Shut up!" he said, interrupting me.

"But…" I was trying to edge my way to the front door while I talked.

"I said to shut up! Get away from that door and sit down on the couch. Do it now!" he ordered when I hesitated.

By this time I was afraid not to obey him, so I meekly sat down. There was something frightening in his expression. The whole thing was weird. He sure seemed normal a few hours ago. What could have happened?

"You couldn't leave it alone, could you." It was a statement, not a question.

"Leave what alone?" I asked timidly. "Richard, will you please tell me why you're here and what's going on? I don't understand what's happening."

"We could have been a good match," he said, "but you wouldn't keep your nose out of it."

He didn't seem to be listening to me. His mind was a million miles away. He was talking to me, and yet he wasn't. It was more like he was talking *at* me. He walked over to the wall where there was still a bullet hole and ran his finger around the rim. He turned and looked at me.

"I tried to warn you off, you know."

"*You* did that?" I asked incredulously. "*You* took a shot at me?" Anger began to replace fear, but I knew I had to keep it under control until Pete got back.

Where are you, Pete, I thought to myself as I quickly glanced at the front door.

"You can forget your boyfriend," Richard said. "He won't be back."

"What did you do, Richard?" I asked quietly. "*What did you do?*" I asked louder as panic began to overtake me.

"Not much," he said casually. "I just made a little adjustment to his brakes. Let's see. I'd estimate that his brakes went out about the time he started down that rather steep hill near his home. You know, the one with all the curves."

"Oh Lord," I whispered. "Richard, he'll be killed."

"That's the idea, darling." He paused and studied me for a moment. His eyes glazed over. There were white lines around his mouth from the tension on his face.

"You had me fooled all along, didn't you. I thought you really cared for me. But you were only trying to get information about Robert. ROBERT!" he yelled venomously. "That little creep got in my way in more ways than one."

What did he mean about Robert? He wasn't making sense, but he seemed to think I should know what he was talking about.

"Richard," I said. "I do care for you. Sit down next to me and let's discuss this calmly. I don't know what you're talking about, but I'm willing to listen."

"Don't patronize me, bitch!" he said through clenched teeth. "You know exactly what I'm talking about."

"Honestly, I don't have any idea about what's going on," I said in exasperation. How could I get through to this guy. I really didn't understand what was going on.

"Come on. I'm no fool. When I saw my button on the table the other night…"

I stole a glance at the coffee table and noticed for the first time that the button was gone.

"…I got worried. But tonight, when you called the missing button to my attention, then I knew you were on to me. I had to wear that shirt so I could be sure."

"But I didn't even know it was your button until tonight, and you explained how you lost it. So what is this all about?" I finally understood, but I couldn't let Richard know. I hoped I was a good actress.

Confusion flashed across his face but disappeared rapidly, to be replaced by a look of weariness. His eyes cleared slightly and he sat down on the chair.

"You really didn't know…" he began.

"How *could* I know it was your button?" I asked. "I'd never seen that shirt until tonight, and I certainly didn't relate the shirt to the button I picked up in the parking area."

"I could have gotten away with it," he said, beginning to laugh. "But now it's too late. Now you know something's wrong and you won't give up until you figure it out. I've learned that much about you. You're tenacious. You'd find out sooner or later." He laughed harder.

Lord, I said in my mind, please take care of Pete. Send your Guardian Angels to watch over him. Don't let him die. Please!

"You're being too quiet," Richard said. "What are you up to?"

"Nothing. I'm just trying to understand. Richard, what happened? Tell me what happened. Maybe I can help," I suggested.

"There's no help for me now. When I heard you mention Becker's name over the phone, I thought you knew. Then you suddenly had to leave. When you mentioned the button, that clinched it."

"What has Becker got to do with you?" I was totally confused by what he was saying. For a second I thought I had the whole thing figured out, but Richard was twisting and turning in directions which I couldn't follow.

Richard hung his head, looking defeated.

"Becker is a man of many talents. I knew he was dealing drugs, and I knew he was a loan shark. Did you know he's a fence too?"

"No," I replied. Becker was a real Jack of all Trades.

"He is. He got rid of some pieces from a few of the digs for me. You'd be surprised how much money people will pay for artifacts so they can put them in their private collections."

"But Richard, why? You come from a wealthy family and you're a prestigious college professor. Why would you need to steal precious artifacts and sell them through a fence? This doesn't make any sense."

"Wealthy family? They disowned me years ago. Father said I was incorrigible. I'd become involved with gambling and lost a fortune. My father bailed me out a couple of times, but I couldn't stop. It was like a disease. Father thought it would teach me a lesson if I had to make it on my own. Good old dad. Always the wise counselor. We had an argument and I ended up hitting him. Then I hit him again. I was out of control. I couldn't stop myself. My two brothers pulled me off, but not before I really hurt him. They covered up for me quite nicely though. It wouldn't do to have a nasty little scandal. A violent son in the Smythe family? Never!"

Violent? Wonderful. I really needed to hear that. If he and his father had a fight over gambling debts, then what could *I* expect. A lot of trouble, that's what.

"But where does Robert fit into all of this?" I asked, stalling for time. I might as well get the whole story while I was at it. Things certainly couldn't get much worse than they already were.

"Robert? Oh." His eyes glazed over again. "Professors don't make as much money as most people think. Certainly not enough to cover the gambling debts. I owed a lot of money, and certain people were becoming impatient. Very impatient. Then, quite by accident, I hit upon a wealth of items out at one of the digs. Priceless items. I kept my students digging elsewhere, and at night I'd go out and take a few things at a time. I felt like I'd found a pirate's booty. I knew there were collectors out there who'd give their eyeteeth for what I'd found. They were a way out for me. I had to steal them. I couldn't let them go to a museum when I needed them so much. Besides, no one would miss what they didn't know existed."

"So you found Becker and began selling them," I supplied. I could pretty much figure out the rest of the story, but I needed time. I'd have to keep Richard talking while I decided what to do.

"Yes. I only intended to sell a few, but I kept getting in deeper and deeper. I didn't have any choices left to me."

"What about Robert?" I asked.

Before Richard could answer my question, the phone rang. I glanced from the phone to Richard, but he seemed to be ignoring it.

"Should I answer it?" I asked hopefully.

"No. Let it be. Whoever it is will think you're out."

But the phone kept ringing insistently. Maybe it was Pete. I could only hope. I'd turned the answering machine off so if I fell asleep the phone wouldn't wake me.

"Answer the damn thing," Richard ordered angrily. "But be careful about what you say. Don't cross me."

"I won't," I said as I picked up the receiver.

"Mother?" I said as I heard her voice. "What do you want?"

"Well, don't be snippy," she replied. "I just called to say hello. Why did it take you so long to answer the phone?"

"I was just coming in the door and I dropped my keys," I lied as I looked at Richard. Thank goodness she hadn't hung up after the usual three rings. Richard nodded his head, indicating that my answer was satisfactory. "I didn't mean to sound snippy, I'm just rushed." I was desperately trying to think of something to say to her that would tip her off to the fact I was in big trouble, hoping she'd catch on and call the police. My mind was an absolute blank.

"Dear," she began, "I've been thinking. Don't you think it's about time you gave up this detective nonsense? I mean, you're just not the type."

"What is the type?!" I snapped at her. Of all times for her to call to discuss my career. "Mother, I can't talk about this right now. There's someone here…"

"Cut it short," Richard snarled.

"I can't talk right now. Let me call you back, Mother."

"Yes, honey, you call me back," she said with an exaggerated sigh. "We'll discuss this when you're in a better mood."

Oh, God! Why couldn't I think of something to say to tip her off. Desperate times call for desperate measures.

"Mother, *call the police right…*"

Richard grabbed the phone and slammed it into its cradle. He grabbed hold of the cord and ripped it out of the wall.

"That wasn't too smart," he said.

"What did you expect? You're scaring me."

"That's the idea," he said smugly. "Now, as to your question about Robert, I'll answer you. We've got time before the police show up. It will take her awhile to figure out what to do. You've confused her, my dear."

He sure seemed willing to answer everything. Maybe he needed to get it all off his chest. I prayed with all my heart that my mother was on her phone calling the police. If Richard was willing to talk, maybe help would come in time. I knew my mother didn't get confused that easily.

"I started sneaking things out during the day at the dig," Richard said. "It seemed, I don't know, somehow more exciting. I told Robert I was going to my car to get some more brushes that day. I stopped on my way and picked up something I'd hidden away. I didn't know that Robert was following me. I opened the trunk of my car, and Robert walked up behind me. I was still holding the artifact.

"He said he had a problem and needed a friend to talk to. He said he needed the advice of an adult instead of one of his school friends. He had that envelope in his hand, the one with his name on it, and he began to explain that it was some type of evidence, but then he saw the artifact and asked me what it was and where it had come from. I tried to lie to him, but that nosey brat took it right out of my hands to get a closer look. He knew there was something wrong. He was one of my best students. One of the brightest. He said something like, 'You're all alike'.

"I couldn't be found out. Do you understand? I *couldn't*! My career, my reputation, everything was at stake."

"What happened next?" I asked, after a very long pause.

"I heard some other students coming. Robert promised me he wouldn't say anything until I had a chance to explain things to him. I'll give him that, he was trying to be fair. He agreed to meet me back at the dig that night. He said he was going to a party, but that he could sneak out for awhile.

"I worried all day long. I'd already lost my family, but more importantly, if he turned me in it would ruin my career. I hoped that I could reason with him. I felt like my whole life was on the line."

Where were the cops. My mother should have reached them by now. If I'd only been able to give her some kind of idea about how much trouble I was really in. And where was Pete? Someone should be showing up to help me. Help *me*? What about Pete? Was he safe? Or lying in a totaled out wreck of a car somewhere. Richard drew me back with his words.

"Robert showed up at ten o'clock that night. I'd told him to meet me out at the dig. I tried to explain to him, but he wouldn't listen. He said I was just like his brother, whatever that meant. He told me he was sorry, but he couldn't let it go. He said he was tired of looking the other way, and he said he had a lot to set straight. He'd have to report me to the authorities."

My stomach tightened up while I listened to him. I pretty much knew what was coming next. My head felt like wrestlers were jumping up and down on it.

"He started to walk away and I grabbed him. He turned and swung at me, but he missed. I hit him in the stomach. He tried to fight back, but he was no match for me. He was too small and I'm in better condition. I hit him a few more times, but the little sniveler said he was still going to call the authorities. I grabbed his neck and began choking him. I realize now that I was out of control. It was like I didn't know what I was doing. We fell to the ground, but I never let go. I didn't mean to kill him, not really. I only meant to scare him, but I couldn't seem to stop. I finally came to my senses and told him to get up," Richard said, tears beginning to run down his face. "He wouldn't get up. I *begged* him to get up, but he wouldn't move. I realized he wasn't breathing. His eyes were open, but he was gone. I'd killed him.

"He must have torn the button off my shirt during the struggle. I guess it fell on the ground when I put his body in the trunk."

The pain in my stomach was being replaced by nausea. He was telling me all of this because he knew I'd never be able to repeat it to anyone. I was going to end up in the same trunk.

"So you put his body in the trunk," I said, again stalling for time. "Then you took him up to the cave?" I was still hoping against hope that someone would show up and help me.

"Yes. I had to drag him most of the way to the cave because I couldn't drive the car all the way up. I had to go on foot and he was too heavy to carry that far. I didn't think anyone else knew about the cave. I discovered it once when I was hiking. I searched his pockets and found that envelope, so I kept it, figuring I could somehow use it to throw the suspicion away from myself. It worked, didn't it."

I nodded, trying to appear calm, but I was scared spitless.

"What about Frank Samuels? Was he involved in this too?" I asked. There was still the matter of his disappearance.

"Never heard of him," Richard replied.

"Oh," I said meekly.

"But now," Richard said, looking deep into my eyes, "I'll have to kill you too. I honestly don't want to, but you found that damned button. You know I have to do this." His voice lacked any emotion at all.

"You don't have to do this, Richard. I believed you when you told me about the button tonight. I never linked it to Robert," I said desperately. "If you'd just left well enough alone, it never would have come to this. We can still work something out. You know I care about you. You're just confused. I wouldn't want to see you hurt."

"Don't patronize me," he said again. "It doesn't become you."

Anger and desperation were racing through my veins. If I was going to die anyway, I might as well go out fighting. The second phone, which was in my bedroom, started to ring. I knew instinctively that it was my mother, but it was too late.

"Well what do you want me to do, Richard? Stand here meekly and let you strangle me too? You may not think much of life, but I do!"

With an unexpected movement I swept my hand across the coffee table and grabbed a heavy candle holder, heaving it at him. It only took him a moment to recover from the blow to his head, but it gave me enough time to unlock the front door and throw it open. He grabbed my arm. Mustering up all the strength I could, I shoved myself against him, forcing him to hit his head on the door jam. He lost his grip on my arm and I turned and ran down the stairs. He was behind me in a flash.

I ran to the nearest car and jumped in, locking all the doors as fast as I could. I was breathing hard and my heart was pounding as I saw his face appear through the window. It was contorted with anger, and I saw something closely resembling what I guessed madness must look like. I realized I was beginning to hyperventilate and tried to regulate my breathing. It was hopeless. My fingers and lips were already beginning to feel numb. The pounding in my head was almost incapacitating.

Richard was running around the car, trying all the doors.

I leaned over on the seat and discovered someone's lunch sack. The lunch was still in it, so I dumped it out and began breathing into the sack. I had to be able to defend myself and I couldn't do it if I passed out.

Richard glanced through the window and began to laugh at me.

"It's not funny!" I yelled angrily, then resumed breathing into the bag.

By the time I began to breath normally, Richard had begun banging on the windows, trying to get at me. The humor of the situation hadn't lasted long. I leaned on the horn, hoping to attract someone's attention. Nothing happened. The horn wouldn't work unless the key was turned on. What a stupid way to design a car!

By that time Richard was rocking the car. I had no idea what he thought he could accomplish, and I didn't think he knew either. In fact, he probably didn't care. I couldn't understand why no one heard the commotion. Why wasn't someone coming to help me? Were the neighbors deaf? I looked at the apartment doors, willing one of them to open. The lights were out. No one was home.

I thought I heard sirens in the distance and hoped that maybe my mother had finally gotten through to someone. It sure would be nice if they were on their way to rescue me. It was amazing how many thoughts could go through a person's head in a matter of seconds.

Richard stopped rocking the car and I looked out the window. He was rummaging through the trash bin. I thought he'd *really* lost his mind until he turned around with an old rusty hammer in his hand.

He smiled at me as he returned to the car and began trying to break the window in.

Was it my imagination, or were those sirens closer. Please God, I thought to myself. Let them be here soon.

The windshield cracked and Richard began swinging with renewed vigor, encouraged by his efforts. I moved as close to the other side of the car as I could. I saw a look of total concentration on his face. I knew he owned a gun and briefly wondered why he didn't just shoot me and get it over with. He didn't want to get caught. He wanted to take me somewhere remote and do the lowdown deed with no witnesses. But banging on the car windows should have gotten as much attention as a gunshot. Of course, he wasn't thinking rationally, and it hadn't gotten any attention anyway. I knew it was now or never.

I threw open the door on the passenger side and began running for all I was worth. It took a moment for him to focus on what I'd done, so I got a small head start. I ran out to the street and tried to yell, but it took too much energy. I kept running.

"SANDI!" he screamed at me. "IT'S ALL OVER."

I heard the gunshot but I kept running. He missed me. I was getting a side ache and my head was splitting. The dizziness hit me like a ton of bricks. Things started to turn black and I fell. I could smell someone's freshly mowed lawn. I laid there for a moment and the blackness began to dissipate. I looked up and saw Richard standing over me. He aimed the gun right between my eyes, no longer aware of what he was doing, not thinking about being caught. I closed my eyes.

I heard the sirens close by and the screech of tires, and then I heard the gun go off.

"Isn't it marvelous to know that instantaneous death means no pain?" I thought, in a dreamlike state. "I was afraid of pain, but there isn't any."

No pain, but I felt a heavy weight on me. I was confused.

"Are you here, God?" I asked.

The weight was lifted off of me and I felt someone shaking me.

"Sandi, are you okay?"

It sounded like Pete, not God.

CHAPTER 21

"Pete?" I cried as I opened my eyes. "Oh Pete! I'm not dead!"

"No, you're not dead, and I'm not God. You're alive and well," he said. "Let me help you up."

"I can't stand. My legs are too weak."

"Sit still for a minute then."

I sat up and looked around. The first thing I saw was Richard, lying next to me. He was very still. My brain finally clicked into gear and I realized that *he'd* been shot, not me. As still as he was, I could see that he was breathing, although shallowly. He wasn't dead. I felt relief. There'd been too much death already. Then I saw Pete talking to Rick. They walked over and stood by me.

"How did you know, Pete? Did my mother call? Why is Rick with you?"

"Your mother?" Pete looked confused. "It's probably the concussion," he said, turning to Rick. "She even thought I was God for a minute."

"We'll talk about it later," he said to me. "Right now I want to get you back up to your apartment."

He helped me up and I turned to look as I heard another siren. It was the paramedics coming to take Richard away. No matter what had happened, I still felt an overwhelming sorrow and loss for Richard. I voiced that thought to Pete and he snorted.

"Sometimes you're too soft-hearted," he said.

When we reached the apartment, Pete got a pillow from my bedroom and I laid down on the couch. Rick knocked on the door and Pete let him in.

"A couple of uniformed officers are following the paramedics to the hospital," Rick said. "I need to know exactly what happened."

I told Rick everything that had transpired, including all that Richard had told me about Robert's death.

"If he'd just left the thing about the button alone, he probably would have gotten away with it," I finished.

"I think that's enough for now," Rick said. "You get some rest and we'll talk some more tomorrow. By the way, I found Frank Samuels. He's been in rehab since shortly after the party where he and Robert argued. It seems he had a pretty heavy drug addiction. He didn't know anything about Robert disappearing, but he said Robert was the one who talked him into getting help. He and Robert talked before they argued, and Robert told him some things about his brother which apparently scared Samuels. I don't know what Robert actually said to him, but I'd patent it if I could."

"Wow! Robert was quite a crusader," I said. "Rick, I know a simple thank you sounds pretty lame, but thank you. I'd probably be the one the paramedics are hauling away if you hadn't shown up when you did."

"Don't thank me, thank Pete. He's the one who saved your life. See you tomorrow," he said as he left.

"Pete," I said when he sat down. "How did you know there was something wrong?"

"My car. I was driving home and it wasn't running right. I tried to pull over to the curb, but my brakes were gone. I turned off the engine, bumped into the curb a few times and rear ended a parked car. The curb and turning off the engine had slowed me down enough so that it wasn't too bad."

"I had the brakes worked on less than a month ago, so I knew there shouldn't have been a problem. I got out and checked. It was obvious that someone had tampered with them."

"But how did you know to come back here?"

"I called Rick for a lift. Between the two of us, we figured the only time the car could have been monkeyed with was while I was here. That's where my brilliant deductive reasoning comes in," he boasted. "I knew it meant you were in trouble. Someone didn't want me to come back. I have to be honest though. I thought it was another one of Becker's men. I never suspected the good professor."

"I got a flash when I saw a button missing from the shirt he was wearing tonight," I said. "It was the same kind of button I found at the dig. He gave me a reasonable excuse for the missing button though, and I believed him."

"I think he took us all by surprise," Pete said, "although I never did like the son-of-a-bitch."

I sat up and Pete moved from the chair to the couch, sitting close to me.

"Do you know if Richard is going to be okay?" I asked.

"Yeah, Rick said he wasn't hurt as bad as it appeared. He'll be able to stand trial. Too bad, if you ask me."

Pete stared at me for a minute. He grabbed me and kissed me hard. So he still thought I was like those other women, huh? He'd have second thoughts about that by the time I was through with him. He sure had lousy timing.

"What's the matter with you?" I asked as I pushed him away. "Don't you think I've been through enough for one night? Or is my current state of vulnerability too much to resist."

"What do you think?" he said angrily as he rubbed his sore lip.

"I'm not one of your so-called groupies," I said, glad that his lip hurt.

"Damn it!" he snapped.

"Pete! Knock it off."

"I was jealous. Okay? Does that make you happy?"

"Jealous!" I said incredulously. "You were jealous?"

"You idiot!" he snapped at me. "I thought you were in love with Richard."

"You're the idiot," I said. "What is it? The fact that I don't trail around behind you like a little puppy dog like the rest of your women? You just want what you can't have. Forget it!" Wow! All the yelling was making my head pound even harder, if that was possible.

"I love you," Pete said quietly, giving me a disgusted look. "Don't you know that yet?"

"Love? You don't know the meaning of the word," I said calmly. "I, on the other hand, know *exactly* what it means, because I love you. Who said that?" My eyes opened wide and I stopped cold, looking over my shoulder.

"You did," he said, grinning. "And I'm holding you to it."

"Not me. Huh uh. No way. That was just a little slip of the tongue. I don't have time to love anyone," I said. "I don't even know you that well."

"Slip of the tongue my…I've never really had time for love either, but sometimes you just have to go with the flow. No one has ever touched me the way you have. I'm not letting you go, and don't even think about trying to get away from me. You need me to take care of you."

"I don't need anyone to take care…"

He pulled me close and kissed me. Not a greedy kiss this time, but a long and tender kiss that sealed our future.

"Smythe is lucky I didn't kill him," Pete said as he gave me a squeeze.

The phone rang. Pete followed me back to my bedroom where I picked up the receiver.

"Hi, mom," I said sweetly, knowing it would be her.

"What's going on there?" she asked fearfully. "I've been trying to call you back because I couldn't hear what you said before you hung up awhile ago, and you sounded really odd. But you didn't answer. I was really getting worried."

"Nothing's going on now," I replied. "Things couldn't be better. I want you to meet someone. Mom, this is Pete," I said as I handed him the phone.

END

ABOUT THE AUTHOR

Born and raised in So. California, Marja worked in the Los Angeles County Court System in both civil and criminal law for over 15 years. She also worked in law enforcement in Oregon, and has drawn on those experiences for her writing. Marja and her husband, Al, currently live in a small farming community in No. Nevada.

.